Summer's CARESS

TIELLE ST. CLARE

ELLORA'S CAVE
ROMANTICA®
www.EllorasCave.com

An Ellora's Cave Publication

www.ellorascave.com

Summer's Caress

ISBN 9781419963919
ALL RIGHTS RESERVED.
Summer's Caress Copyright © 2007 Tielle St. Clare
Edited by Briana St. James.
Cover art by Syneca.

Electronic book publication August 2007
Trade paperback publication 2011

SUMMER'S CARESS

෨

Trademarks Acknowledgement

‫ℰꙻ

The author acknowledges the trademarked status and trademark owners of the following wordmarks mentioned in this work of fiction:

Energizer: Eveready Battery Company, Inc.

Chapter One

ဆာ

"Wait, hold on, hold on." Rebecca cocked her head to the side, trapping the phone against her shoulder as she juggled purse, briefcase, shopping bag, Chinese food container and soda cup in her hands. She pulled the key from the lock and blindly reached for the doorknob. Once inside, she sighed, knowing she was mere feet from dropping some of her burdens. She lowered the bags to the floor and pulled the phone back to her ear. "Okay, I'm here."

Taylor laughed. "If you'd make more than one trip, you wouldn't have so much trouble."

Rebecca smiled. Taylor knew her so well.

"Yes, but this way is such a challenge. I feel like I've really accomplished something when I don't drop anything. So, forgetting my lazy tendencies, did the client like her living room?"

Taylor's small interior design company was just getting started so every client was a new challenge and a new story.

"In the end, yes, she loved it. Said she was going to recommend me to her friends. Ugh. If they are all like her, I'm not sure I want the business."

Rebecca wished she could be so cavalier about new clients. She and her business partner had been building their company for two years. They were succeeding but they hadn't come to the point of being relaxed about losing a client.

She rolled her head to the side and tried to loosen the constricted neck muscles that made nodding almost impossible. God, she needed a break. Or a least the anticipation of a break.

"What are your plans for the weekend?" she asked.

"It's Tuesday and you're already looking forward to the weekend? That's not good."

"It's been a long week already." One trainer had quit and another had taught the wrong course to the wrong client. It was going to take most of the week to untangle that situation.

Running into her ex-boyfriend hadn't helped. Not that it had been traumatic or distressing. Maybe that was the problem. Rebecca had seen him and his new girlfriend at lunch and had even stopped by their table to visit. She'd felt no spark, no pain, not even a memory of why she'd dated him in the first place. They'd been together for six months. Surely she should have felt something. Of course, maybe he was right and she was just too cold. Too emotionless.

"Anyway, this weekend? You guys coming into town?"

Taylor and her men—Mikhel and Zach—lived about ninety minutes north in a house on a lake.

"Probably not. The boys—" as she called her lovers, "have decided that we need a hot tub on the back deck. So that's the project for the weekend."

"They're going to build a hot tub?"

"Oh no." The sarcasm that laced Taylor's words made Rebecca smile. It was good to hear the humor in Taylor's voice. When she'd first taken up with two guys, Rebecca was afraid she would lose her best friend. She didn't see Taylor as often as before but they kept in touch and Taylor hadn't lost herself in the relationship. "They have the hot tub picked out but now the deck isn't right, so this weekend, they are taking apart the deck so they can rebuild it so it will support the hot tub."

"Ooh, sounds like fun."

"It's going to be a mess. Even Trey agrees with me."

"Trey?"

Taylor paused. "Yes, you remember Trey, right?"

Rebecca winced even though no one could see her. How could she forget Trey?

"Tall, blond, gorgeous? Oh yeah, I remember him."

Unconsciously, she licked her lips as she thought about the one time they'd met. His eyes—bright green and terribly wicked—had met hers, assessing, observing. She'd seen a flare of heat in his stare, one that made every female hormone in her body go on full alert. The kind of fire that warned she could be naked and bent over the nearest flat surface in seconds. Just the memory of his stare made her pussy flutter. If he'd made any sort of move, given *any* indication that he intended to act on that burst of lust, she would have been all over him. Hell, she'd have dragged him out of the house and fucked him in the woods, but after that momentary flash, it was gone. Not faded or hidden but brutally crushed.

Oh but that hadn't stopped her. She'd flirted and teased him all night, practically chasing the man. In response, he'd backed as far away from her as was physically possible. Not her finest hour.

She cleared her throat. "Trey's helping with the deck?"

"Probably." Taylor hesitated. "He's been hanging around a lot lately. Oh, listen, I've got to go. Zach's flapping his arms like insane chicken. I think that means that dinner is ready."

"Okay, well, have a good night."

"You too. Ta!"

"Ta!"

Rebecca flipped her cell phone closed and sighed. Taylor was going off to have dinner with Zach and Mikhel. And Rebecca was going to eat cold vegetable lo mein.

A twinge of jealousy she wasn't proud of sparked in her chest but she quickly dismissed it. She was thrilled that Taylor was happy. And if sleeping with two men was what made her content, more power to them. Rebecca didn't want two men. Hell, she wasn't even sure she wanted one. They tended to be more trouble than they were worth.

She just wanted something different. Something to shake up her life.

* * * * *

Rebecca stared at the narrow road that curved to the left and the slightly wider version that bent to the right. The last time she'd been through here there had been a gate across one of them giving her no choice in direction. Her previous visits had been made during the daylight and when it wasn't raining. Of course, it hadn't been raining when she'd started out. The summer storm had caught her by surprise and slowed her progress, delaying her arrival until after sunset. Everything looked different in the dark. The trees that bent over the road gave it a definite creepy forest feel.

This is just perfect. I'll show up on Taylor's doorstep, late, soaking wet...and with no invitation to be there. It had seemed like a fine idea when she'd started out two and half hours ago. Getting out of town, spending the night and part of tomorrow with her best friend. Rebecca just couldn't bear spending another Friday night at home, working.

But she hadn't called ahead to warn Taylor. Hadn't wanted to be told it wasn't a good night for a visit. She'd *needed* to get out of town. She could only hope that Taylor was home and heaven forbid, wasn't involved in some wild orgy.

Rebecca shook her head. She didn't really think Taylor, Mikhel, Zach, and wow, maybe Trey, actually had orgies but the possibility lurked in her brain.

With a chuckle, she guided her car to the right, pretty sure that the left road would take her to the far side of the lake.

Lightning flashed and brightened the sky, giving the trees a threatening feel for just one moment. Back in darkness, with only the power of her headlights, she inched along.

Her car slowed to a creep but she kept going forward, crouching low to help duck under the overhanging trees.

She sighed with relief when the trees widened to the gravel pad that served as driveway and parking lot. Her relief turned to dread.

The corner that normally held Taylor's car was crowded with three vehicles, probably Zach's and Mikhel's. Three other cars sat near the front door.

Great. I've interrupted a party. She pulled her car off to the side, sliding under some low tree branches. She killed the engine and sat for a moment. Taylor obviously had guests. *God, what if it really is an orgy?*

Rebecca grabbed the steering wheel, silently slapping herself for not calling ahead. How mortifying.

Hi, I know I wasn't invited, but can I crash your party?

Great intro.

Lightning crashed again and Rebecca shivered. The night was warm but the air in her car was blowing cold. The light shirt and shorts she'd put on to fight the summer heat suddenly weren't enough coverage.

Well, there was nothing to be done. She couldn't drive back. If nothing else, she needed to use the bathroom.

With a sigh, she opened her door and stepped out. She'd forgotten an umbrella so she was just going to have to run for it. Her feet landed in a puddle that reached over the soles of her tennis shoes.

She slammed the car door and ran across the gravel driveway, the pounding rain instantly drenching her. She stopped on the front step and knocked. Stepping back, she stared at the wild sky. Dark except where sparks of lightning illuminated it.

The door behind her popped open. She spun around and gasped. Trey. Looking gorgeous, and more arrogant than before. He smiled. The movement changed his face — making it more sneering than sexy. He barely glanced at her face. His eyes dropped down to her body, and stayed latched onto her chest. The smile turned into a leer and she realized the rain had turned her white t-shirt into a sheer, soaking wet glove that clung to her breasts. She shifted beneath the lecherous stare but he didn't react.

How disappointing, she thought.

"Nice," he said and the voice startled her. That wasn't Trey's voice. She blinked and looked again. He looked like Trey, enough to be his twin, but it wasn't the same guy. The hair was a little more yellow and those bright blue eyes had to come from colored contacts. He raked his gaze down her body while he licked his lips. "Mikhel didn't tell me he was providing *snacks*."

Rebecca crushed her lips together and resisted the urge to cross her arms over her breasts. She wasn't going to let this man think he'd managed to intimidate her.

"Well, he didn't tell me he'd taken to letting assholes into his house either, so we're even."

The lecherous light in the man's eyes flipped to rage. "Listen, bitch, you don't—"

"Who is it, Marcus?" Now *that* was the voice she remembered.

Marcus didn't move, but she saw the muscles in his neck tense up. With a final glare, he straightened and turned around.

"Don't know. She didn't give a name." He walked off, leaving her standing in the rain.

She scraped back her hair, which had begun to drip on her face. When she looked up again, Trey filled the doorway. God, he was just as stunning as she'd remembered.

His hair—longer than Rebecca's—was thick and straight, falling to the middle of his back. On another woman, Rebecca would have been jealous—her red curls just couldn't compete—but on him, she wanted to release it from the tight band that held it tied back, letting the thick strands slide through her hands, her fingers gripping, holding him over her. She almost whimpered as the delicious fantasy filled her head, distracting her. An interesting flutter in her pussy followed and Rebecca squirmed beneath his intense stare.

He blinked, as if he couldn't believe his eyes. Then his gaze, too, tracked down her body, his eyes widening when he saw the outlines of her breasts.

A strange thing happened. Instead of internally cringing as she'd done with Marcus, her body tingled with pleasure. Her nipples tightened and pressed harder against the lace of her bra. She was sure they were poking against her t-shirt.

Trey's mouth dropped open and he looked as if he'd been punched in the gut. The heat in his eyes that she'd seen before returned, flooding across her skin like liquid fire. So hot, it looked as though his eyes were glowing red. His tongue teased the inside edge of his lip as if he was imagining her flavor. The movement was unconscious and so sexual that it only made her want to offer herself up for his tasting.

She took a deep breath and the movement seemed to shock him out of his stare.

"Oh, I'm sorry. You're soaking. Come in." He stepped back, his eyes popping back to her face and staying there.

Warm rain or not, Rebecca wasn't going to refuse the possibility of getting dry. She stepped inside. The narrow hallway didn't give them much room to maneuver. Rebecca turned, facing Trey as she slipped by, the tips of her breasts brushing against his chest. The light caress translated into a hot hard lick on her clit and she gasped.

Wow. If just touching the man causes that kind of reaction, imagine what actually fucking him could do. Oh, the wicked little devil in her mind was back, tempting her. No, she'd vowed to be nice, polite and impersonal to Trey. In keeping with that vow, she pushed by him and stood, dripping on the carpet while he shut the door.

Voices echoed from the living room, reverberating into the small entryway. Rebecca mentally winced. She *had* interrupted a party.

13

"Is Taylor —"

"You should —"

They both spoke at the same time. And both stopped.

"Go ahead," Trey said, though she noticed the heat she'd seen in his eyes was gone. He was a master at controlling himself and shuttering his emotions.

"Is Taylor around? I didn't mean to interrupt."

"She is. Let me get her." He walked past her and stopped where the entryway met the main hall. "You should probably stay here." He looked pointedly at her chest, as if that explained his statement.

She waited until he'd turned the corner and looked down. Damn, he was right. Between the rain wetting her t-shirt, the thin lace bra she'd put on this morning—which was sexy but didn't do much to contain her breasts—and the tight points of her nipples, she looked like a walking sex show.

"Rebecca?" Taylor's voice preceded her by seconds as she turned the corner. "What are you doing—wow, we need to get you a towel."

Rebecca laughed. "I was just thinking that." Now she crossed her arms over her chest because it was one thing to refuse to be intimidated. It was another to stand in front of friends with her breasts all exposed.

"I'll get it," Trey volunteered, leaving Taylor and Rebecca alone.

"You're soaked. Is everything okay? You're not hurt?"

Rebecca winced. "No. Just wet. And a little embarrassed. I was just looking to get out of town for a few —" *Days.* "Hours and you said I was always welcome and so I decided to drive up. I didn't mean to crash your party," she said, trying not to feel a little hurt that she hadn't been invited. Taylor had her own life and friends that didn't include Rebecca.

But Taylor rolled her eyes. "It's not exactly a party. Just a few guys. Mainly friends of Mikhel."

"Well, I don't mean to interrupt. If I can just dry off and use your bathroom, I'll hop in my car and drive home."

"No!" The intensity of Taylor's rejection soothed Rebecca's feelings. "I want you here. And you can't leave in this weather." Trey appeared with the towel. He barely glanced at her when he handed it over and there was no indication, even a residual hint, of the lust she'd seen in those first few minutes. He nodded toward Taylor in a low respectful way — almost like a bow — then backed out.

Rebecca clutched the towel, curious at the strange interaction between Taylor and this gorgeous man. Once Trey backed into the hall, the spell was broken and Rebecca rubbed the towel over her hair, evening out some of the clumps and squeezing out the water. She'd only been in the rain for a few minutes but the power of the storm had soaked her. She ran the towel over her arms and legs. The cool air in the house chilled her even as it dried her skin.

"Come on in." Taylor stepped back. "Uh, you might want to wrap that towel around you until we can get you dried off. You walk in there like that and not a single male will listen to a word I have to say."

Rebecca laughed but took Taylor's advice and looped the towel around her body and under her arms, hooking it in front. "Right. Like Mikhel would ever look at another woman."

"Oh, I don't doubt that he looks, but he doesn't dare touch."

She said it with such confidence and love that Rebecca couldn't help but be jealous.

They walked into the living room and instantly became the center of attention. Eight pairs of male eyes turned to them. She recognized Trey, of course. He was deep in discussion with Mikhel. When they looked up, Rebecca realized she was the subject of that discussion. Marcus, the creep who had answered the door, was sitting on the couch, his legs spread wide, as if he was offering himself to whoever passed by, or showing off what he had. Rebecca didn't even bother to look. Big cock or not, he was a big dick and she didn't have time for that kind of male posturing. Two men stood beside Zach. They looked over with curiosity and masculine interest but Rebecca felt no threat from them. Two others stood off by themselves — twins. Exact copies of each other. They looked faintly familiar but she didn't have a chance to explore that as Taylor led her forward to Mikhel and Trey.

"Just hang here for a second, Rebecca, I need to chat with Mikhel."

Mikhel nodded and followed Taylor into the kitchen. With a tip of his head, Mikhel called Zach to go with them, leaving Rebecca alone except for Trey. Rebecca forced a smile.

"Thanks for the towel."

"No problem."

She nodded, then looked at the twins — smiling awkwardly. Normally she had plenty to say but part of her concentration was on the discussion occurring in the kitchen. She knew it was about her. What? Did Taylor need permission for Rebecca to visit? Was Mikhel that controlling? There was no way to deny he was a dominant man.

"How was the drive?" Trey said. "The rain must have slowed you down." They were reduced to talking about the weather. Hmmm, not a good sign.

"It wasn't so bad when I started. I almost made a wrong turn on the road here. I almost turned down that little road that leads across the lake." That seemed like a safe topic. "I've never been over there. Is there anything there?"

"A cabin," Trey answered, his lips tightening, as if there was more than he was saying.

"Does anyone stay there?"

"There's a new owner, Deacon Crowley. He's been there quite a bit since he bought the place. He's just planning to use it as a weekend retreat."

"Nice guy?"

Trey shrugged. "I have no idea. Never met him. He's a doctor of some sort."

"But you've never met him?" *Then how do you know he's a doctor? And why do you seem to know so much about him?* She didn't ask the questions but she didn't need to. Trey answered anyway.

"I did a background check on him."

"On a neighbor who lives over a mile away? That's a little paranoid, isn't it?"

"I call it being aware of my environment."

The way he said it—cold and intent—sent a shiver down her spine. It combined with the chill in the air and she realized she was quite cold.

And she still really had to go to the bathroom. Just about to ask if she could use the restroom, Taylor returned. Her smile was a little tight and Mikhel didn't look pleased, but Taylor didn't look threatened or cowed.

"It's all set. Let's get you settled in your room." Taylor grabbed her arm and pulled her up the stairs.

Rebecca had stayed at the cabin before but Taylor passed the room she'd previously slept in. When Taylor saw her hesitate, she shrugged. "That's Trey's room now."

"Trey?"

"Yes, he's living here."

Wow. *Is he sleeping with Taylor too?* The idea didn't sit well. Not that Rebecca expected her odds to improve with Trey but Taylor already had two men. Did she need to strip the entire male population?

And, how did Taylor get all the gorgeous men? Not that she wasn't pretty and fun and probably sexy, though Rebecca had never thought of her that way. But it seemed strange that after years of dating mediocre, bland businessmen, Taylor would suddenly become a magnet for bad-boy male flesh.

Taylor must have sensed the direction of her thoughts because she laughed and shook her head. "No, I'm not sleeping with Trey. God forbid. The two I have are sometimes two too many. I certainly don't need a third."

Still a little uncomfortable with the idea that Taylor regularly had sex with two men, Rebecca just smiled.

"You can stay in this room." She pushed open the door. A large bed dominated the room, straining the small space. But the blue and teal bedspread brightened things up. "So, here's the deal," Taylor started. "We have this...thing tonight. 'We' being me and the guys downstairs. It's an RSVP kind of thing so I can't ask you along."

"No stress. I really should have called." *Really, I should have called. Next time I'm going to call because this is so weird.* Though it certainly felt less uncomfortable now that she was away from the staring male eyes.

"No, I'm glad you're here. I've been meaning to invite you, but with everything going on..."

"Everything?"

"Oh, just stuff. Trey moving in. This thing tonight." She waved hands as if to dismiss the topic. "Anyway, we're going to leave in a bit and we'll be back really late. So you've got the house to yourself. There's plenty of food downstairs and movies and that outrageously huge TV that Zach installed. Have a good time, and then tomorrow you and I will dump the guys, go into town and have lunch, goof off." Taylor winced. "Sound okay?"

"Sounds great." And it did, because after her awkward entrance, having the night to herself was sounding better and better. But first a shower. And another more pressing need. "But I really, really have to go to the bathroom."

Taylor laughed and released her. "Right through that door. Take a shower if you want to warm up a bit."

"I will." Rebecca spun around and hurried into the small half-bath. There wasn't a tub to lounge in but that was okay.

She'd never been much of a lounger. After she used the facilities, she washed her hands and stared in the mirror. Total drowned rat. The lights also illuminated her white t-shirt. Damn, she really had been flashing her tits at Trey. As another shiver assaulted her, she stripped off her shirt and dropped it on the floor. A shower was sounding better all the time. She undid the button of her shorts and let those fall as well.

After her shower, she would hang them up. She groaned. What was she going to put on until then? She needed Taylor to grab her overnight bag before they left. Rebecca opened the bathroom door and hurried out—slamming to a stop, her shoulder connecting with something hard, thick and solid. Large hands snagged her out of the air as she bounced and fell backward. Stunned, she stared up—into Trey's eyes.

Her heart caught her throat as he looked down at her. And for just a moment, Rebecca understood how a rabbit felt in the claws of an eagle.

Chapter Two

ℰⓄ

She blinked and tried for a coherent thought—any thought that didn't involve dropping to her knees and placing her lips...or him dropping to his knees and—she shook her head. "Umm, sorry."

He nodded and his fingers gripped her upper arms. His eyes flashed and eerie red but instead of fear, warmth spread across her skin. His gaze fell, dipping into the space between her breasts. The front clasp of her bra dug into her flesh as she took a deep breath, straining the limits of her demi bra. It wasn't the most comfortable bra she owned but she wore it when she needed to feel sexy. And she'd needed that today.

Trey didn't speak. He released her arms and she thought he was going to back away. Instead, he trailed one finger down the inside edge of her bra, leaving a path of heat, as if he was made of fire. Rebecca opened her mouth, trying to grab enough oxygen, but afraid to startle him. She didn't want anything to interfere with his touch. His eyes tracked the same path as his finger, watching as he touched her skin, captivated by the sight.

His finger stopped at the front clasp and Rebecca held her breath. With a quick flip of his thumb, he popped the tab open. The sides of her bra pulled back, the wet lace clinging to her nipples as it separated.

She held her breath as he pushed the two cups apart, baring her breasts. His fingers skimmed along the outer curves, pushing the material away until she was completely naked before him. New shivers crisscrossed her skin, delicious and hot. The heat swelled inside her.

"Beautiful." It was low and sexual—a whisper of sound from his lips.

Rebecca stepped closer, craving his taste. She pressed up on her toes, leaning in, offering her mouth, needing a response to know that all this heat wasn't coming just from her. A deep growl rumbled from his chest—and she felt the sound in her nipples, tingling little vibrations that made her ache. His eyes flashed as if he sensed her reaction and he bent down to meet her.

The first brush of his mouth was soft. Not hesitant, but as if he wanted to give her a chance to escape. A tendril of fear spiraled through her—not that he would hurt her, but that once she tasted him, once she'd had him inside her, nothing else would compare.

But even that wasn't enough to make her pull back. The temptation to taste him, to have him, was too strong. She opened her lips and flicked her tongue out, a fleeting caress to his upper lip. A calling to him.

He stared down at her, frozen, his body trapped in the wicked tension that held them both.

Her heart beat three times before he moved, bending to her and locking their lips together, his tongue plunging into her mouth. No soft, gentling kisses. He took, dominated. Consumed. The powerful lure of his kiss grabbed something inside her core and dragged her closer. Her hands reached behind his head, holding him in place, needing the power that flowed from him. He groaned as her tongue twisted with his and the harsh bite of his teeth on her lower lip created new fire in her pussy. God, she wanted his mouth on her.

His hands tightened on her ass and he pulled her to him, stepping into the caress and pushing her back against the door.

The hungry desperation of his kiss sent a spike of need and pleasure into her core. She sank her fingers into his hair and held him to her, trying to keep up with the sensations zipping through her body—his lips, his tongue, the slow pulse of his cock against her.

Trey dragged his lips away, leaving her with a not so gentle bite to her lower lip. She chased his mouth, needing more. The delicious flavor of his kiss lingered, the intoxicating taste addictive. He whispered another kiss on her lips, then moved lower, sinking his teeth into her shoulder. The bite was almost painful but after a brief second, he pulled back. He stared at the place on her shoulder, his eyes glowing, his breath ragged, as if he was struggling to control himself.

She thought for a moment that he'd succeeded and would retreat—then he raised his eyes. Deep in the green depths she saw that strange red glow, as if the desire in him had turned into a physical presence. Warmth flooded her pussy and she squeezed her knees together, needing pressure to ease the ache that throbbed through her sex.

His lips tightened at the edges as he fought his internal battle. With a low groan, he leaned down and scraped his teeth across her shoulder, a warning and a caress. He licked the same place, soothing and healing. The hot stroke swirled through her core. She grabbed his arms, keeping herself upright as the hunger sapped her strength.

His hand released her ass and roamed, sliding between her thighs. She had no choice but to move into his touch, spreading her legs. He lifted his head, enough to look at her, to watch as he skimmed his fingers beneath her panties, through the tight curls protecting her pussy. He watched her, his eyes daring her to draw back. Her chest constricted and she fought for each breath, but there was no way she could move, except to get closer, wanting him deeper.

The first brush of his fingers pulled a gasp from her as he slipped into her slit, one thick finger touching her. Heat poured into her skin. She tipped her head back against the door, trying to breathe, focus her scattered thoughts. He seemed to take it as an invitation and tasted her neck, light kisses and sensual licks, tripping across the tightly strung muscles as he eased that lone finger into her pussy.

"So hot," he whispered against her skin. "So tight. I'm going to fuck you." The soft tones turned to an intoxicating growl, pure power rippling from his throat. "Sink into this hot little cunt, fill it." As he spoke, he fucked his finger into her, deep long strokes, strokes that promised more. Her pussy clenched around his invasion, wanting it all. He dragged his teeth across her skin, up, until he nipped at her earlobe, each tiny bite consuming her. God, it was like he was eating her alive. "Come inside you, until all you feel is me." He rubbed his thumb along her clit, teasing her with the wicked stroke.

"Yes." Her agreement slipped easily from her mouth. The slow steady pump of his finger inside her sent all thoughts out of her head. He accepted her lips, driving his tongue back into her mouth. The heady double assault—his kiss and his finger fucking her pussy—swelled inside her until she was moaning and rocking her hips against his hand, pushing him deeper.

He snapped his head back and growled. He pulled his finger out and Rebecca cried out at the loss.

"Don't worry, honey. I'm not done with this sweet cunt. Not yet." The promise weakened her knees.

Unable to resist, to stay passive any longer, she slid her hand between their bodies and cupped his erection, squeezing lightly. He growled into her mouth, nipping and kissing her lips, her jaw. He pulled her hand away and shifted until his erection was between her legs, her thigh wrapped around his hip. His fingers splayed across her ass, holding her steady as he slowly pumped forward. More promises, more temptation.

"That's where I'm going to be," he whispered. "Inside you. Fucking you, until you're screaming my name."

Yes. She could no longer speak.

His teeth scraped the nape of her neck, the sharp stinging bite perfectly timed to the pulse of his hips, his erection rocking against her clit. She cried out and clung to him, needing more. Needing him inside her.

With that sexual warning, he ground his cock against her, a slow seductive circle that massaged her clit. She gasped and Trey grunted, a satisfied masculine sound.

A light tapping vibrated the door behind her.

"Rebecca? We're going now," Taylor called through the door. Rebecca heard the voice and tried to respond, but Trey's cock was so perfectly positioned, just there, a little more and she could… "Will you be okay?"

"Fine! I'll be fine. Have fun!" *Oh God, just get out of here. Let me…*

His thumb replaced the hard ridge of his cock, rubbing a slow circle around her clit. It was just the right touch. Her pussy clenched and she heard him groan as he leaned into her, his mouth again moving her to neck. Bright shards of pleasure sparkled through her pussy and she felt her knees tremble.

She whimpered as he rubbed his teeth across her skin. He didn't bite but she felt the smooth sharpness of his canines — long and fierce. Her clouded mind tried to tell her they didn't feel normal, but at this moment she didn't care. She wanted to feel every part of him.

He pushed against her one more time, as if he couldn't quite make himself leave her.

Then abruptly, he stepped back. A few long blond strands had come free from his ponytail and hung loose around his face. The hair acted as a shield, hiding his eyes, muting his expression. But still Rebecca trembled. There was something different about him. Almost wild. The brutal control he had over his emotions was at a thin edge. He raised his eyes and stared at her.

"I'm not someone to play with, Rebecca." His words sounded strange, muffled. "You'll get more than you want."

She straightened. She'd never liked anyone — particularly a man — telling her what she wanted, what she should or should not do. And she sure as hell hadn't been playing. "I'm not so sure about that." She lifted her chin to prove her defiance.

He didn't seem to notice. "I am." He reached past her for the doorknob. He opened the door, forcing her to step aside. "Lock your door when you go to bed tonight, Red." She'd always hated being called "Red" but something about the way Trey said it made her heart pound faster. Still she wasn't about to take orders from him.

"Why? Is the boogie man going to slip into my bedroom?"

His face was mostly turned away but she saw the edge of his mouth pull up into a sexual, dangerous smile. "Not the boogie man." He glanced at her. "The big bad wolf."

Trey flicked his hair back out of the way and tried to calm his breath as he jogged down the stairs. Damn, something about Rebecca just spun him up, almost out of control, faster than any woman he'd ever known. Damn, he'd almost bitten her. As it was, he hadn't been able to resist nipping her skin, marking it.

The wolf inside him growled its desire. The animal had scented her the first moment they'd met and hadn't released its interest. Unlike the werewolves of popular literature, the wolf didn't choose an ideal mate with the human falling into perfect love. The wolf was an elemental creature. It hungered on a purely basic level. Trey had learned through brutal experience that while a wolf might crave a female, the human connection didn't necessarily follow.

In this case, Trey approved of his wolf's choice. Rebecca was one hot little piece of female flesh. A sweet little fuck, he was sure.

He rubbed his fingers together, remembering just how wet she'd been—hot, tight. God, what it would feel like to drive his cock into her.

Maybe, in the right time and place, he'd get the chance to find out if fucking her was anywhere close to the fantasy his imagination had created.

But that time was not today. Not with the full moon rising. And it sure as hell wasn't going to happen in his Alpha's spare bedroom.

Trey entered the living room and found Mikhel, Taylor and Zach waiting along with their guests.

Marcus, Trey's cousin, was leaning against the dining room doorframe, smirking when he saw Trey come in. As though he knew what Trey had been doing, and with whom. But Marcus was always smirking so it was difficult to tell when it meant something.

Erik and Stephan stood to the side. Max and Jax, Mikhel's brothers and identical twins, were already out on the deck. The bond between them was strong and they kept mostly to themselves.

Mikhel had invited his brothers and the other males to join in the full moon run. Without it being expressly said, Trey knew they'd been invited with the intent that someday they might be welcomed into Mikhel's pack, as Trey had been. All the males here tonight were either unaffiliated with a pack or so low in rank that they'd never rise to any power.

"Sorry," Trey apologized. "I had something I had to do."

"No problem. Let's go." With Mikhel leading the way, the group walked out the back door and onto the covered deck. The rain was still coming down in sheets. Trey shivered. He hated getting his fur wet, but not even the rain was enough to dissuade him from making this run. The moon was too high, too strong. His wolf needed the release.

Taylor pushed open the huge golf umbrella she'd brought. Trey smiled as Zach took it from her hand and held it for her, covering her and Mikhel. She snuggled close to Mikhel, giving Zach space to slip under the shield as well. They were three bodies used to being close to one another.

When Trey had been contemplating joining Mikhel's pack, Mikhel had explained the relationship between the three of them. It was a condition of joining the pack that he be willing to accept the three-way mating. It didn't bother Trey, except for a little spark of jealousy now and then.

He stepped off the porch and felt the warm summer rain splash down. If Rebecca hadn't been upstairs, he was sure they would have used the house as their base, leaving their clothes there and returning to the dry building when they were done. But with the arrival of the human, they were going to use a small shelter that stood just to the east, a short distance inside the forest. Not as comfortable, but safer for everyone. Mikhel and Zach owned most of the land that surrounded the lake which gave them a safe place to run on nights like this.

"That little bitch has a fine rack on her." Marcus' low comment accompanied the distinct leer in his voice.

Maybe it was the fact that Trey had just had his lips on hers and had had the opportunity to caress her breasts and knew just how fine they were that made him so irritated by Marcus' remark.

Or it could be that Marcus just irritated him.

"She's a friend of the Luna's. I'd be careful how loud you say that."

Marcus scoffed. "She's not *my* Luna."

And not likely to be, if Trey had a voice in who joined their pack.

The little group arrived at the shelter. The males slipped inside and began to strip. Trey kept his clothes on, guarding the others as they made the transition—the only time a werewolf was truly vulnerable.

Clothes were dropped—some neatly, some in piles—and bodies began to change. Mikhel wasn't the largest of the group but it was obvious in wolf form that he was the strongest. Zach turned into a sleek gray animal. Trey had a feeling Zach was a nasty fighter—small, but vicious if he needed to be. When the twins changed, the difference between them was obvious. One was black, the other gray.

Trey watched as each man took on his second form. Within moments, the small space was filled with seven wolves, Trey—and Taylor. Mikhel opened his mouth and gently bit down on her wrist, tugging her close. She laughed and petted the animal. With that greeting, the wolf tipped his head back and howled. The others followed suit. Trey felt the sound rise inside him as well but he brutally grabbed the wolf's desire to run and reined it in. Soon, he promised the animal. *Soon.*

As the howl disappeared into the night, Mikhel took off down the path, Zach behind him. The others followed and disappeared in the darkness.

Trey knew the routine. The group would run for several hours, letting their wolves play in their natural form with others of their kind. Trey envied them this run but knew he couldn't leave. Not with their base an open shelter. If they'd been at the house, he would have stripped off his clothes and run with his Alpha.

"You can join them," Taylor said, almost as if she'd heard his thoughts. "I'll be fine just waiting here."

Though she couldn't turn into a wolf herself, she still liked to come on the runs. Mikhel and Zach would run for a while with the other wolves then they'd break off and return, playing with Taylor. What went on when the three of them disappeared into the forest, Trey didn't know, but they always returned looking tired and extremely satisfied.

But until Mikhel and Zach returned, Trey would stay here.

"I'll just wait until the Alpha or the Beta comes for you."

Taylor laughed. "What do you think is going to happen?"

Trey shrugged. "Nothing." It was true. With the cabin so isolated and well concealed, it was rare that they had campers or hikers come through. And certainly not on a night like this. All sane people were snuggled up in their beds, preferably with a hot body beside them, beneath them. *Rebecca*. She'd be the perfect rainy night bedmate—sexy and sensual.

The thought made his cock harden and he groaned softly, trying to keep the sound hidden from Taylor. She was the type to ask about it and he didn't want to lie to his Luna. Nor did he want to tell her he was having dreams about fucking her best friend.

"See? Go, run. I can see you want to."

Trey shook his head, not wanting to get into a full debate with his Luna. In Pack hierarchy, he was the Guardian. Rank-wise, that put him just below the Beta. Of course, their pack was so small, Trey had no one below him.

"Do you know what Mikhel told me was my primary duty when I joined the pack?"

"Pack secrecy?"

Again Trey shook his head. "Your safety. That, above all else."

He could see he'd surprised her, maybe even worried her a bit, so he smiled to ease the tension. "Then of course, Mikhel had a whole list of other things I have to do."

She laughed as he'd hoped she would. "That's Mikhel. He likes things organized."

Trey nodded. That suited him fine. He liked a little regimentation in his life as well. Kept things from getting too wild. He'd had enough of that growing up. From the outside, the little pack he'd joined would never be called normal, but Trey was pleased with his choice. Mikhel and Taylor seemed to have a solid relationship. It involved a lot of sex—that part was kind of hard to miss—but there was something more. They actually seemed to like each other, spent time together that didn't involve being naked. And Zach seemed to be a calming influence on both of them.

Trey didn't understand it, but it worked for them.

"I hope Rebecca staying here is okay."

The comment startled him. "Of course, Luna, she's your friend."

Taylor laughed. "No, not that. I know the last time she was here, she kind of tormented you. A bit." She winced like she was caught between loyalty to her friend and apologizing. "She just likes to tease."

"I'm sure she does."

"And I think you confuse her."

"Me?" Trey told himself not to be intrigued by this conversation. He was not interested in pursuing a relationship with Rebecca. Or not one that included more than a few nights of fucking.

"Yes. Usually men, if they don't fall all over her, at least respond to her. She's just got this power to attract them. But you seem immune to it."

"So that makes her want to catch my attention even more?" Great. He'd become some kind of trophy to a human man-eater.

"No, that's not it. I think she just finds you interesting. But if she gets on your nerves, I can talk to her. I don't know if it will help. Rebecca's pretty stubborn about what she does."

Trey smiled. Taylor was trying to protect him. It was really kind of sweet. "No worries. She and I understand each other."

At least he hoped they did. After that scene in the bedroom, he might have just confused things.

They talked softly as the rain pounded down. Trey kept watch and felt the time pass. In the distance he heard barks and wolf howls, animal sounds that called to his soul, that begged him to join them, but he had a duty first and he could wait, would wait, until his Alpha returned.

The soft padding of paws across wet ground drew Trey's attention and he straightened, putting himself on alert, making sure he knew where Taylor stood in relation to the approaching wolf. True, it was probably a friend, but it paid to be cautious.

Two wolves ran down the path and Trey recognized them as Mikhel and Zach. Mikhel ran into the covered enclosure, his fur drenched, and sniffed around Taylor as if to assure himself that she was unharmed. Then he turned to Trey. Mikhel reared up on his back legs and planted his paws on Trey's chest, marking his shirt with two muddy paw prints. The wolf licked Trey's neck and growled his thanks.

Trey laughed and pushed the animal down.

"You're welcome, Alpha. And you're filthy." The wolf danced around, visually laughing. There was such joy in being in the animal form and wolves liked to play.

Knowing he was free to make his own change, that Mikhel and Zach would stay with Taylor, Trey stripped off his shirt and folded it. He reached for his jeans and remembered that Taylor was nearby. He turned away, giving her his back.

"No need to be shy," Taylor laughed. "I don't mind."

Trey smiled over his shoulder but didn't turn around. Modesty wasn't one of his virtues but neither was he going parade himself naked in front of his Luna, particularly not with his Alpha nearby. He stripped off his jeans and put them with his shirt.

The moon was high and the power flowed through his body. With a sigh, he released the wolf inside him and let the animal take control.

His bones stretched and cracked, changing, his muscles adjusting to the new form. His face extended forward and he felt his teeth break from his jaw. The world changed to black and white and the scent of the ground filled his head. He put his nose to the soil and breathed in, letting it consume him. His wolf howled its pleasure.

A friendly nip on his ear sent him forward. He played for a moment with Mikhel and Zach and with a farewell growl, took off, heading down the path.

All thoughts except the basic instincts of the animal disappeared.

* * * * *

Rebecca scraped her drying hair back away from her face. The shower had warmed her up. No, actually the little necking session with Trey had warmed her up. She'd been burning by the time he'd walked away.

She wandered through the living room, watching the storm rage. The lightning seemed to have passed and all that was left was rain. She stared into the darkness, searching for answers.

What was she going to do? Take the chance and leave her door unlocked? Had Trey even been serious? The possibility of fucking him renewed the delicious little tingles in her pussy and she had to walk to distract herself.

He'd seemed to be warning her. But did she want to be scared off? With a few caresses and some wicked kisses, she'd come. It boggled the mind to think what the man could do if he put his mind to it...if he had a proper bed and time. Not that up against the wall hadn't been yummy.

The memories seized her body and she groaned. She wanted more. So much more. But Trey wasn't an easy man. He wouldn't be an easy lover.

Growling with frustration, she grabbed a flashlight off the counter and headed toward the back door. An umbrella sitting by the door made her smile. Perfect. She stepped onto the deck and flipped up the umbrella. She needed to move and the storm was a perfect match to the turmoil surging inside her.

The rain pounded on the top of her umbrella but the sound soothed her as she left the porch and walked across the backyard, heading toward the lake path. Water kicked up from the grass and splashed on her bare legs. The weak light of the full moon, barely visible through the rain and clouds, guided her along the trail. She had no option but to walk slowly. The dark and the rain made the path slippery but the thrill of being outside within the power of the storm was too much temptation to resist. The flashlight beam helped illuminate the large tree roots that crisscrossed the path.

She picked her way along the path until it opened up before her, revealing the lake. Her breath caught in her throat. It was amazing. Beautiful and terrifying in the same heartbeat. Waves rocked against the sandy beach and tiny white caps formed in the deeper water. The wind swirled across the surface of the water, sending cold air onto her skin.

Stepping closer, she took a breath and lowered the umbrella, letting the rain beat down on her. It was chilly and shocking but she laughed. She just gotten dry and here she was wet again.

She tilted her head back. The drops splashed onto her face, tickling her cheeks, landing on her tongue. God, this was so what she needed. A little freedom, the feel of the rain on her skin.

A low growl rumbled from behind her and Rebecca straightened. The sound was close. Taylor had mentioned that there were wolves in the area but she'd said they never came near humans.

Moving slowly, so as not to startle whatever was behind her, Rebecca started to turn. She looked over her shoulder, aware of a large, bulky figure standing inches from her back. Before she could identify the person, an open hand slammed into her cheek, knocking her almost to her knees. Her cry rang loud in her own head. Strong arms wrapped around her waist and jerked her back against a male body. A bare hard cock pressed against her backside. The naked body and the inherent threat shocked her into action. She twisted, fighting the painful hold, kicking behind her, her heels connecting with the man's shin. He grunted but didn't release her.

"Feisty bitch, aren't you? You even smell like him. He wants you. Bad. Won't he be sad to know you belong to me."

Pain lanced her shoulder as if he'd stabbed her with a dozen sharp knives. Fire poured through her veins. The rain smothered her scream and she knew no one would hear her. Spots formed in front of her eyes as she fought for breath. He only squeezed harder, pressing his body against hers, one hand tearing at her blouse. The material ripped and hung from her shoulders.

Her attacker released her, shoving her forward. She hit the ground hard, her cheek smashing into the sand as oxygen flooded her lungs. The brief respite gave her mind time to work. She glanced over her shoulder, but couldn't see her attacker clearly, only that he was huge.

Laughter followed her to the ground. "Poor boy's going to be so disappointed he didn't get to have you first." She latched onto the words, the sounds, locking them into her memory. The threats were strangely muffled, as though his mouth was full of rocks. "I'm going to fuck you and every part of you will belong to me." The vicious voice strengthened her resolve. She wasn't going down without a fight.

She curled her fingers into the sand and waited, fighting the pain in her shoulder and throbbing in her cheek. The man drew close, sinking to his knees. She waited until he was almost to the ground and kicked, both feet, right at his head. She felt one connect with something solid—his skull—and the other with softer tissue. The gurgling sound made her think she'd hit his throat but she didn't take time to check. She was on her feet and running, heading for the lake, water splashing across her legs.

Cold invaded her core as she ran but she didn't let herself stop. She couldn't. Whoever, whatever that thing was, he was behind her. Coming after her.

Chapter Three

ʂ

Deacon pushed back the hood of his slicker and peered through the driving rain. There was little hope of seeing the wolves tonight. Even wolves would have better sense than to be out in weather like this. At least he liked to think they did.

But still, he wasn't going to miss a chance to see them. A few hours ago, he'd heard their howls and had set off to find them. They were elusive creatures but fascinating. If they were out in the rain, it would be interesting to see how they dealt with it. Where they went to get warm and dry. Or if that even mattered to these animals. They weren't typical wolves, he'd already decided that. His best guess was that they'd been raised in captivity before some well-meaning person had released them to the wild. Whether they would be able to survive was another question.

He'd only seen them a few times but once they'd been very close to a woman. She hadn't been frightened, had actually seemed to be talking to them. He shook his head at the memory. What was she thinking? Even if they'd been raised in captivity, there was still something of the wild animal in them. And wild animals deserved respect and distance.

His feet sloshing through the high water at the edge of the lake, Deacon continued his hike back toward his cabin. It was late and he was wet. Not even the rubber rain suit could keep him completely dry.

The bright light illuminating the front porch of his cabin made him sigh. It would be good to get back inside, dry off and watch the rain from the other side of the window. He swung his flashlight beam back and forth across his path.

A shock of white stalled him. It took a moment for his mind to process what he was seeing. It was a body. He trained the light and hurried over. Specifically, it was a woman. Her long hair was floating in the lake water, her face pressed into the sand. A nasty bruise marked her jaw and, damn, there was blood across her cheek and along her shoulder.

Deacon's mind cleared and his training kicked in. He felt for a pulse. Strong and steady. He ran his hands down her body, doing a quick check to see if there were any obvious injuries. He didn't like to move her, but he couldn't leave her lying in the water. Even in midsummer the lake water was cold, and she'd get hypothermia.

Placing his hand at her back, he slowly rolled her over. The woman groaned as he moved her but her eyes remained shut. Where the hell had she come from? He looked up to see if anyone else was around but they were alone. In the middle of nowhere. A single light flickered from the far side of the lake. Was it possible she lived over there? He hadn't met his neighbors yet. He'd chosen the cabin for its solitude.

Not that it mattered now. His cabin was much closer and he had to get her warm and dry and look at her wound. He knelt and scooped her up in his arms, amazed at how light she was. Or maybe it was the adrenaline running through his veins. Murmuring what he hoped were comforting sounds, he carried her through the rain, up the two stairs that led to his front door and inside, kicking the door shut behind him.

Without stopping he headed straight for the bedroom. Balancing her in one hand, he stripped back the comforter and laid her on the sheets, her skin pale against the dark fabric.

She moaned again and her head rolled to the side as if she was fighting some internal battle. The movement bared her neck and he saw the wound clearly—four distinct puncture marks—like an animal bite, only it looked too crisp, too clean. Blood leaked from the wounds but they were starting to close.

Deacon took a moment to strip off his rain slicker and grabbed his handy-pack from the living room. Years ago he'd gotten into the habit of carrying a small kit with him whenever he traveled, just a few supplies. He didn't know if it would be enough. As he hurried back into the bedroom, he grabbed his cell phone. The cabin didn't have a landline. He looked at the tiny phone and sighed. No service. Service was sketchy on the best of days, but with this storm, there was little chance he'd get a call out. He tossed it aside.

He'd examine her first. If she was hurt badly, he'd have to attempt the roads and hope the bridge three miles away wasn't washed out. The realtor had warned him that heavy rains frequently closed the bridge. At the time he hadn't cared. If he was cut off from civilization for a few days, all the better. But now, he was regretting that decision.

He opened his bag and pulled out the stethoscope. Her heartbeat was steady and strong and her lungs didn't sound clogged. If she'd gone into the water, it wasn't long.

He stopped and looked at her. A bruise was forming on her cheek—it looked like a handprint. Her blouse was open and scratches marked her stomach and between her breasts. Holy hell. She'd been attacked. But by who or what he couldn't tell. He quickly scanned her body and didn't see any other marks except for the wound at her neck.

He pushed her head to the side and looked at it. It was an animal bite. If he didn't know better, he would say it was a wolf bite, but wolves rarely attacked humans. And even if a wolf did attack, he would have gone for the thigh or belly. Something within reach. How the hell would the animal have gotten high enough to bite her shoulder?

Deacon pushed his confusion aside and focused on the wound. Animal bites were well within his purview. He cleaned the wound and covered it with a bandage. The bleeding had almost stopped but she'd probably end up with a scar.

The cold and wet was his next problem. Taking a deep breath, he began to strip the soaked clothing from her body. He pulled her shirt down and off, dropping it beside the bed.

The white shorts followed. Her shoes, which he assumed had once been white, were covered in mud. He yanked them off as well. Leaving her dressed in bright pink panties and bra.

The low-cut bra pushed her breasts up and together. His fingers twitched as he looked at her, needing to reach between those luscious mounds and undo the front clasp. His cock twitched in his pants and he cursed. What was he thinking? She was hurt, wounded and freezing, and he was getting a hard-on staring at her. Don't be an ass, he mentally slapped himself. *You're a professional.*

But in his practice, he definitely didn't see bodies like hers.

That was no excuse. He really needed to get her completely naked and dry her off. Girding himself to ignore any temptation, he reached down, needing both hands to pop the clasp. The sides of her bra separated, pulled apart by the weight of her very fine breasts. Her nipples were tight and hard, no doubt from the cold but, damn, they were inviting. Heavy, deep breaths filled the room and Deacon realized the sound was coming from him.

Great. Lusting after an unconscious woman. Can you sink much lower?

Unfortunately, he knew he could. Because he still had to pull off her panties. He rolled her over and wiggled the bra straps down her arms and off. Almost there.

She sagged back onto the mattress when he finished manipulating her body, naked from the waist up. Just a tiny scrap of pink.

Damn it, just get on with it, he commanded his reluctant body. Only it wasn't his body that was reluctant. It was his mind. The temptation was too great. Not that he was going to hurt her or touch her or do anything physical to her. But staring at her naked, unconscious body was invasive enough. And he needed to keep himself in check.

Grabbing every professional ethic he had like a shield, he hooked his fingers into the waistband of her underwear and pulled, sliding it down, revealing her pussy. Neatly trimmed light auburn hair hid her sex from his sight. As he tugged, her legs moved, one knee bending, opening her thighs just a hint. Deacon jerked his gaze upward. Her eyes were open, staring at him.

"I'm sorry. I was just trying to get you naked." He gulped. "I mean, get your clothes off you. Your wet clothes. So you could warm up."

Her only reply was to groan and shift on the bed. "Cold," she muttered, her eyes dropping closed.

"Yes, I know. I'll get you warmed up." The sudden threat that she might wake up slapped the lecherous tendencies out of his system. He stripped down the panties and threw them on the rest of the pile. He had a washing machine so as soon as she was settled, he'd throw her clothes in. Give her something to wear once she woke.

He grabbed a towel out of the bathroom and wiped down her skin, struggling to keep his actions mechanical. After drying her off as best he could, he piled on the blankets and cranked up the thermostat. Being July, the night was relatively warm but the rain added a touch of coolness to the air. And her being in the water wouldn't help.

He paced the side of the bed, considering an attempt to drive her to the hospital. She didn't appear to have any other wounds, just the animal bite. He touched her forehead. She didn't feel warm. Or cold. He stepped back and stared. She was pretty and had a delectable body. As much as he tried to ignore it, his cock was responding. He placed his hands on his hips and released a disgusted sigh. It had obviously been too long since he'd seen a naked woman if an unconscious one was causing this kind of reaction.

* * * * *

The forest passed by her, the sights and scents a blur as she ran, the ground inches beneath her nose. She wanted to stop and savor the experience but too soon she felt her body changing, expanding.

The black and white world turned to color and she saw herself standing in the moonlight, the lake shimmering behind her.

Where's the rain? There should be rain. But even as she recognized the wrongness of the vision, the thought drifted from her mind. *Wind brushed against her skin, cooling it, teasing it. Moonlight painted her naked flesh, so bright it became a physical caress.*

Her hyper-senses went on alert and the weight of someone's stare pressed against her back. She turned, slowly, searching for the gaze that stroked her body. He was near. She knew it was male and that he'd come for her. She walked deeper into the forest. He waited for her and she needed him, her body craved him.

The moonlight guided her forward, leading her to a small clearing. Two men waited, their faces blurred, their bodies bare and hard. Her pussy clenched and she felt the lightest brush against her clit. Yes, she would have them both.

The world shifted. She lay on her back, the damp grass teasing her hips, her lovers over her. Four hot hands skimmed across her flesh. Two mouths, licking and sucking her breasts. She arched her back, moving into the caresses, loving each touch and wanting more.

"Yes," she moaned as one of her lovers licked between her thighs, tightening her clit with one delicate swipe of his tongue. Her hands caressed the hard bodies that touched hers, absorbing their heat, needing them inside her. As if they heard her plea, a cock filled her, hard and thick, sliding deep until she couldn't take any more. The other lover didn't leave her. He continued to kiss her breasts, biting gently on her nipples until she thought she would scream with the painful pleasure. She opened her mouth and the tip of his cock was there, teasing her lips. A fierce hunger filled her and she sucked the thick shaft between her lips. Yes. More. She wanted more.

The cock in her pussy began to move, slow and forceful, each penetration and retreat sliding across her clit, moving perfectly. A howl filled her head as they both screamed toward climax. She came seconds before he released inside her, his cum filling her, sending her pussy into another jolting orgasm.

Rebecca came awake as the violent climax rocked her body.

Gasping and fighting the seductive lethargy that followed, she forced her eyes open, instantly aware that she was in a strange place. Heavy blankets crushed her into the soft mattress, practically strangling her with their weight. Pushing back the thick layer, she groaned. The muscles in her shoulder ached as she moved. She dragged in a much needed breath and realized one other fact. She was naked.

In a strange bed and naked.

"Okay. What's going on?" She briefly considered that she'd taken Trey up on his offer of wild sex, but if that was the case, why didn't she remember any of it? No way. If she was going to have sex with Trey, she wanted to remember it.

Groaning, recognizing that it was much more than her shoulder that ached, she sat up, swinging her legs over the side of the bed.

The door popped open and a strange man walked in.

"Aii!" She screamed and moved at the same time, grabbing the blankets she'd just removed and covering her body. The stranger stopped in his tracks.

"You're awake."

"Yes. Who the hell are you?"

"I'm Deacon Crowley."

Didn't tell her anything. Wait. She'd heard the name before. Trey had said something. This was the neighbor. A doctor of some kind, he'd said.

"I found you at the edge of the lake. You'd been attacked or hurt. Something."

Following the line of his gaze, she touched her fingers to the base of her neck and felt the thick bandage. And winced at the tenderness beneath. She ran her fingertips across the material.

"It looks like an animal bite."

"Animal?" Rebecca tried to think back, flipping through her evening to find when her memory stopped. She'd gone walking in the rain and had a vague recollection of someone's voice—then pain and nothing.

"Yes." He nodded, but didn't move any closer. She could tell he was trying to give her space, make her feel safe. "How are you feeling?"

Rebecca did a mental scan of her body. Her muscles were sore and she could feel the strain in her neck, annoying but nothing particularly painful. But something was different. It was as if there was a silence in her mind, a distance between her and the world. Weird, she thought with a shake of her head.

"I'm fine. I feel okay."

"What's your name?"

She smiled. "I'm Rebecca. Rebecca Rhodes. I'm staying with friends at the lake."

"I thought you might be."

"Where am I?"

"On the other side of the lake."

She nodded. "How did I end up all the way over here?"

"It's only a mile or so."

"Yeah, but how..." Her courage wavered and she clutched the blanket like a lifeline. "I don't know how I got here." She'd lost time. The memories were hazy and dark. Surely she should remember. Thunder interrupted her thoughts. "The storm is still going on."

"The emergency radio says we have another couple of hours."

She shivered, dark memories of cold and wet creeping up her spine. "I should go." She started to stand but realized her legs were wobbly and sank back down.

"You're welcome to stay for a bit. Until the rain lets up." She must have eyed him suspiciously because he shrugged. "Or I can loan you a raincoat and send you on your way."

"Uh—"

"We can call your friends and let them know you're okay and where you are. They're probably pretty worried." He offered her the cell phone.

"They weren't home when I left." Oops. Probably wasn't best to admit that. Just in case he *was* an axe murderer. "But I could leave them a message."

"That's a good idea. And maybe you'd like to take a shower? I did strip you." The edge of his mouth kicked up in a shy smile and his cheeks started to turn red. He was blushing. "I'll confess that right now. And I dried you off. But if you're still cold, you could take a shower. I'll fix something to eat and then you can decide." With that, he backed toward the door. If he was an axe murderer, he was going out of his way to make her comfortable. "Towels are in the cupboard behind the door."

"Where are my clothes?"

"Washing machine."

Wow, he does laundry too. She took a moment to really look at him. His dark hair was cut short, very crisp. From where she was seated, he looked a little taller than her but he wouldn't tower over her. His shoulders were broad and his arms looked strong beneath the long-sleeved shirt he wore. He looked comfortable and solid. Like a woman could lean on him, rely on him. He wasn't physically stunning like Trey but his face was interesting. As though he smiled a lot. Somehow that seemed comforting.

"I'll just let you clean up. Come out whenever you're ready." He waved vaguely toward the closet. "Rummage around. Find something to wear until your clothes are dry."

With that, he backed out of the room, leaving her alone. She took a moment to look around. There was nothing frightening or creepy about the place. Just like the man who lived here, it felt comfortable. After a few minutes, she tried standing again and found her legs steadier this time.

The tiny bathroom was as rustic and undecorated as the bedroom. Very utilitarian. Alone, she dropped the blankets, started the shower and stared into the mirror. A bruise decorated her right cheek. She wiggled her jaw as she fingered the mark. A twinge of pain but nothing major. She closed her eyes and searched her memory again. A bright burst of pain — a voice and a growl.

With a grunt of frustration, she pushed the sound away. It would come back. She looked at the rest of her body. Three scratches ran across her stomach but no other marks. Except for the bite. Gingerly she peeled back the edge of the bandage. Two puncture wounds pierced her skin, high on her shoulder. She twisted around and saw a matching pair on her back. The red wounds looked ugly — scabbing over already. *Damn, I wish I could remember how this happened.* Sighing, she replaced the bandage and climbed into the steaming shower, letting the hot water pour over her skin, careful to keep her bandage from getting wet.

As she washed her hair, heat pulsed from the wound on her shoulder and sank into her stomach, warming her from the inside, reminding her of the orgasm that had woken her. What a dream. She smiled. Sex with two men. It had to be Taylor's influence.

The water turned cool but Rebecca didn't feel it. With the heat flowing from her body, she was surprised she wasn't making the room steam up. She decided it was time to get out when her fingers wrinkled.

Stepping out of the shower, she grabbed a towel off the stack and brushed it down her arm. It was a very male kind of towel, worn and soft from years of use. The kind a woman would have thrown away or hidden in the garage for messy clean ups. Still, the texture brought out interesting tingles that radiated into her body and settled in her core. Sensations that made her think of Trey and his wickedly delicious mouth and the slow lick of his tongue. She groaned and felt her eyes droop closed. Hands and lips—sucking and stroking her nipples—her clit. The dream. One fucking her from behind while the other filled her mouth. Her mind filled in the faces and bodies of her dream lovers—Deacon and Trey. Heat shot through her pussy and she grabbed the counter to keep her knees from collapsing.

A couple of deep breaths and she was able to stand straight. She looked in the mirror. Her nipples were tight and hard, her skin pink, almost flushed. Unable to resist, needing to feel an actual touch, she thrummed one nipple with her thumb, gasping as the delicate stroke sent a shock into her pussy. Squeezing her thighs together only made the ache worse. Heavens, what was happening to her?

"Did you drown?" Deacon's voice called through the door, followed by a light rap of his knuckles on the wood.

"I'm fine. I'll be out in minute." *Once I get my hormones under control.*

He didn't speak again, but she could sense that he'd walked away. Ignoring the sensitivity of her skin, she dried off quickly and peeked out of the bathroom door. The bedroom was empty. Wrapping the tiny towel around her, though it didn't quite close at her breasts, she followed Deacon's instructions and dug through the small chest of drawers for clothes.

She came up with a long flannel shirt and a pair of sweats that had been cut off at the knees.

He was clearly a man without a woman. She'd have dumped this pair of shorts the minute she'd seen them.

But at least she wouldn't naked.

She rummaged around and found a comb and a new toothbrush. Everything in the bathroom was distinctly masculine. Clearly Deacon wasn't planning this as a love nest. Unless his lovers were male.

She chuckled at the thought. That would be a sad thing for females everywhere.

She scraped her fingers through her hair, pulling it back and fluffing it. Not that she was primping for Deacon. He was just a nice man.

With really strong arms and tight powerful quads. Thick hard muscles that would hold up to long hours of deep thrusts, making her come over and over again.

More heat flooded into her pussy and she whimpered. What was wrong with her? She wanted sex and she wanted it now.

Chapter Four

℘

Her host was standing in the corner of the cabin that was probably designated the kitchen. It wasn't much more than an alcove with a tile floor but it worked. He was stirring a pot, concentrating on it with such intense power that Rebecca knew he was giving her space. And that he'd probably been trying to keep busy so he didn't look as if he was waiting for her.

The whole idea was quite sweet.

"Thanks for the shower," she said.

He looked up, his eyes widening when he saw her clothes.

"Is this okay?" she asked, holding up the end of the shirt.

"It's fine. I'm glad you found something."

She was glad the shirt was long enough to cover her ass because it was obvious that Deacon's butt was smaller than hers. The stretchy material of the sweatpants was molded to her every curve.

"Did you have a phone?"

"Yeah." He lifted his chin toward the small living room. She followed the direction and saw a cell phone sitting on the reading table. "Help yourself. Service comes and goes but it was there a minute ago."

With the rain pounding outside, and feeling relatively safe inside, Rebecca was in no rush to trudge to the other side of the lake. She dialed Taylor's cabin and waited as the machine picked up. Wandering to the far side of the cabin, she left a message saying where she was and that she was okay.

She closed the phone and walked back across the room.

"Would you like some breakfast?"

She looked at the clock. It was almost two in morning and Deacon looked tired. He'd no doubt been watching over her for most of the night. She'd left Taylor's place sometime around nine to walk to the lake. It was the hours in between that she couldn't quite remember. She walked her mind through the night—the lake, a voice and an animal's growl.

"Are there any wild animals around here?" she blurted out as Deacon moved to the refrigerator.

"Some. There are some wolves who roam the area."

Rebecca nodded, remembering that Taylor has spoken about the animals. "I forgot about the wolf pack."

Deacon began to scramble eggs, then stopped as if he suddenly realized he was cooking for someone else. "Is scrambled okay?"

"It's fine."

He nodded and went back to what he was doing. "I wouldn't exactly call them a pack. It's a small group. I've only ever seen four or five together." He shrugged. "They might just be passing through. I haven't been able to get close enough to distinguish any markings."

"You sound like a researcher."

He smiled. "Just a hobby. The concept of the wolf pack is interesting. They have a certain structure, organization. It's fascinating how they form an integrated group, but still live as individuals."

"You do know a lot about wolf packs."

He shrugged and dropped slices of bread into the toaster. "As I said, it's kind of a hobby." Rebecca watched as he scrambled eggs and made toast to go with it, bringing the light meal to the table before joining her. He didn't say much but she felt surprisingly comfortable around him.

That strange hollow feeling inside her seemed drawn to him. She ate the eggs and toast, enjoying the flavor, but feeling something was missing. She wanted more. She looked across the table at Deacon. He glanced up, meeting her gaze. A shot of warmth surged into her chest. The heat sank into her core, settling in her sex before drifting into her limbs, making her fingertips tingle and her toes curl. She licked her lips, wanting more than the taste of eggs on her tongue.

She wanted to Deacon. The revelation came to her as a whisper and built inside her. She wanted her mouth on his skin, his cock between her lips and then between her legs. Without realizing that she'd moved, she leaned forward, easing her pussy against the hard vinyl chair. The slow movement was a distant caress to her clit. Not enough. She forced her gaze back down to her plate.

"Uh, so what hospital are you with? Or do you have your own practice?"

"Hospital?"

"I assumed you were a doctor. Stethoscope and all." She hitched her thumb toward the open bag.

"Oh, I am. I have a practice I share with three other doctors."

"And I heard one of my friends say you'd just bought this place?" She left her voice hanging, hoping he would fill in the empty space. He did, talking about his desire for a retreat. A quiet place on the weekends. Heat continued to boil in her body until she had to undo the top button of the blouse, desperate for cool air across her skin.

She tried to focus on what Deacon but her mind kept leading her astray. Thoughts much more basic kept filling her head — images of her kneeling, with Deacon pounding into her pussy from behind. Another cock in her mouth, a slow slide, so different from the hard fuck. God, she needed that. Needed to be fucked. She squished her lips together to crush the groan that threatened.

She dragged her hair back away from her face, letting the long strands slip through her fingers. Even that soft caress was savored and magnified by the hunger flowing through her body. She watched him, sitting across from her, just out of reach.

Desperate for some kind of relief, she turned in her chair, separating her knees and shifting until she straddled the corner. Keeping watch out of the corner of her eye to make sure Deacon didn't notice, she pushed her hips back, curving her spine and rolling her pussy against the vinyl chair. The subtle movement teased her clit and it was all she could do to suppress the groan. Keeping her motions slow, she sank back and repeated the massage to her clit. She grabbed the bottom of her shirt and ground it between her fingers, crushing the fabric and using it as an anchor to keep from reaching for her breasts. They ached. Her whole body ached. She needed to come.

"Rebecca?"

Deacon's concerned call snapped her attention back to the table and she realized she must have made a noise.

"Are you all right?"

She nodded, not trusting herself to speak. Not knowing what words would flow out of her mouth if she gave herself free rein. She might demand he fuck her.

The thought should have shocked her but she couldn't shake the desire.

She was just so hot. She tugged on the collar of the shirt, wanting to strip off the fabric and stand naked in a breeze. Deacon's eyes dipped down and she knew she was flashing him a bit of cleavage. Her breasts normally attracted a fair amount of male attention. It usually caused her more irritation than pleasure, but the sight of Deacon's gaze heating up made her nipples tighten. The light brush of flannel teased the peaks even more. God, she had to be sweating by now.

"You sure?" he asked. "You're looking a little flushed."

She nodded. "I'm just a little warm."

"You might have a fever." He stood up and came around to her side of the table, placing his hand on her forehead. It was all she could do not to turn her head and lick his wrist. His warm masculine scent wafted toward her, making her stomach rumble—with a completely different kind of hunger. "You don't feel hot," Deacon said.

That's because he isn't on the inside my body, she decided. *If he were inside me, he'd feel the heat.*

"It doesn't feel like a fever." She wondered if Deacon noticed how breathless she sounded. Wondered if he could hear the sex in her voice. And would he even care. "I just feel like I'm wearing too many clothes." She tugged on the shirt again, needing the air on her skin. God, she needed to strip.

He took a step back, as if he was intent on giving her space—but there was a fire in his eyes as he watched her that made her insides melt. He was going out of his way to be a gentleman and she couldn't take advantage of him. No matter how much her body wanted it.

Her gaze dipped to his neck. It was almost as if she could hear his heart pumping. She licked her lips, wanting to taste him, sink her teeth into his skin and mark him.

No. This was wrong. Obviously the possibility of sex with Trey earlier lingered and the attack was causing her mind to get confused. Overwhelmed. She was much too practical, too logical for this. The sexual sensations were just because she was in a strange place and looking for comfort. That had to be it. She pushed back the chair.

Deacon's hand curled around her forearm to help her stand. Heat spread from the impersonal touch, flowing up her arm, pulling her already tight nipples to painful peaks. The sudden shock made her want to whimper.

She pulled her arm out of his grasp, needing to get away from him before she did something really stupid, like rub her breasts against his chest.

"Maybe I should lie down." That sounded good. It sounded better with Deacon lying on top of her.

"That's a good idea."

Yes, it was. Deacon, on top of her, inside her, thrusting deep and hard.

She turned and started for the bedroom, stopping after two steps. "Or I could just go back across the lake." Maybe that was the answer. Getting away from Deacon. "I'm throwing you out of your bed by staying here."

"It's no problem. I'll crash in front of the fireplace." Lightning crackled outside the window. "And I think we're in the height of the storm. Now might not be the best time to go." He nodded toward the bedroom door. "You just try to rest, and if you need anything or this heat doesn't pass, let me know. I'll check on you in a bit."

Her body was a confused conglomerate of relief and desire — wanting him but knowing she shouldn't have him. He was a complete stranger. He could be dangerous. Only she didn't feel threatened. She felt sexual, her body strong, powerful.

She offered a weak smile and retreated into the bedroom, immediately stripping off the sweatpants. Rebecca went to the window and opened it, needing some relief. It was such a strange heat — not a hot flash but warmth welling inside her. Warmth that needed pressure and contact to ease it.

She leaned her head against the window frame and stared out into the night. Random bursts of lightning illuminated the trees surrounding the cabin, then disappeared, leaving the world in darkness. The hunger continued to expand inside her as she watched the night. Her body responded to the storm, moving with the heartbeat of the rain, slow swings of her hips, her hand slipping across her stomach, teasing the very top of her mound. Fearing the cataclysmic reaction if she touched her clit, she retreated, moving up to cup her breast. The nipple pressed hard against her hand, craving some attention. She tightened her grip, creating a gentle, almost painful pinch to her nipple. The low sound of her groan reverberated against the window.

What is wrong with me?

With a moan, she spun away and went to the bed, stripping back the blankets and lying down on the night-cooled sheets. Her sigh echoed through the room and returned to her as a breath across her skin. She stared up at the ceiling, listening to her body, analyzing every response, every need that surged through her veins. She needed something. Needed something inside her.

Biting her lip, using the delicate pain to keep her focused, she pulled up the hem of her shirt, spread her legs and shoved her finger into her pussy. There was nothing sexual about the caress. It was mechanical, practical. She needed relief. The penetration was a subtle shock to her wet pussy. The tight passage closed around her finger. Her back arched and she tried to reach deeper. This was no time for a slow, exploring masturbation session. She needed to come. Now.

She pumped her finger in and out, trying to find the touch. All she needed was one orgasm and the desperation would pass. She was sure of it. Heat poured off her skin and she tore at the shirt, opening the buttons, leaving her breasts bare. With her free hand, she squeezed and pinched her breasts, trying to ease the ache in her nipples. God, it wasn't enough. The finger fucking her pussy only made it worse.

Deacon. She needed Deacon. Her body strained, as if responding to the mental cry.

No. She wasn't going to demand sex from a stranger just because her body had gone haywire. She took a shallow breath and concentrated. She could do this. She'd made herself come before. She could do it now.

Deacon. She dropped her head back onto the pillows and changed tactics, picturing him above her. It wasn't a hard fantasy to create. His warm brown eyes staring down at her as he pumped in and out, slow and steady, solid.

A groan rolled from deep inside her chest and she pressed deeper, slow but with power, brushing her thumb across her clit as she worked her finger in and out. It was good, so good — but still not enough.

Frustration built as her mind battled the desperate need of her body. She ground her teeth together. She was trying too hard. She knew this. Passages from sexual self-help books clogged her brain—that masturbation should be about pleasure and exploration, not a hard drive to come. Tears formed at the back of her eyes. She needed this. She needed to come.

But her own touch wasn't working. She squished her lips together to crush the snarl that threatened. She would do this, she would...

Movement teased the edge of her vision. Her body froze, instincts she didn't know she possessed preparing her to flee or face this new intrusion. With only a shift of her eyes, she glanced toward the door. There was a gap between the frame and the door and she realized she hadn't closed it fully.

A shadow filled the thin space. Deacon. He was there, watching.

Heat flooded her pussy and the rush of moisture coated her hand. Groaning, she met the new liquid with a push of her fingers, sinking two into her pussy, savoring the thicker penetration. Her attention split between the steady thrust of her fingers and the man watching her.

It was strange, but she could sense his hesitation. As if he wanted to watch, but knew he shouldn't. Such a gentleman, she thought with a smug smile—but not so much that he was willing to walk away.

Her watcher made her body tingle. And she performed for him, letting the soft sounds she usually kept contained free. Sweat made the skin between her breasts slick. She flattened her palm and rubbed a slow circle around her tight nipple, groaning as the caress slid into her cunt. She spread her legs wider, knowing he could see her pussy from the doorway, opening herself and pumping her hips up, meeting the slow downward thrust of her fingers.

Yes, that's it. She was close. And she wanted Deacon to see her come. Glancing up, she saw he was still watching, as if the sight made him unable to move.

Faster and deeper, throwing her hips up again and again, she pushed her fingers deep inside her. With her other hand, she rubbed her mound, tight fast circles against her clit. She stared at the door, his tension and hunger vibrating through the barrier. Perfect.

A delicious sparkle began in her sex and she rubbed harder, pushed a little deeper, wanting more. Her cry shattered the silence as the tight pressure in her pussy released. Moisture covered her fingers and the delicious lethargy seeped into her limbs. A low groan escaped her lips as she dropped back onto the bed, her hand lingering between her legs, drenched in her pussy juices.

* * * * *

Deacon stepped away from the door, trying to calm his pounding heart. What was the matter with him? He'd heard noises coming from the bedroom, sounds of distress, and had thought to check on her. But the house was old and the doors didn't close well. He'd glanced inside, just to make sure she was okay, and had seen her.

Then he couldn't make himself walk away. No matter how he tried, his body wouldn't respond to the command. The sight of her, those slim fingers dipping into her wet, pink cunt had been too much for him to resist.

He reached down and adjusted his cock, giving his erection one quick stroke and considered jacking off. He certainly had a fantasy hot enough to make him come. What he really needed was a cold shower, but that meant going into the bedroom, or standing out in the rain. He wasn't going to do the first because he wasn't sure if he'd make it past her sleeping body. And he wasn't going to do the second because he didn't feel like getting soaked.

Not that a cold shower would help. The image of Rebecca, her lush body spread out on his bed, would linger in his mind.

Forcing his feet to move, hoping to work off some of the extra energy, he cleared the dishes they'd used for their meal and spread out his sleeping bag in front of the fireplace. He considered building a fire but it was warm outside. Not even the rainstorm could cool it down completely.

Besides, his body was burning up. He stripped off his shirt but left on the shorts. If he had to get up and check on Rebecca in the middle of the night, he didn't want to be naked. Plus, the constriction would help keep his cock in check. He hoped.

He threw a light blanket over his lower body and lay back, staring up at the ceiling.

Rebecca, moaning softly, her fingers shunting in and out of her pussy.

Deacon groaned. He'd always had voyeuristic tendencies, loved to watch women touch themselves, pleasure themselves. Loved to see slim fingers sliding into a pretty pink cunt.

His most recent lover hadn't understood his desire to watch. When he'd asked her to masturbate for him, she'd told him to rent a porn movie. Deacon had let it pass but knew then and there, the relationship wouldn't last.

Porn didn't do much for him. He liked to watch — then he wanted to touch.

He wanted to see a woman finger-fuck herself, making her pussy wet and slick and then he wanted to take over, pushing *his* fingers inside her, his tongue and finally his cock. Riding her slow and deep.

He draped his arm over his eyes, trying to block out the image of Rebecca in his head. It didn't work. She was still there. Still naked.

He sensed the movement before he heard it. Slowly he lowered his arm and saw her, standing at his feet. Her lips hung slightly open and the long loose curls of her red hair hung around her shoulders. She still wore his shirt. It was unbuttoned, revealing just the inside curves of her breasts — and creating a perfect frame for her pussy. Closely trimmed red hair covered her mound and even in the weak light he could see the moisture that still clung to her skin.

He forced himself to look up, into her eyes. "Rebecca?"

"I'm still so hot. I need you to cool me down."

Chapter Five

ഇ

He should protest. He knew he should, but as she stepped forward, stopping when she got to his hips and slowly lifting her leg over him until she was straddling his body, he couldn't make his mouth work. She didn't take off the shirt and somehow that made it even sexier, that her breasts were still hidden, still tempting him.

She slowly sank down, the pure sexual hunger in her body giving her a sensual power that squeezed Deacon's cock like a fist.

Wet heat brushed against his bare stomach as she spread her legs a little wider and pressed her pussy against his skin.

"I'm hot, Deacon," she said again.

He swallowed and his mind latched onto his training. "Maybe you have a fever. I should take your temperature."

She laughed and shook her head. "My mother could tell if I had a fever just by putting her hands on me." She grabbed his hands and pulled them to her body, placing his palms flat against her stomach, the tails of his shirt fluttering across the backs of his wrists. "Do I feel hot to you?"

"God, yes." He winced at the passionate response. "I mean—"

She laughed again and leaned forward. His hands slid around her back, forming to her hips and the upper curve of her ass. The slow steady press eased her pussy tighter against him until he could feel all the warmth and heat flowing out of her.

A crinkling sound chimed next to his ear and he glanced over. In her hand, she had clutched a condom, obviously collected from his stash under the bathroom sink. He'd put it there when he'd moved in on the off chance he might have the opportunity to bring a woman up here—the real estate agent who'd handled the sale had seemed interested—but he hadn't expected this.

Rebecca clearly did. If he was going to stop this—and some gentlemanly part of him told him that he should—he had to do it now.

"Listen, honey—" The endearment rolled off his tongue as she placed a kiss on his jaw.

"Hmm, I like that. Honey." She whispered a kiss across his lips, another on his cheek. "That's how I feel. All warm and melty. Like I want to just melt all over you."

An invisible band seemed clamped around his throat, making speech impossible. She ran her open mouth across his skin—not kissing him, more like she was learning him with her sensitive lips. Finally, she returned to his mouth, the whisper kisses gone. She placed her lips against his and pushed her tongue inside.

God, yes. Deacon closed his hands over her ass and pressed her down as she sank her hands into his hair and held him in place, ravaging his mouth with her hungry kiss. Some sane portion of his mind protested but her taste and power silenced it. She drew back, nipping his lower lip, leaving a gentle imprint of her teeth on his skin.

As if pleased that she'd marked him, she returned, commanding, demanding another kiss. And Deacon couldn't fight her desire. Or his own. He clamped one hand on her head and turned her, just a little, giving him deeper access as he seized control of the kiss, his tongue plunging in her mouth. She whimpered and he feared he might be frightening her but she made no move to draw back, only pressed closer, her breasts hot against his chest.

Long, delicious moments later, she dragged her mouth away, licking and kissing a short path to his ear.

She nipped at the lobe and whispered, "I saw you watching me."

His whole body froze. Fuck. He'd been mentally debating whether or not to tell her that he'd seen her. Now he had no choice.

"I'm sorry, I—"

"I liked it." She pushed herself up. Deacon let his hands fall to the sides, not wanting to hold her if she wanted to escape. "Did you like watching me?" She trailed the fingers of one hand down the center of her body, between her breasts, across the gentle curve of her stomach and to her pussy. "Did you like seeing me touch myself? My fingers moving in and out of my pussy?" He didn't answer. Couldn't. He watched as she dipped her hand between her legs, her fingers disappearing into the sexual shadow that tempted him.

She withdrew her hand and watched him, waiting until he looked up at her. Then she grabbed one of his hands and slowly pulled it to her, easing it between her thighs.

"Did you wish it was your fingers fucking me?"

"Yes." The response was ripped from him as she pressed him deeper, guiding him until he slipped into her opening.

He pushed forward, going deeper, sliding up into her cunt. She tipped her head back and moaned, letting her hand drop away. "Oh yes. You feel so much better than my own hand."

Her hips began a slow roll, moving forward and back, fucking her pussy onto his finger. She lifted up onto her knees, giving him more access, and herself more room to move. He pulled back only long enough to add a second finger and then drove both back into her body.

"That's it," he encouraged as she moved hard against him. He held her hip with his other hand. He watched her for a long time, wanting to see all of her. "Open your shirt."

Her eyelids fluttered and she stared down at him, her eyes clouded by sensation. But she peeled back the edges of the shirt, revealing her breasts. The smooth mounds were perfectly sized to fit his hands. The tight pink tips were hard and straining forward. Waiting for his mouth, his teeth.

"Good, honey. Now, touch them, squeeze those pretty tits."

A shiver ran through her body, into her pussy, gently contracting around his fingers. His chest tightened as he imagined what it would feel like to be buried in that sweet cunt when she came. He pushed his fingers up to meet her downward thrust, sinking deeper into her, drawing out a long sexy groan.

Breathless, she reached up and cupped her breasts in her hands, squeezing, following his orders.

"That's it, honey," he whispered, loving the sight of her fingers caressing her skin, the tight peak of her nipple — pink and hard — appearing as she slowly moved her hands in circles. He swiped his tongue across his lips, wanting that peak in his mouth, wanting to suck on her, swallow her. All thoughts of stopping disappeared. God, he needed to fuck her.

She pumped up and down, riding his fingers hard until he could feel her body was close to coming.

"No." She placed her hand on his and slowly eased his fingers from inside her. "I'm about to come."

"Good."

She laughed and shook her head, looking down at him with eyes that almost looked as if they were glowing. She pulled his hand up, the scent and sight of her pussy juices coating his skin, drawing it to her mouth. Her tongue flicked out, the very tip slipping across his skin. Then she placed his fingers on her chest and dragged them down the center of her body, leaving a trail that he wanted to taste, wanted to follow with his tongue.

"I want to come," she whispered as she lifted her hips. "When you're inside me." She backed up until her knees were outside his. She dropped her head to his chest and pressed light kisses across his skin, a damp little lick on his nipples. He grabbed the sleeping bag beneath his hips, fighting the urge to grab her.

His mind was spinning. Fuck, she hadn't even touched his cock and he was on the verge of coming.

She worked her way down his body, her lips branding his flesh as she tasted him. Her hair teased his skin and he scraped his fingers through the soft strands, letting that little caress slide into his body as she kissed the space right above his shorts.

She lifted her head and stared at him with those wild glowing eyes. Something strange must have been happening to the light because her eyes almost looked red—like an animal in the dark. She blinked and the vision went away.

As he watched, she laved her tongue across his skin, one long stroke. Then she began to work the button and zipper of his fly.

Her heart pounded as she eased the zipper down and the edges of his shorts spread apart, pushed up by his erection. Unable to stop the impulse, she bent down and placed a kiss on the mound contained by his underwear.

Yes. She wanted him. Needed to feel him. With his help, she slid the shorts and boxers down. His cock sprang out and Rebecca couldn't contain her gasp. The gasp turned to a groan as she imagined putting him inside her. She wrapped her hands around his shaft, barely able to contain him. He was long—not too much, just a little more than she was used to— and thick. Very thick. Her pussy fluttered as if panicking a little at the thought of this cock sliding inside.

But she wanted it. She'd dreamed of men like him—of taking a large, hard cock into her body. Unable to stop herself, she smoothed her hands up and down, caressing and petting the thick shaft.

"Damn, honey, you need to stop." The strain in his voice made the temptress in her come out. She never would have believed it of herself. She'd always thought of herself as a sexual creature, but this was something completely different. Some foreign craving or power that moved through her, like the storm that raged outside was somehow pulsing through her body. Nothing could compete with the desire, the pure animalistic need to fuck him.

Feeling like an elemental goddess, she stared down at his gorgeous body — tight hard muscles, strong and powerful, and so hard. For her. He would service her well. She bent over and raised the tip of his cock to her lips — placing one open mouthed kiss on the thick crown. The sparks that erupted from his eyes lured the hunger that was surging through her veins. She couldn't wait any longer. She needed this cock, *his* cock inside her.

She pressed up onto her knees and placed his thick shaft to her opening. Pausing just a moment, teasing both of them. She eased the round head to her pussy, feeling her moisture drip down, coating her hands and his shaft. She slicked the warmth down his cock, drawing another hot groan from deep inside him.

"Do you want me to fuck you?" She spoke the words as she pressed him into her, letting just an inch slip inside her. The sensation caught the words in her throat but she waited, wanting to hear his hunger as well as her own.

"Yes."

She rubbed her hand down his cock, teasing him, loving the way he fought against his own desire. She could see it in his body. In his eyes.

"Come inside me?" she teased, pushing him just a little farther.

"Yes, damn it." The tight controlled voice had turned to a growl, low and warning. "Fuck me. Now."

The command grabbed something deep inside her, refusing to release her until she complied. Searching for breath, she spread her thighs and sank down, letting his thick, hard length slide into her. He stretched her, almost to the point of pain. But it felt so good, too good to stop.

His hands grabbed hers, holding her as she slowly, slowly took him into her body.

"That's it, baby. Take me. Let me inside this sweet cunt. Oh yes, you feel so good, honey."

His words were like subtle caresses to her pussy, easing her way until she felt the tight curls that surrounded his cock mesh with hers. Her breath filled the air as she adjusted to his width inside her. His hands slid up and down her sides, soothing her, relaxing her.

It felt so good, so right. She lifted her eyes and stared at the luscious body beneath her, the tight ripples of his stomach, hard strong muscles of his chest. But it was the pulse in his neck that drew her attention. She licked her lips, wanting that tight skin between her teeth.

A surge of joy, pleasure, something sparkled from up inside her and she giggled, loving the way the sound filled the room. She placed her flat palms on his hard stomach and pressed her hands up, easing her body forward, testing his flesh as she touched him.

"You feel good inside me," she whispered. She leaned down and placed a kiss on his mouth, intending a light caress, but he didn't let her escape. He drove his tongue into her mouth, consuming her in that kiss. Showing her how he wanted to fuck—strong and hard.

Yes, she would have that. Soon, but now she would enjoy him. Feel him slide in and slowly out of her pussy.

Fighting the urge to sink beneath his commanding kiss, she pulled back, scraping her teeth across that seductive place at the base of his neck, leaving a tiny mark on skin. Satisfaction curled through her chest as she stared at the mark. Yes, she would claim him, mark him so the world knew he belonged to her.

He turned his head, putting his hand at the back of her neck and tried to draw her back to his mouth, but she laughed and shook her head, sitting up, out of reach.

"I want to fuck," she whispered.

The breathless sound of her voice was a caress to his cock — that and the demand behind it.

The pure sensuality of her seduction had a drugging effect on his senses, allowing him to release control. Soon, when she was done with her fuck, he would have her. He would turn her over and pound into her.

"Yes," she answered as if she heard his intent.

But he didn't get a chance to reflect on the strange connection between them. She began to move, slowly lifting her hips, allowing his cock to slide almost out of her pussy before she sank back down, squeezing every inch inside her tight cunt.

"Oh my." She stared down at him. "You feel..." As if the words were too much of a challenge, she let the sound fade into a groan and moved again. Riding his cock. "So good." She didn't stop to speak, just kept up the slow, intoxicating ride.

Deacon rubbed his hands across her thighs, hips, breasts, needing to feel all of her, captivated by the sensation of her skin. He fought the urge to flip her over and fuck her, instead offering himself for her pleasure. He stared up in fascination, watching her body move, the steady shimmy of breasts as she went a little faster, a little harder, driving him deeper. His mouth was dry with the desire to taste her nipples, to lick and suck, while her pussy squeezed his cock.

Rebecca reached down, placing her hands on his chest, her fingernails becoming little claws as she scraped then down. The sharp bite of her nails drove the pleasure hard into his cock. He couldn't stop his groan — or pressing his hips up, punching the last inch into her.

Her delighted gasp and the way her eyes popped open drove him to repeat the motion. She watched him, holding herself steady as he levered his hips up, trying to get deeper. It wasn't enough.

"Fuck this," he snarled softly, placing his hand on her ass to keep his cock buried inside her as he rolled over. Her laughter sparkled through the air as she landed on her back, halfway off the sleeping bag he'd been using for a bed.

Her arms wrapped around his neck and she pulled herself up to him, kissing him, using her dainty tongue to tease him. "Fuck me," she whispered against his lips and he knew this was what she'd wanted all along. Him above her, hard and pounding inside her.

He pulled back and slammed forward. She cried out and fell back against the floor, her body arching into his, taking him deep.

"Yes," she moaned as if she'd finally found what she needed.

He pushed into her, groaning as her cunt grabbed him, held him. God, he wanted to stay inside her forever, fucking her sweet pussy. But he couldn't last much longer. The need to come was too great. Cautions rang in his head but were silenced by the soft whimpers drifting from Rebecca's throat, the quiet way she begged him to fuck her, come in her.

Some vague notion struck him—that he wasn't wearing a condom—but nothing could make him stop. He wanted to come in her, mark her with his cum.

He grabbed her hips and plunged inside once again, determined to feel all of her. Her pussy contracted around his cock, sweet squeezing along the full length, dragging his cum from deep inside. With a shout, he filled her one last time and let his body release.

Breathless, his heart pounding, Deacon held himself still, sinking down on her. Rebecca dropped her head back onto the thin cushion and savored his weight. It was perfect, the male felt good and right inside her. He belonged to her.

Needing his taste on her tongue, she stretched up and snagged his lower lip with her teeth, biting down. He was delicious but it wasn't enough. She needed more. Following her down, he kissed her, driving his tongue into her mouth. Feminine pleasure unfurled in her chest as he commanded a response. She gripped his back, letting her nails bite into his skin. He grunted and thrust forward, his cock still hard inside her.

The stroke was perfect, sliding against her clit, the gentle penetration reignited the hunger in her sex and illuminated the desire to claim him.

"Come inside me," she whispered against his lips. "Again. I want to feel you come in me again."

The drowsy satisfaction in her chest disappeared as he drew back and began a slow long thrust into her cunt. The strong muscles of his throat called to her. Rebecca pushed herself up, scraping her teeth along the tight skin between his neck and shoulder. Her mouth felt strange, her teeth too big. She wanted more than a delicate little love bite. Unable to fight the need, she opened her jaw and bit down, his flesh giving way to her teeth.

Deacon cried out, his body arching into hers. A long hot splash poured deep inside her. Savoring the sensation of his cum pulsing into her, she lapped at the four tiny wounds she'd left on his neck, satisfied that he was hers. That anyone who looked at him would know he belonged to her.

Deacon fought against the lassitude that threatened, holding himself above her, inside her. Fuck, he'd come inside her. Twice. What had he been thinking? Hell, he hadn't been thinking. From the moment she'd come into the living room, all he'd been able to do was react. Even now, after he'd come twice, he was almost hard. A few strokes and he would be ready to fuck her again. His cock twitched at the idea. Deacon knew staying inside her was a bad idea, but he couldn't remember why. And clearly his dick didn't think so.

He started to pull out, unable to hold this discussion while he was buried in her pussy, but her legs clamped around his waist and held him. Too much a gentleman to fight, he raised his head, expecting some sort of condemnation, recriminations or, God-forbid, triumph to stare back at him.

What he hadn't expected was desire.

Her lips were open, pink and swollen from his kiss. Her eyes blazing with renewed need.

"Don't leave me," she begged. She pumped her hips up, fucking herself on his cock, controlling the motion. She tipped her head back and closed her eyes as if his cock sliding in and out of her pussy was the center of her world. He groaned and fought to keep himself still, to hold himself in place for her pleasure. She scraped her fingers down the front of his chest, the bite of her nails marking his skin. The whispered pain was too much for his cock and he thrust down, meeting her upward pulse, going deep, afraid he was hurting her. "I love the feel of you inside."

Her hot eyes watched him, commanding him, demanding that he fuck her. And something inside him rose up, wanting to satisfy her. It was impossible. That he'd come twice was shocking enough but there was no way he could be hard again.

But his cock wasn't getting the message. He felt his dick swell and couldn't stop the groan that escaped his throat. He grabbed her hips and pulled her up, driving into her pussy. Her breasts rocked in rhythm with his thrusts, tempting him, calling to him. He bent down, holding her still, holding her close for his mouth, and wrapped his lips around one tight peak, sucking deep, feeling her pussy tighten around him as he drew on her. God, she was delicious.

He wanted to lick her and taste her forever.

She slid her fingers into his hair and held on. She arched into his mouth, giving him more of her breast. He moaned and gently bit down. Her pussy clenched, pulling him deeper. The urgency of before was gone and all that was left was the steady desire to feel her, all of her. Experience every inch as he pushed deep inside her. Her body moved in time with his, slow steady thrusts up as he penetrated her wet slick cunt.

"Yes, Deacon," she moaned, holding him. "Again. I want to feel you again."

He resisted the urge to drive hard into her. He knew he would come again, but he wanted her with him. He slipped his hand between their bodies, sliding his thumb into her slit, finding that sweet spot that made her gasp.

"That's it, baby. Let me feel you come. Squeeze my dick as you come." He continued the slow steady thrusts — and gently rimmed her clit, teasing her with each strokes.

Power flowed through him as her body responded — straining, fighting for more. Yes. That's what he wanted. Her hips lost their steady rhythm and she fucked herself, frantically pumping against him, fighting his grip. Deacon grabbed her ass and held her still, still buried deep inside her. Round female flesh curved perfectly in his hand and he squeezed, holding her tight to him.

"Deacon, please." The sound of her begging was like hot honey coating his body.

He held her in place and slowly began to fuck her — again, hell, had he even stopped? Each pulse sent him deep inside, shallow little thrusts that squeezed every inch of his cock. The pressure was too intense to escape and Deacon knew he wouldn't last long. Even the fact that he'd just come didn't seem to matter — his cock was hard and ready, so ready to burst inside her. But he had to bring her with him. The stretched tension in her body told him she was almost there.

Dragging himself away from the edge, he levered his hips back, loving her gasp as he pulled out of her, as if she hated the thought of him leaving her cunt.

"I'm not going anywhere, baby," he reassured her. "Let me just..." His words faded as he slid his thumb into her slit, massaging her clit. Hot liquid drenched his skin as he eased his thumb in slow sweeping circles around the tight bundle of nerves. Her breathy cry slipped into his soul and he knew the sound would follow him through his life — the seductive gasp as she found her pleasure. Keeping his cock inside her, he continued slow, full penetrations, giving her all of him even as his gently worked her clit.

Her fingers gripped his shoulders, not the wicked claws from before but frantic feminine bonds to hold him.

"So sweet." He placed his mouth on hers, not a real kiss, just sharing breath, rubbing their lips together. Her lax lips moved with his, following him, capturing him. The delicate bites of her teeth followed, harder, as if her patience had run its course.

Holding his thumb in place, he thrust his cock hard into her, pressing down on her clit so she felt the full stroke. She cried out and the red lights reappeared in her eyes. The low growl that rumbled from her throat urged him on, harder and deeper. He fought to keep a section of his mind apart, so he could make sure she came before he spilled inside her.

But the seductive grip of her cunt was too much and he was too close to coming. Thankfully she cried out and soft ripples worked the length of his cock as the contractions of her orgasm squeezed him. That delicate touch was enough and he shouted, thrusting into her one last time, spilling his cum into her pussy.

* * * * *

Trey flicked his hair away from his face and tried to suppress a shiver — and his impatience. The rain was pounding down on them. It wasn't as noticeable in wolf form. The animals were more adapted to the foul weather than the human form. The whole group had returned. Trey had caught up with Erik and Stephan and run with them. Marcus and Mikhel's brothers had eventually joined them and the six wolves had dropped into the natural rhythm of their animals.

Their wolves needed the society of their own kind and the run had loosened any tensions Trey had felt before.

Well, almost any. The urge to have Rebecca under him lingered but he figured that would be a steady craving until it either happened or she found another to mate.

Mikhel's howl had called them back. The wolf had no concept of time, feeling only the rise and setting of the moon. They'd run back, meeting at the shelter. Trey had changed first. As the new Guardian for Mikhel's pack, he was the last to change into wolf form and the first to change out of it.

He watched as Mikhel and Zach transitioned. The two men stood apart from each other as they pulled on their dry clothes, their eyes avoiding contact. The men were lovers, but tonight, there was a distance between them after the run. That was disconcerting. Tensions in the Alpha pair — or trio — would echo through the pack.

Trey surreptitiously monitored Taylor, knowing she would reveal any tension between her lovers, but she seemed serene. A slight agitation made her gaze unsteady, but the rest of her body was mellow and relaxed. Mikhel finished dressing and went to stand beside Taylor, curling his arm around her back. Zach, instead of moving close to his lovers as Trey had expected, stepped back, moving away, but his eyes never left the place where Mikhel's hand rested on Taylor's hip.

Mikhel almost appeared to be deliberately ignoring Zach. The strange behavior of his Alpha and Beta sent Trey's nerves on edge. He tracked Mikhel's stare — which was locked on his brothers as they made their transition. He seemed to be watching, waiting for some reaction from them.

And the reason for the distance between Mikhel and Zach became obvious. Mikhel's brothers didn't know he and Zach were lovers...and the Alpha wanted to keep it that way.

Trey took a deep breath, gathering as much information as he could, and caught the smell of both the Alpha and Beta

71

on Taylor. It was possible the twins wouldn't notice—wolves were unfailingly polite—but he decided to assist his Alpha.

"If you guys want to go on up, we'll be right behind you," Trey said to the twins. The brothers looked at each other and nodded and stepped out of the shelter where Trey knew the scents of Taylor, Mikhel and Zach wouldn't be as intense. He glanced at Mikhel. Mikhel nodded his approval and his thanks.

From Taylor he received only a blush. Not wanting to embarrass her, he looked away.

Marcus and Erik were the last to transition. Marcus blatantly bared himself to Taylor as he came back to human form. She glanced coolly at him, then turned away, her disinterest a blatant rejection.

Marcus saw the reaction but only grinned. Trey sighed. They were cousins—though they looked enough alike to be brothers—but they'd never been close. Trey was dreading the moment when Mikhel would ask for his opinion about letting Marcus into the pack. Family loyalty was strong but his loyalty to his new Alpha had to take precedence and he would have to be honest...Marcus would not make a good pack member. He was too selfish, too dangerous. The man liked to stir up trouble.

Once everyone was dressed, Trey led the way back to the house. Lights glowed in the downstairs and in Rebecca's room upstairs. His cock twitched inside his jeans. A full moon run always made him horny, but the thought of Rebecca—naked and waiting in a warm bed—made it almost intolerable. He picked up the pace, until they were almost jogging. He didn't worry about explanations. The pounding rain was enough of an excuse.

He tried to rein in his wolf but the remembered scent of Rebecca's cunt made the animal nearly uncontrollable. Trey ground his back teeth together. He wanted to taste her, to sink his tongue into her and capture all that hot liquid in his mouth.

Feel those sexy little shivers on his tongue. His cock leapt in his jeans. Not even the soaking rain helped his hard-on.

They walked into the house—the twins were in the kitchen toweling off. Despite the rain, everyone was in a relaxed, cheerful mood. Getting the chance to run, full out, in wolf form was a special treat that none of them got the opportunity to indulge in very often.

Taylor walked through the kitchen and offered coffee to everyone.

Part of Trey hoped the group would accept—it would give him time to remember that he really didn't want to fuck Rebecca. That crawling into her bed tonight was a really bad idea—especially with the power of the full moon so strong in his veins.

Despite his mind's open acknowledgment that not having Rebecca was the wise thing to do, his cock had other ideas and twitched with pure excitement when all Mikhel's guests declined the offer of coffee and headed for the door. Max—one of the twins—said he and Jackson had a long drive and exited within moments. Marcus and the others followed shortly thereafter, leaving the house almost silent.

As the various cars drove away, the tall clock in the hall chimed four. Four in the morning. Too late to crawl into Rebecca's bed? Hell no. His wolf growled its agreement.

Trey watched as Zach, Mikhel and Taylor headed for the stairs. The sexual looks he'd witnessed during the walk back had turned to blatant caresses. The three of them would no doubt be locked in their room until well past noon. That wouldn't be enough time—not nearly enough—for him to sate himself on Rebecca's luscious body, but it would be a start.

The brutal desire was all that held him in check. It was strong, too strong. Too consuming. If he crawled into her bed, he wouldn't want to leave. He'd want to mark her. Claim her.

The full moon was straining his control—he could almost feel the pleasure of sinking his teeth into her flesh. The temptation was almost as great as sinking his cock into her pussy.

But then, when the full moon lust was gone, he'd be stuck with her. And she him.

As he locked up downstairs, he talked to himself, mentally shoring up his defenses — defenses against his own desires. The battle inside him raged even as he went to his room and took a shower, drying off quickly and tugging on a fresh pair of jeans.

The empty bed held no appeal. He couldn't force himself to lie down. Despite the hour, the moon was still strong, still pulling on him.

That, combined with the fact that Rebecca was two doors away, made his cock twitch.

Even knowing he would regret it, he went into his bathroom and grabbed a condom, then grabbed two more, and shoved them in his pocket. She'd been willing, he thought. He just had to make sure he wore a condom and that he kept his teeth away from her. Either could begin the binding he had to avoid.

He closed his bedroom door quietly behind him. The master bedroom was across the hall and he just tipped his head that direction to make sure everything was okay with his Alpha. A soft feminine cry followed by a chorus of masculine groans made him smile. Yeah. His Alpha was fine.

Turning his back on their room, he walked down the hall, trying to keep his senses in check. His wolf was already scrambling and clawing to reach the surface, to be near the female, but Trey restrained the beast.

He stared at her door for a long time, knowing what waited for him on the other side. Not even the threat of future regrets could stop him. His fingers shook as he silently twisted the doorknob, easing the door open, not wanting to startle her. The weak light was bright enough for his eyes. Bright enough to see her bed was empty. That it hadn't been slept in. Sniffing the air, he tried to track her scent. The delicious perfume of her skin lingered, but it was faint, muted by hours. He poked his head into the open bathroom, knowing before he checked that the room was empty.

Not wanting to panic the house, he checked the other spare room and downstairs. Her car was still in front of the house...but Rebecca was gone.

Chapter Six

ୡ

The scent of the earth filled her body, becoming a part of her soul as she breathed it in. The subtle caress of the grass beneath her skin was like a thousand fingers touching her, each blade a delicate tease that kept her alive.

Hot hands smoothed up her skin, cupping her breasts, lightly pinching her nipples. The warmth from his touch counteracted the chill of the morning dew, heating her body from the inside.

She opened her eyes and saw him—Deacon and...another. Another man stood behind them, watching Deacon touch her. The mist blurred his identity but she somehow she knew him. She definitely wanted him. Wanted these men to touch her, wanted them inside her.

Please. She didn't know if she said the word aloud, but the heat swelled across her skin, spiraling down into her pussy. Her mysterious watcher stared with eyes that glowed red. His lips opened and she could see his teeth—long and sharp. Dangerous. Not human. But she wasn't afraid. She wanted those teeth on her.

Touch me. The mystery man heard her command but stayed just out of reach. Just out of sight.

Deacon's hands slid between her thighs, cupping her sex, letting his fingers dip into her pussy, drawing her attention from the watcher. She knew the other man was still there but she couldn't resist the caress of her lover. She groaned and arched her back, moving into his touch.

"Deacon," she moaned. She came awake, realizing she'd said his name aloud. Her eyes popped open and she stared up—into Deacon's chocolate brown eyes, heated with lust, and a bit of confusion as well—as if he didn't understand how he came to be there. Just like her dream, his hand was between her thighs. She looked down his body. His cock was hard, pressing against her leg.

She stared at the four marks on his shoulder. Marks she'd made. The wounds were already healed over, leaving pink, new scars.

Panic and satisfaction battled for supremacy in her emotions. Satisfaction that he was marked and claimed. *The other bitches will know he belongs to me.* That internal dialogue just added to the panic. It was like another voice in her head. And how had she bitten him? She ran her tongue across her teeth. They weren't sharp enough to make that kind of imprint.

But she'd done it. She reached her hand up and touched the wounds. Her fingers teased the skin and Deacon groaned. For a moment she thought she'd hurt him but then she felt his cock twitch against her thigh. Wanting to give him more of that pleasure, she pushed up and placed her mouth on him, running her tongue across the scars. Sexual tension whipped through his body and he pumped his cock against her, as if he couldn't fight the urge to move. To fuck.

She turned her head and he met her, their mouths connecting and joining. The commanding stroke of his tongue made her imagine his mouth on her pussy, licking and tasting. She started to draw back, ready to make that command, but a heavy pounding from the other room locked the words in her throat.

Deacon's head snapped back. He blinked as if he was being forcibly dragged back to reality. He paused, listened and seemed to identify the sound.

"I'd better get that." He pushed himself off her and rolled out of bed, grabbing his shorts off the chair and putting them on. He winced as he adjusted his cock inside his clothing. "It's probably your friends."

Friends? Rebecca sat up and looked out the window. The sun was up. The rest of the night had passed and at some point, the rain had stopped. *Damn. Those friends.*

"You're right."

The impatient knocking repeated and Deacon started toward the door. "I'll get your clothes. They should be dry by now." He didn't look at her as he walked away.

Embarrassment and loss filled her chest. Poor man. She'd practically pounced on him—hell, *practically* nothing. She *had* pounced on him in the living room, giving him little choice but to fuck her. And then she'd bitten him. She still didn't understand how that was possible but she couldn't deny that it had happened. She distinctly remembered sinking her teeth into him, and the bone deep satisfaction that had followed.

For both of them. He'd shouted and come inside her seconds later.

After her third orgasm—eek, was that even possible?—they'd a taken shower together. But it seemed her body wasn't done yet and she'd wanted him again. Deacon had responded, taking her against the shower wall, hard and fast.

She placed her hand on her stomach, still able to feel him inside her, the lovely way he stretched her.

She'd come back to herself as Deacon was rinsing water across her skin. She'd been too exhausted, too dazed for it to be awkward. Deacon had carried her out of the shower and into bed. She vaguely remembered him trying to leave, telling her she needed to sleep but she'd been determined and had pulled him down beside her, refusing to let him escape.

Alone for the first time in hours, she caught her face in her hands, trying to hide from her memories. So much of what had happened during the night was completely out of character and poor Deacon had gotten the brunt of it. Not that he hadn't enjoyed parts. She smiled. There'd been no denying his pleasure at fucking her.

Masculine voices rumbled from the far room and Rebecca instantly recognized the new arrival. Trey. *Remember him? The man you were thinking about fucking.*

She stared at the door for a long time, almost expecting it to pop open and Trey to storm in, demanding an explanation. The door remained closed. Of course it did. Trey was too controlled for such a display. Besides, he had nothing to be jealous about. It wasn't like they were lovers. Yet.

She grabbed Deacon's shirt and pulled it on. Knowing that she was blushing, she opened the door and stared at the two men in the other room.

Instantly the dream crystallized in her brain and she knew—Trey was the other man, the one watching as Deacon fucked her.

Moisture flooded her pussy as she imagined the two of them, loving her body, touching her with hands and lips, fingers and cocks. Her knees wobbled and she grabbed the doorframe to hold herself steady.

She took two long deep breaths and fought the desperate sexual hunger that gripped her. Her body ached from taking Deacon inside her through the night and her mind was a mass of contradictions—and all she could think about was fucking these two men.

Trey looked at the human who had let him into the tiny cabin. The man was a little shorter than Trey and with a slighter build. But he looked fit—for a human. And there was a sharp intelligence in his eyes that warned he was on guard.

Rebecca's distinct scent had led Trey to the cabin. He'd been slower than he'd wanted, needing to stay in human form to track her, in case he'd needed his cell phone. Now he'd found her.

The human seemed resigned when he'd finally answered the door and introduced himself. And now Trey knew why.

A delicious sexual scent surrounded Deacon—a perfume that Trey recognized. The hairs at the back of his neck stood up. His jaw muscles tightened, pulling his lips back.

"Where's Rebecca?" he demanded through teeth that were growing.

"I'm right here, Trey." Her call snapped his head around and he sniffed the air again, searching for any sign of danger or threat. Only sex and desire filled his head.

She stood in the doorway to the bedroom, dressed in a long flannel shirt, looking small and fragile—sexual and tempting. Her lips were slightly swollen, showing the marks of long hard kisses. A delicate flush covered her skin as if she was embarrassed to be found in this situation. His body moved forward, needing to be near her, protect her.

"Are you all right?" he asked.

"I'm fine." She accompanied the response with a nod. The oversized shirt slid off her shoulder and he saw the bandage, blood dotted the white patch. Rage that someone would harm her roared inside him but he fought it back, closing his lips and breathing deeply, barely containing the fury. As he inhaled, a second smell assaulted him. Werewolf.

He glanced at the male. He was human. His scent gave him away.

The werewolf scent was coming from Rebecca. Faint and growing.

"What happened?"

His harsh question seemed to startle her and Rebecca put her fingers to the bandage. "I was attacked. By an animal."

"And a human," Deacon inserted. When Trey looked at him, he came forward. "The bruise on her cheek has faded, but it had definite signs of a hand. And you said you heard a voice, right?"

Rebecca agreed. "I don't remember much beyond that. Just waking up naked in Deacon's bed." The blush returned to her cheeks as she looked at her lover. Trey's cock twitched in response to the pink in her cheeks. Wanting to be the cause, the source, of her shy pleasure.

"I found her at the edge of the lake."

"And Deacon's been taking great care of me."

I'll just bet, Trey silently sneered. He listened to their voices but his mind was on the cold hard facts. Rebecca had been bitten by a werewolf. And even now her body was changing. Making the transition.

Well, the sex made a lot more sense now. The newly created werewolf often came into being craving sex — particularly in females. In males the reaction was more dangerous, more violent.

Rebecca's wolf was driving the sensual part of her, demanding her satisfaction, needing to be fucked.

And she'd found a male to do it.

He looked over at Deacon. The human seemed to sense his stare and returned it, almost daring Trey to accuse him of something. But red stained the base of his neck as if he was fighting a blush.

Trey casually scanned the man's body. His cock was hard and pressing against his shorts, but that was to be expected. After all, Rebecca was barely dressed and practically panting with the need to fuck. Ready to dismiss him as nothing more than a temporary source of sex for Rebecca's wolf, Trey finished his observation, looking back up. A spot of shiny skin caught his attention. Two scars. Newly healing. He recognized those marks. No doubt there were two more, on Deacon's back.

Fuck. She'd bitten him.

He had to separate them. Now, while the bond between them was still weak. It would be uncomfortable for both, but it had to be done.

It wasn't Rebecca's fault. She probably hadn't even known she was biting him. The wolf had been in control. Being a nascent werewolf, she didn't have the strength or power to

81

actually change the human, but she'd marked him. Claimed him. That explained his erection. His body was responding to Rebecca's desire. The thick cream that was coating her thighs was tempting the human, practically demanding a response.

"We need to go. Now."

"Uh, okay." Rebecca's eyes got a little wide and Trey realized he'd been a little abrupt. He tried to smile but was pretty sure he'd failed.

"Taylor's probably worried."

"I left a message on their phone."

Trey silently cursed. He hadn't thought to look there. "Well, we should probably get going."

Rebecca nodded and looked at Deacon. "My clothes?"

"Right."

He disappeared into a side room returning seconds later, not giving Trey any chance to speak to Rebecca alone. Deacon handed her a neatly folded pile of clothes and she disappeared into the bedroom.

Trey watched the door close behind her. What was he going to say to her? How was he going to explain it?

The simple answer—he wasn't. He needed to get her back to the house. Mikhel would deal with it. She was officially part of his pack now.

Trey smiled grimly. When he'd been invited to join Mikhel's pack, coming in as the Guardian, two things had been explained clearly to him—that Taylor, Mikhel, and Zach were lovers and if he found the three-way relationship offensive, he shouldn't join. And that the pack would stay small. Mikhel didn't want to lead a huge crowd. He wanted a few, loyal wolves surrounding him.

Well, his pack had just grown by one.

Rebecca appeared moments later, looking rumpled and full-on sexy. His mouth watered and Trey could only hope he wasn't drooling. He glanced at Deacon and saw the same stunned, hungry look on his face. There was just something about her — particularly when she looked a little off balance.

And God, Trey wished that he'd been the one who'd made her that way — that it had been his hands scraping through her hair. His lips, marking hers with harsh deep kisses.

Needing to break away from the enticing sight before him, he spun around. "Let's go," he commanded to Rebecca.

"Uh, well, I guess we have to leave."

Trey heard the tension at the edge of Rebecca's voice.

"I'll just be outside," he said, deciding to give her a moment to say goodbye. But his gentlemanly urges didn't move him past the front door. He stepped onto the porch, shoved his hands into his pockets and stared out at the lake.

And listened.

"Umm, well, I—I don't really know what to say. I mean…" Rebecca said.

"Don't worry about it." Deacon's voice was gentle and comforting. And made Trey want to growl.

"About last night—"

"Rebecca, we both know it was…I don't know…a moment out of time."

Trey rolled his eyes and wished he had a cigarette. He'd quit smoking six years ago, but damn, if ever there was a time to have one, it was now.

Rebecca laughed. "Well, whatever it was, thanks." Her voice dropped to a whisper and Trey knew without turning around that she had her lips pressed to Deacon's ear. "I will always remember the feel of you inside me."

A low groan sounded from the room and Trey felt a mirrored response in his cock. God, what that woman could do with just a few words.

He tapped the heel of his boot on the porch, reminding her that he was here. Waiting. He wasn't going to look back.

He wasn't. Fuck, he had to. He turned his head and stared into the cabin. The couple was engaged in a kiss that drained the blood from Trey's upper body.

Rebecca was curled around Deacon, her arms over his shoulders, her fingers in his hair, her thigh pressed to his hip. Deacon's hand had a firm grip on her ass, holding her close, his cock no doubt nestled against her pussy. Trey could only imagine the heat that was rolling from inside her cunt, pouring into Deacon's skin.

A hot breathless moment passed between them as their mouths hovered inches away from each other. As if they were fighting their own desire, slowly they separated their bodies, until only their hands were touching. And their eyes. God, Trey had never seen anything so sexual as the way Rebecca stared at Deacon.

He knew it was the wolf inside her, coming alive, but still the power of that stare squeezed his cock.

"Bye." Her voice seemed to hang in the air, filling the space between them.

"Bye."

She spun around and stalked out of the cabin, walking past Trey, as if she knew she had to leave now or she'd never escape.

Deacon stared after her, then tilted his gaze up to meet Trey's. The two men glared at each other for a long time, rivals for the same woman.

Lifting his chin, Trey silently said goodbye and went after Rebecca.

Her heart was pounding in her chest and her lungs felt tight. God, it was almost painful to leave Deacon. She forced her feet to keep moving forward, knowing that if she gave her body the chance, she'd spin around and go back to him. Drag him back to bed. Take his cock into her mouth and swallow his delicious heat. She'd work him hard with her lips and tongue.

It was easy to imagine his response, the tight way he held himself, fighting for control. Until commanding her to fuck him was too much to deny.

Heat exploded inside her and more liquid soaked her already damp panties.

A low heavy growl sounded from behind her and Rebecca froze. That sound. She recognized that sound. From the attack.

Slowly turning, she looked behind her and saw...Trey. But that didn't make any sense. That wasn't a human noise. The fierce glint in his eye gave her shivers for a different reason.

"Did you hear that?" she asked.

"Hear what?" He must have recognized the panic in her voice because he came to her side, stopping inches from her, putting his body between her and any danger.

"That growl. That's the sound I heard last night."

A strange emotion—embarrassment?—flickered across his face but he shook his head.

"I didn't hear it." He put his hand to her back and nudged her forward. "Do you remember where the attack took place?"

"Sure. At the lakeshore."

"Show me."

He was alert and aware as she led him around the lake to the place she'd stood last night. The bright sunshine made the water sparkle—such a different sight from the dangerous waves she'd seen last night. The rain had cleaned the air, making everything fresh. She took in a long breath—letting the newness fill her. It seemed as if her senses were stronger. Almost as though she could taste the air around her.

"Uh, it was here." She pointed in the general direction of where she'd been standing. "I was watching the lake. Heard something—" She pointed at him. "That growl. And then something hit me." She touched her cheek at the memory but there was no pain now. "I remember pain in my shoulder — that must have been when I got bitten and I fell. I think I kicked whoever it was and then I ran."

"You didn't see who it was?"

She shook her head. "No. There aren't a lot of people around here, are there?"

"No." But she could see the thoughts in his head. The cabin was isolated and the lake well hidden. With private land surrounding most of it, there weren't many people who came here to camp.

That meant either a stranger had come into the area...or it was one of the men she'd seen at Taylor's house last night. Where had they all gone last night? On foot. In the rain.

Definitely something she needed to pry out of Taylor today. Though, in truth, she'd have tales to tell herself. Sex with a stranger. Wow, that was a fantasy she'd never known she'd had. She was too cautious, despite her often outward appearance otherwise.

And it had been great sex with a stranger.

"Let's go," Trey said, tipping his head toward the path that led to Taylor's cabin. He walked past her and she caught a whiff of his scent — pure, masculine. The faint traces of his shampoo lingered along with the smell of the rain. He smelled yummy — like she could lick him all over and savor every taste.

She followed him, her senses bombarding her with stimuli. It truly did seem as if she smelled and tasted the world differently this morning. And felt. Her clothes were scratchy against her skin, irritating, and the heat that had overwhelmed her the night before was returning. She wanted to strip off her shorts and shirt and... She stared at Trey's ass. And get fucked. By him. By Deacon. Both of them.

The house came into view and the sight jolted her from her thoughts. Good thing, she decided. The last time she'd gotten this hot and bothered, she'd ended up masturbating, with Deacon watching.

Taylor appeared on the back deck, her face lined with concern.

"You're back. Thank goodness." She trotted down the steps and wrapped Rebecca into a tight hug. "We heard your message but I'm still glad Trey was out looking for you." She pulled back and looked down at Rebecca, her head tilting to the side as if she was trying to work out some confusing problem or dilemma. "Are you all right? Something's diff—"

"We should go see Mikhel," Trey interrupted. Taylor reluctantly dragged her gaze away from Rebecca to Trey. The big man's eyes were filled with warning. Rebecca didn't understand it but Taylor nodded.

"And I'm sure you want to take a shower, or something." Taylor looked at Trey as if seeking his advice.

That irritated Rebecca. "I'm fine. I showered at Deacon's." *I showered* with *Deacon.* She kept that information to herself. Her stomach rumbled. They hadn't eaten except for the scrambled eggs early in the morning. Though she knew it was impolite, she had to say something. "I'm starving, though."

"Yeah," Trey agreed. "We should probably see if there's any of that steak left from last night."

Taylor shook her head. "Rebecca's a vegetarian. She doesn't eat meat."

"She does now," Trey muttered.

Confused by that comment, she was more shocked by her own reaction—because a steak actually sounded really good.

"Can you get Mikhel?" Trey asked.

"He's upstairs," Taylor said cautiously. "I'll go get him." She looked up. "Thanks for finding her." She walked away, leaving Rebecca and Trey alone again.

He'd been searching for her. Hadn't known that she was safe.

"I don't think I've thanked you for coming to find me."

Trey shrugged. "No problem."

But she knew it was more than that. If she guessed correctly, he'd started looking for her while the rain was still pounding down.

"Well, thank you." She moved in close, to give him a brief kiss, a mere brush of her lips on his cheek. Just a thank-you kiss between friends of friends. That was all she intended, or so she told herself. Her lips whispered against his stubbly cheek. The subtle caress sent a zing down her spine and she wanted more. His body was strung tight, as though he was bracing himself for an attack—or fighting the urge to reach for her. She leaned in and kissed him again, closer to his mouth. And then again, putting her lips on his. He hesitated for only a moment, then a groan rumbled through his chest and he turned his head, opening his mouth as he meshed their lips together, driving his tongue inside in one slick move.

Hot hands clamped down on her hips and pulled her snug up against him. The pressure of his body, the connection of his hard cock against her pussy made her cry out. He captured the sound in his mouth and cupped her ass in his huge hands, rubbing her against him, teasing her clit with a wicked cock massage.

Her head swam as he kissed her, drawing her breath inside him. She wanted him. Here now. She needed his cock inside her. A low growl echoed inside her own head, demanding that she have him.

"Trey!" Mikhel's sharp call jerked Trey back, leaving Rebecca a little wobbly. He didn't immediately let go of her—she was sure she would have collapsed if he had—but he stepped back, taking away the delicious seduction of his mouth and warmth of his body. She leaned forward, intent on having him again, but his hands held her away.

The shock that he was actually having to hold her back was enough to break through the lust that was again pumping through her veins. What was the matter with her?

She looked up and saw Mikhel, Taylor and Zach standing on the deck, watching them. Taylor's mouth was open and Mikhel was watching as if he expected Rebecca to turn into some kind of monster. Only Zach seemed calm, almost amused.

"What?" she asked. "It was only a little kiss."

With a flip of her hair, she stalked past the small group and into the house, thrilled that her knees held steady. Because despite her announcement, that had been so much more than a little kiss.

Trey stood before Mikhel, Zach and Taylor and tried to contain his blush at being caught with his tongue in Rebecca's mouth.

He brushed his hair back and walked up onto the deck, watching Rebecca as she went inside. The sensuality that flowed through her body had little to do with the burgeoning wolf inside her and all to do with the sexual nature he'd recognized the first time they'd met. It was captivating. Dangerous.

The upside to this whole insane mess was that he could fuck her now and not worry that they would be locked together forever.

"Zach, could you go with Rebecca and help her find something to eat? She's liable to rip our kitchen apart searching."

Zach shrugged but looked to Mikhel for a nod of approval before he went inside, leaving Trey with Taylor and Mikhel.

"So, what's going on?" Mikhel demanded, the light in his eyes expressing his irritation.

The sheer dominant power that radiated from inside the Alpha werewolf caused Trey to lower his eyes. "I apologize for interrupting but we've got a problem."

"And that is?"

"Rebecca has been bitten."

"By what?" Taylor asked.

"A werewolf."

Mikhel stared at the ground for a moment then nodded. "I thought something was different about her. When?"

"Last night. I found her across the lake in that cabin." He shook his head to answer before they could ask. "Not him. He's human. Though now he's a bit of a complication as well."

"How is that? Did he recognize what was happening?"

"I don't think so. But Rebecca bit him. While they were...making love."

Taylor drew back and blinked both her eyes. "Rebecca doesn't even know him. She wouldn't have sex with some guy she doesn't know."

"The wolf growing inside her has certain urges she might not know how to control. Might not be *able* to control."

Mikhel looked at his mate. "Remember when I bit you, that night in the forest? The bite—particularly in females—translates into sexual need and hunger. You had already been exposed to me and Zach so the transition wasn't quite so abrupt."

"She had sex with this guy?" Taylor's surprise soothed a little of Trey's jealousy.

"That's the least of our worries," Mikhel said. "First is, what do we do about him now that she's marked him and second, who the fuck bit her?"

Trey relayed what Rebecca had told him about the attack but neither male could come up with an option on who or why one of the wolves who'd been on site would bite her. The rain had washed away any lingering scents that might have identified the werewolf.

"Taylor, you should tell her," Mikhel announced.

"Me?"

"She's your friend."

"Yes, and she's going to think I'm crazy if I tell her she's about to become a werewolf."

"It has to be done."

Taylor glared at Mikhel and Trey had to admire her courage. Of course, it was obvious from the affection between them that Mikhel would never hurt her. She felt completely safe defying the Alpha.

"You tell her. It's your pack."

"Yes, but she's your friend, and she doesn't like me in the first place." Trey noticed Taylor didn't bother to deny that fact.

Finally she sighed. "All right. I'll tell her. Just give me a little time to think about what to say, okay?"

Mikhel nodded then directed his gaze to Trey as if asking for his approval. Trey shrugged and nodded. He didn't care how or when Rebecca was told. Only that she was told soon. The wolf was coming alive in her body and she needed to understand the strange sexual urges that came with it.

His body hummed with the image of Rebecca, standing in the human's cabin, the scent of sex and desire surrounding her like a spiral of smoke, luring him closer. Casually he turned his body away. There was no need for his Alpha to know he got hard just thinking about their new little werewolf.

Chapter Seven

ℰↄ

Trey took a swallow of his beer and headed to the living room. He'd taken a run around the lake, keeping to his human form but needing the movement to expend some of the energy that burned through his muscles. The sun was long set, the house quiet and the moon rising in his veins. The full moon was waning but it was only one day old and the power remained.

He turned the corner, walking through the dining room. He heard the masculine moan and feminine gasp seconds before his foot hit the living room carpet. In the two months he'd lived here, he'd become familiar with the sound—Mikhel and Taylor. That meant Zach was probably around as well.

Trey retreated, not wanting to interrupt his Alpha, but the sounds without the sight only made it worse. The low, sexual whispers and moans sparked his imagination—giving him too many options about what was happening on the other side of the wall. From there, he inserted himself and Rebecca into the fantasies and he was instantly hard. Not that he'd been "un-hard" for much of the day. Seeing her with Deacon, then feeling her tongue in his mouth. God, just licking his lips reminded him of her taste. And he wanted more. A lot more.

And he could have it. He knew he could. In fact, fucking her would probably be a good thing. The strange component in werewolf sperm that bound *human* females to males would ease a newly turned werewolf. It would lessen some of the cravings. That would be best for the whole pack.

He scoffed. *How noble. Fucking her for the good of the pack. That's about as lame an excuse as I can think of. I want to fuck her because I want to fuck her.*

The one benefit to her having been bitten—besides the rabid sexual need she was experiencing right now—was that if he came inside her, he wasn't going to bond with her. Whatever that compound in his sperm was, it didn't form a connection to female werewolves. If he wanted to create a bond with Rebecca, he'd have to bite her and he had enough control not to do that.

"Please, Zach, please."

"Soon. I just want to taste you."

The low, whispered conversation was like a fist in Trey's gut. He couldn't stand there listening and there was no other way to the stairs except through the living room. The *occupied* living room.

What the hell was he supposed to do? He was new to this pack and didn't know the rules. Hell, he wasn't even sure there were rules.

He poked his head around the corner and almost moaned. There was Taylor, kneeling beside the couch. Her long flowery skirt was thrown up, over her ass, revealing the round tight cheeks. Her legs were spread. Trey looked, unable to resist the sight. Zach was propped up beneath her, his mouth on her pussy. The slow pump of her ass back and forth told him that Zach had his tongue inside her passage. Seductive groans filled the room and emanated from Zach as he tasted her sex.

Trey licked his lips, imaging his mouth on Rebecca's cunt. Driving his tongue into her pussy. He'd had a sample yesterday. Today, the newly created wolf was ravaging her senses and his was clawing to return to the woman it wanted to claim. God, he wanted to taste her. Fuck her.

She'd been so hot when he'd touched her yesterday, but there had been no time to linger, savor, the way Zach was doing to Taylor's cunt.

He let his eyes wander over the tableau before him. Zach working his mouth hard on Taylor's pussy. Taylor, almost naked, her head buried in Mikhel's lap.

Trey watched, couldn't stop himself. The seductive slide of her mouth up and down Mikhel's cock was an almost palpable sensation to his own dick. Hours of denying his cock any relief—from the moment he'd walked into Deacon's cabin and seen Rebecca, smelled her sweet pussy juice coating the human—had taken its toll. His control was at an end.

Taylor licked and sucked Mikhel's cock, her pink tongue a wicked temptation with every stroke. Her moans joined Zach's—growing louder each time she filled her mouth with cock.

"Oh, God, baby, that's so good." Mikhel slid his fingers through her hair, lifting the strands away, almost as if he was giving Trey a better view. She pressed down and the hard shaft disappeared into her mouth.

Trey felt his fingers bite into the wood of the doorframe. His cock was rock solid and read to fuck—but he didn't want to join his Alpha and his lovers. Hell, if anything would get him killed, it was approaching Taylor in a sexual way. In *any way* except with pure respect.

No, his hunger wasn't for Mikhel or Taylor. It was for the woman upstairs. Watching the bodies before him just made the ache to fuck her worse.

He glanced at the stairs, wondering if he could make it without being noticed.

Unlikely. Mikhel was too aware of his surroundings.

Finally Trey decided he had two options—hide out in the kitchen until they finished, which from the whispers and groans could be awhile—or he could slip upstairs.

He took another swallow of his beer and placed the bottle on the dining room table.

With eyes lowered, he slipped from the dining room, across the corner of the living room, to the stairs. When he reached the first step, he glanced at Mikhel, feeling the need to see if his Alpha was watching.

Mikhel stared down at Taylor as she swallowed his cock again, then slowly lifted his gaze. He raised his chin in masculine acknowledgement that he'd seen Trey and approved of his subtle departure.

Trey bowed his head, a movement he rarely did but one that seemed appropriate on this night. When Mikhel nodded again, Trey turned and continued up the stairs.

He hit the upper landing and stopped. The smell of sex permeated the upper floor.

Rebecca.

His cock leapt and Trey groaned, fighting the pull to his body.

Trey grabbed the edge of his door, but the lure of her sex was too great and he found himself stumbling down the hall. He paused at her door, hoping there was some way to fight this. Some way he could break free. The pure temptation of this woman made her dangerous.

He tried to breathe but every breath was filled with Rebecca — her scent, her taste, her power.

Animal hunger radiated through the door and grabbed at him like claws, pulling him deeper.

Without knocking, he pushed the door open. His cock pulled up, fighting the confinement of his jeans. The rebellious organ wanted her cunt, wanted to be inside her.

He tensed — his mind conjuring the image of her naked, her legs spread wide, her pussy dripping with moisture, the tight round peaks of her nipples pink and straining for his mouth.

He looked at the empty bed and froze. Empty? Where the fuck...? He let the question die as he opened the bathroom door. She wasn't there either. That meant she'd left the house. He didn't stop to wonder how she'd slipped out with no one noticing her. He spun around and ran down the stairs.

Rebecca was out there, alone, with a quickly emerging wolf inside her. The moon was still strong—strong enough to tempt a nascent werewolf. He didn't even question her destination. She was heading toward her human lover.

Trey went back downstairs, ignoring the lovers on the couch as he slipped by, and headed for the back door. Once on the porch, he inhaled, breathing in the night air. The faintest hint of Rebecca lingered but it wasn't enough.

He took off his shirt and unbuttoned his jeans, dropping the clothes in a messy pile on the deck. With a deep breath, he let the wolf's image fill him and asked the animal to share his form. Muscles pulled and stretched and within seconds he was a rider in the wolf's mind. He sniffed the deck. Immediately Rebecca's scent flooded his head.

The wolf growled its triumph and took off in a run.

* * * * *

The water sloshed across the top of her feet—cool and calming—and allowed her a moment of peace. She stared down at her naked legs. She'd left her shoes behind. Left them back at the cabin. The soles of her feet ached but even as she stood in the lake she could feel them healing.

The almost full moon glanced off the smooth lake surface, leaving a bright white streak down the center of the water. Rebecca stared at the moon's reflection for a long time. It called to her. Not to plunge into the deep lake but to let its power inside her. To let the energy of the night become a part of her.

Another rush of heat pulsed through her pussy and her whimper filled the night air. Her senses were hyperaware. Sounds and scents came at her from all directions. She slid her hands into her hair and tugged, letting the light pain focus her mind. Her body was out of control. She'd hidden in her room all afternoon. Somehow facing Taylor was too much—and seeing Trey was out of the question. It made her think about kissing him, licking him, wrapping her lips around his cock and sucking, long and deep. She moaned as the light lake breeze fluttered through her hair.

The cravings—for Deacon and Trey, for sex, for some male inside her body—had finally driven her from the house. And now, here she was, at the lake. She didn't remember getting here. She wore only the fitted t-shirt and panties that she'd put on after her shower.

Footsteps whispered from her right and she froze, listening closer. She heard four distinct pads on the ground...then it changed and there were only two.

The sounds became human—the deeper breath, the heavier weight.

Faint memories from the previous night filled her head and she tensed, preparing for another attack.

Slowly she turned to face the sound. Trey stood at the entrance to the pathway, naked, his cock hard and erect.

Her mind tried to process the fact that he was naked in the woods but all she could focus on was that deliciously hard rod between his legs. She wanted him. Wanted the male inside her. The pulse in her sex turned from a steady throb to a pounding need.

A distant corner of her conscious tried to scream its protest but the rest of her mind and body moved forward. Trey stepped out of the shadows. A faint sheen of sweat covered his chest and she licked her lips, wanting to taste, wanting him in her mouth.

Red covered her mind as she moved closer, her steps gaining speed until she was there, close, almost able to touch him. She sniffed the air and smelled him—the warm masculine scent seeped into her pussy, making it clench, ache.

Her teeth felt strange inside her mouth, long and too big, but even as she thought it, the concern disappeared. She wanted his skin beneath her mouth—her teeth penetrating his flesh, sinking into him.

Her muscles contracted and she leapt forward, landing hard against him. He caught her weight and stumbled back but he didn't go down. She wrapped her legs around his waist and felt her fingernails nip into his skin. She opened her mouth and leaned down, scraping her teeth across the bare flesh of his neck. She raised her head and licked her lips, preparing to taste him.

Trey shook his head.

"No, baby, no biting. Not tonight." Not to be denied, she tried to lean down. Again he stopped her. "If you try to bite me, I won't fuck you."

Her lower lip bent down into a pout and she stared at him. She growled, the sound erupting from deep in her chest, so foreign and frightening that it jolted her from the frenetic lust that consumed her. She looked around. It took a moment to realize she was in Trey's arms, her legs wrapped around his waist.

Trey's hands held her tight against him, his strength supporting her. "Are you all right?" he asked.

She nodded and tried to loosen the tight grip of her legs but as she squirmed, delicate jolts shot into her pussy and she pressed forward, grinding her mound against his cock.

"Oh fuck," he moaned. The hunger in his words called to hers. She had to have him now. She reached down and tugged on her underwear, intending to slide them down her legs. The material ripped in her hand. Moonlight highlighted the bright white panties. How had she...? The curiosity died as Trey's cock teased her entrance, nudging against her pussy. The thick head slipped into her and she squeezed her legs, trying to drive him deeper.

The world shifted as he dropped to the ground, his knees sinking into the soft sand. Hot hands lifted her until she was perfectly positioned. His eyes locked on hers and for a moment, neither breathed. Then he pulled her down, driving his cock hard into her. Their cries shattered the night's silence as he filled her.

The hunger roared inside her. She needed to have him, mark him. She pulled him closer but he fought, shaking off her silent command. She growled and tried again, but still he resisted.

"Control it, Rebecca." His command barely penetrated the red fog that surrounded her. Red with lust and fury. He belonged to her. She needed to claim him. Her lips raked back from her teeth and she stretched forward. His neck with that tempting, pulsing beat, stayed just out of reach.

He shook her, snapping her head up. "Rebecca." This time his voice broke through and she stared at him, actually seeing him. He was inside her, his cock hard and deep, but it wasn't enough. "You have to control the animal, Rebecca. You cannot bite me. Do you understand?"

Part of her mind—the corner that still held logic and reason—couldn't comprehend what he was saying. But she understood control. And in an instant of clarity she realized that if she gave into the strange desire to bite him again, he would pull out. And she couldn't have that.

She nodded, unable to find the words. Confusion and hunger swirled through her skull.

"Kiss me, sweet," he whispered, soothing. "Let me taste that pretty mouth of yours."

Feeling almost shy, she leaned forward and offered her mouth to him. Her lips opened and the warm rich taste flowed on her tongue. She groaned and licked, wanting more.

Trey's hands cupped her ass and slowly lifted her up, sliding her almost off his cock before easing her back down, filling her again. Rebecca dragged her mouth from his, dropping her head onto his shoulder as he worked his cock in and out of her pussy. Hot hungry whispers filled her head— how tight she was, how delicious her cunt was, that she was made to be filled by his cum. His voice was low and seductive, weaving around her until the words filled her head and flowed through her body.

The wickedly slow fuck went on and on, her body moving in time to his guidance, rocking up and down on his cock.

A delicious scent filled the air — hidden beneath the smells of sex and sweat. Rebecca licked her lips, wanting more. It was sweet and familiar. She opened her eyes and stared into the darkness. Hungry male eyes watched as she rose and lowered her pussy, Trey's cock disappearing time and again inside her cunt. Deacon. Watching from the shadows.

Part of her recognized that she shouldn't be able to see him in the darkness but she dismissed the logic and concentrated on his stare. He'd watched her before, when she'd touched herself. Now, he was watching her fuck Trey.

Her eyes pierced the dark shadows that held him and she could see his hand moving across his groin, rubbing. He was hard, squeezing his cock as she fucked, imagining it was her pussy holding him. She licked her lips, wanting his cock in her mouth, wanting more. Trey's hands gripped her hips hard and he pulled her down even as he thrust his hips up.

Knowing that Deacon watched, that he was masturbating as they fucked, sent a hot rush of moisture to her pussy.

"That's it, sweet," Trey whispered. "Show him. Let him see my cock inside you."

Lost in the purely sensual world, she followed his commands, leaning away, arching her back, her hands digging into the sand behind her, and pressing harder, grinding Trey's cock deeper, each stroke reaching far into her. She let her head fall back and released a cry into the night. Yes, this was what she needed — Trey coming inside her. His strong hands lifted and held her as he fucked her hard, each stroke pounding against her clit with delicious fury. Energy and sex surged through her chest as she opened herself to the night.

As if he could sense her rising orgasm, Trey rubbed his thumb across her mound, adding a touch of pressure, just enough. "Very good, baby. Let me feel you come. Squeeze my cock when you come. Let me feel that sweet cunt."

His guttural growl and light touch threw her over the edge and she screamed — the pounding pleasure breaking free in her pussy and spilling over, sliding into her limbs in strength stealing waves.

Trey's groan followed seconds later. Hot pulses poured inside her as he continued to thrust through his climax.

Only Trey's strength kept her upright. He pulled her forward so she was draped across his chest, his hard thighs beneath her ass. The delicious scent of his cum and Trey and Deacon surrounded her.

Dazed with lingering traces of her orgasm and the power of Trey's cock still hard inside her, she found the strength to raise her eyes and peer into the darkness. Deacon's gaze met hers, held her stare — like a man captivated by the vision before him.

She opened her mouth and slipped her tongue across her upper lip, trying to taste him in the night air, loving that she had the power to command his desire. The movement seemed to drag him forward. He stepped out of the shadows. He seemed to fight each step, hoping to resist, but not having the strength. Arriving at her side, he dropped to his knees and took her head in his palm, pulling her mouth to his, driving his tongue between her teeth. She moaned as his other hand cupped her breast, tweaking the nipple, pulling, just a little too hard. The pain became just another caress.

Heat and pressure filled her pussy and she realized Trey was still inside her, fucking her, short, shallow thrusts that rubbed deep inside her.

She ripped her mouth back, gasping for breath. Deacon didn't seem to mind. He raked his teeth across her neck and moved down, kissing and licking as he explored her breast with his tongue. He moved in wicked circles, closer and closer until he covered her nipple, sucking the tight peak into his mouth.

Her nails bit into Trey's side and Deacon's shoulder as she fought to control the sensations. The scent and taste of these two men melded into her body, consuming her.

Trey bent down, keeping his cock inside her, and latched onto her other breast. The two men worked in silent unison, sucking and gently biting, until she thought she would scream, until she begged to come. Trey worked her clit, his thumb slipping into her slit and rubbing, light and steady, faster and faster.

"That's it, baby, come for us."

She was pretty sure that it was Trey speaking but her mind was too overwhelmed to distinguish. Every sense was illuminated, electrified as they touched and tasted her.

As if by agreement, both men bit down, gently, on her nipples. The double shock sent her body back, her clit pushed against Trey's touch and she cried out, another orgasm flowing through her body.

She came back to herself to find Deacon's lips on her neck, Trey rubbing soothing caresses up and down her back. She reached and pulled Deacon's mouth to her, scraping her fingernails across his chest as they kissed. Vaguely aware that she was tearing through Deacon's cotton shirt, she stripped the tattered pieces away and ran her hands across his muscles. Leaner and sleeker than Trey, his body fascinated her. She wanted to explore each inch with her tongue.

Trey lifted her up, pulling out of her.

The loss of his cock made her cry out in disappointment. The cry turned to a snarl and she flipped her hair back, baring her teeth at him.

He returned the stare, his eyes filled with warning. "Control it, Rebecca," he commanded. The threat was implicit in his words. Control or she got no more of him. Fighting the creature inside her, she lowered her gaze and felt Trey's hand on her hair, comforting her.

"Don't worry, baby, I'm not done with your cunt yet," he vowed. He sat up and caught her at the back of her head, pulling her close for a long, drugging kiss that made her dizzy. Deacon's mouth covered her nipple and sucked as Trey drew the air from her lungs. When he finally pulled back, she knew she was weaving and was thoroughly glad she was already kneeling. She put her hand on Deacon's shoulder to stabilize herself.

"On your hands and knees, sweetheart, I want that ass pressed against me when I sink into your pretty cunt again." The raw tone of Trey's voice filled her already crowded head with temptation and hunger. "And our friend here probably needs your lips wrapped around his cock. Suck him off, baby."

Her body seemed out of her control and Trey's to command. Every word he spoke, she craved. She wanted Deacon's cock in her mouth, wanted to feel all that hard flesh on her tongue, his cum sliding down her throat. She licked her lips and turned, scraping her teeth across Deacon's neck, down his tight chest muscles, sharp little bites, loving the way her teeth marked his skin.

Yes. Her male would wear her mark.

Tension tore at each muscle as she worked her way down his body—hot kisses interspersed with almost painful bites. She'd bitten him earlier—he hadn't noticed the four puncture wounds until long after she'd left. It didn't make sense. A woman—hell, a human—should never have been able to make a mark like that. But little about the day had made sense. After she'd left, he'd spent the day alternately hard and harder, as if his cock was continually being teased.

And then as the night fell, he'd felt the compulsion to go out, to find her. Fuck her. He hadn't expected to find her being fucked by someone else—that blond god who'd collected her from his house—but he hadn't walked away. Couldn't. The sight of her enjoying the cock inside her had been too enticing and he'd stayed, watching, stroking his own erection in time to her fucking. He hadn't come. Even through the afternoon, when he'd tried to jerk himself off, he couldn't come. He wanted to spill inside her. Wanted to feel her cunt gripping him when he released.

He stared at the soft red curls draped across his thighs and couldn't resist sinking his hand into the luscious mass, guiding her down. God, his cock was hard, straining against the fly of his shorts.

He froze as her fingers went to work on the button and zipper that contained his erection. Every light stroke through the thick material was an electric jolt to his cock, tormenting him. He slid his hands through her hair, letting the strands slip between his fingers as she bent over and placed a kiss on the tight mound of his cock. Heat poured from her lips and he could feel her breath against his skin. She teased him again with a whisper kiss, tempting him. Little witch, he thought.

He ground his back teeth together but couldn't hold back the command. "Take it out and suck me," he ordered. She glanced up as if she was startled by the sudden dominance in his words. Her eyes blinked and a flicker of red filled the pupils. For a moment he thought she might ignore his order but then she licked her lips and lowered her eyes. She eased him from inside his shorts and stroked the thick shaft. The delicate caress was made of fire.

Deacon braced his knees deep into the sand, holding himself still, fighting the urge to force her head down, to jam his cock into her mouth.

"That's it, baby," Trey whispered as he caressed her back. "Show him how you missed his cock all day."

She seemed to be following Trey's every direction. Ten sleek fingers caressed Deacon's cock as she guided the tip to her mouth and laved her tongue across the head.

His groan rose into the night as she licked him, soft swipes of her tongue. He lifted his stare, unable to resist watching Trey.

Deacon knew himself to be straight, had never considered fucking another man, but he could also recognize a tight male body. The moon illuminated the beach and revealed Trey's naked form. Hard muscles that came from work and genetics—not hours spent in the gym—lined his chest and stomach. Confused by the path of his thoughts, he looked down, instead watching as Trey caressed Rebecca's back.

His hands were darker than her skin as he rubbed his palms across her hips, her ass. He pressed his thumbs into the split of her ass and slowly slid his hands down. Rebecca's hips rolled, moving with the caress. Though he couldn't see precisely what Trey was touching, Deacon knew when he came to her rear entrance.

Her body tightened and she flinched. Trey raised one thumb to his mouth and licked it, getting it wet. He looked across her body, his eyes locked onto Deacon's.

"Rebecca, have you ever been fucked in the ass?" he asked as he slowly returned that thumb to her entrance and pushed forward. "Ever taken a cock up your ass while another fucked that sweet pussy?"

Rebecca shook her head, her curls teasing the tops of Deacon's thighs. Her soft whimper caressed his skin, sending a bright shock of hunger into his groin.

Trey pressed forward. "Relax for me, sweet, let me in. Good." Trey smoothed his other hand down her back. "Nothing more tonight. You're tight, but soon you'll take us. One in your cunt, the other sliding into this tight ass."

Deacon felt his cock grow harder, watching Rebecca's ass get slowly penetrated, knowing that Trey was preparing her for them. He could almost feel it, as if he was the one getting fucked.

A night bird screeched overhead but Deacon ignored it. He was too captivated by the sight before him, Rebecca, on her knees, that sweet ass curved and reaching for the sky. He didn't know how he came to be here, what drew him on, but he knew he couldn't resist. Couldn't fight the hunger that roared inside him. Her mouth was soft and sweet, tasting and exploring. Heat followed every stroke of her lips. She worked her way down the length of his shaft, teasing flickers of her tongue — like electric butterflies caressing his dick.

Trey pulled his hand away, wiping his fingers on the tore edges of Deacon's ruined shirt. Then he moved between her legs, his hard cock stretching toward her pussy.

Deacon watched as Trey held himself, fitting his cock to her entrance then slowly pressing in. Rebecca's moan massaged his shaft as she accepted Trey into her cunt. Deacon could practically feel the slow penetration. A moment passed when all three were frozen breathless, then Trey began to fuck. With another groan, Rebecca returned to her oral loving of Deacon's cock. She licked and stroked, harder now, teasing him until he couldn't stand it anymore. The need to thrust was overwhelming, to be the one fucking her. He cupped her head and held her in place as he pushed his hips up, nudging his cock against her mouth. She opened her lips and took him inside, gagging when he pressed too far.

He murmured his apology and struggled to remain still. Now that he was inside her, it was enough. He watched as Trey fucked her, the glitter of her pussy juices coating his cock, visible each time he pulled out. Deacon licked his lips, wanting those juices on his tongue, wanting it all. Needing to fuck and be fucked.

Trey looked at him. Pure male sexual desire poured out of his eyes, but Deacon knew the hunger wasn't directed at him. It was for the woman that knelt between them, the woman they shared and both wanted. To the point of near madness.

Rebecca's hips rocked back, meeting a deep hard thrust. Her pleasured groan reverberated into his cock and Deacon punched his hips up. "Yes," he cried, gripping her head and holding her in place as he worked his cock in and out of her mouth, matching Trey's rhythm. The wet sounds of Trey's cock pounding into her cunt seduced Deacon until it was all he could hear. His senses seized control—touch and sight. The sweet suction of her lips as she took his cock. The vision of Trey fucking her.

The combination was overwhelming and he shouted, pressing up, going a little deeper, his cum shooting from his cock. Her throat convulsed as she swallowed him, carrying his cum into her body. As if the sight of his orgasm inspired Trey, he began to fuck her harder, driving into her until both Rebecca and Trey cried out, their bodies caught in the delicious strain of coming.

As the strength left them, they collapsed onto the sand, Trey behind Rebecca, her pale skin delineating his from the shadows. Deacon watched—his body sated, his mind racing. This was completely insane. Here he was. Fucking a woman he barely knew. On a beach. In the middle of the night.

The sensibility that had gotten him through most of his life urged him to stand up, walk away.

Rebecca opened her eyes and looked at him. Some illusion from the moonlight made her eyes appear red. She reached out, her hand curling around his cock. The traitorous organ leapt into her hand. The edge her mouth curled up as if the sight pleased her.

"Fuck me," she whispered. The soft sound was a demand that his body couldn't refuse and he moved stretching out beside her, bending down to lick the tight points of her nipples, knowing that he would come inside her.

His body was hers to command.

Chapter Eight

∞

Monday morning, Rebecca jumped out of bed, determined to return to normal and forget the weekend, though five minutes into being conscious she realized that *forgetting* wasn't an option. She'd just have to ignore that it happened. A quick call to Taylor last night had made things worse. Taylor kept insisting that she had to talk to Rebecca, face-to-face.

The thought made her cringe. Taylor knew about Trey, there was little doubt about that. And she probably knew about Deacon. Did she know about both together? Not that Taylor was one to criticize but... Rebecca gulped down her tea and tried ignore the pounding in her head. Taylor had at least known Mikhel and Zach when she'd taken them as lovers.

Rebecca had fucked two men who were practically strangers. And she'd fallen on them like a starving dog offered a bone.

Even worse, she'd run away. While they were sleeping. Exhausted but chilled, Rebecca had awoken on the beach, Trey on one side, Deacon on her other. It had taken some subtle moves but she'd extricated herself from between the two men, slipped into Taylor's house, grabbed her bag, her purse and her car keys and had escaped before anyone was awake. When she thought about it, she cringed, but there was no way Rebecca could have faced Taylor — or Trey or Deacon for that matter — after what had happened.

When Taylor had pushed to get together for lunch, Rebecca had been vague and promised to call when she had a moment. And if she had her way, she would be jam-packed busy for the next decade and never have to face her friend. She dropped her forehead into her hand. And she'd had sex on the beach—wow, was that a drink?—near Taylor's home. How creepy was that? Unprotected sex.

The realization caused a slow roll in her stomach. She'd have to call her doctor today. Get an appointment. She wasn't worried about pregnancy. She had the Pill for that. It was all the other nasty possibilities. God, she'd never had unprotected sex with a man unless they were in a confirmed, long term monogamous relationship. Even then, she was pretty condom happy.

Where had that logical, sensible woman gone over the weekend?

She rolled her shoulder back. The stiffness in her muscles was gone and so was the bite mark. If she hadn't seen it herself Friday night, she wouldn't have believed it was possible. Must be something strange with her metabolism. She never healed that quickly.

With a busy day ahead, Rebecca got to work early and threw herself into her job as a training planner. They had a new client looking for a full-blown proposal so she buried herself in that. It worked. Mostly. It was only when someone asked how her weekend had been that she blushed and stammered "fine".

Having run herself ragged, she fell into a deep dreamless sleep Monday night.

Tuesday it began. The weekend still loomed large in her memory but she was determined, *determined*, to put it out of her mind. Her body wasn't quite so willing to let the experience go. Midafternoon, her skin started to tingle and by the end of the day, the professional, efficient suit she'd worn to the office felt like a straightjacket. She worked through it. That night she dreamed of sex and running naked through the forest.

Thoroughly irritated by her dreams, on Wednesday morning she dressed in a less formal pantsuit-blouse combination. But still the weight of her clothes was too much. Her skin was so sensitive and by the afternoon, she wanted to strip and let the air conditioning in her office run across her naked body. She restrained. She was a professional after all. But as she walked into her house, she peeled off layers and pulled on the lightest weight nightgown she could find. Cranking her air conditioner to "high" helped, but only if she stood right in front of the thing—then her nipples got hard and, hell, she almost came just from the blowing air.

With only her nightgown weighing on her skin, the excess stimulation turned from an irritant to a seduction. Every touch of cloth or brush of air felt like a caress, a male hand stroking her. The whispered touches moved through her body, settling into her core until she thought she had to be burning up from the inside out. Every movement was a new tactile experience—and every sensation seemed to flow right to the center of her body. Just the process of walking through her house made her pussy ache.

By the time she went to bed, the need to come refused to be ignored any longer and she pulled out her vibrator, using the fantasy, uh, memory, of Deacon and Trey—one in her mouth, the other slowly fucking her pussy—to help her orgasm. The bright, sharp release eased her enough that she could sleep. But that night her dreams were again filled with sex. The dream repeated—the forest, the earth beneath her as she ran, chased and captured by two wicked lovers. Deacon and Trey, whispering to her, calling her name as she fucked them. They wanted her. They belonged to her.

Thursday began where Wednesday left off—the feel of clothing against her skin almost too much for her to bear. Desperate for some kind of relief, she wore a long loose skirt and short-sleeved shirt. Didn't help. She spent the day hypnotized by the seductive brush of cool air against her legs. Her breasts were heavy and ached to be touched, kissed, bitten. She groaned as she remembered both men, their lips on her nipples, licking and sucking until it was almost enough to make her come. She inhaled deeply to calm the sensation but that only made it worse. Every breath scraped her nipples across the delicate roughness of her lacy bra until she thought she'd go insane. With a growl of frustration, she threw down her pen and stormed to the bathroom. Once inside the restroom, she ripped open her blouse and took off the bra.

Standing in the bathroom stall—topless and out of breath—she listened to the hungry voice in her head. She needed her males. Needed to be mounted and fucked. She squeezed her breasts—her own touch making the cravings worse. She closed her eyes and whimpered, the sound somehow helping her keep control. This was not like her, but she would get through it. She had to. Holding that determination firmly in her mind, she forced herself to put her shirt back on, thankful that it was almost the end of the day.

Crushing her bra in her fist, she folded her arms beneath her breasts, walked back to her office and sat down. The presentation for tomorrow's meeting was almost complete. Just a few little tweaks and they'd be ready.

She stared at the graphics on her computer screen and tried to focus but images of wild, animalistic sex stalked her. And they weren't just fantasies. They were memories. Deacon and Trey, hot, hard bodies pressed against hers, one thick cock deep inside her pussy, the other rubbing and sliding against her ass, as if he was asking permission to fuck her there.

A faint cracking sound yanked her from her thoughts and she looked down. The pen she'd held had snapped and was leaking ink.

She tossed the broken plastic into the garbage and wiped off the smudges that had spilled on her desk blotter. Something was definitely wrong with her. She considered the idea of calling her doctor again. She'd seen her doctor Monday and there seemed to be no lingering effects of the weekend— except the pounding urge to fuck. What was she supposed to say? "Doc, I'm so horny, I could scream. All I want to do is fuck and I seem to have developed super strength."

Yeah, it sounded stupid even in her own head, much less speaking it aloud.

No, she would work through this herself.

Tormented, frustrated, and practically drugged on the myriad sensations racing through her body, Rebecca raced home and went straight to bed, taking her vibrator with her. It took three orgasms to calm her body enough so that she could fall into the dreams.

Friday morning, she stumbled out of bed, exhausted, feeling as though she actually had spent the last six hours fucking. Despite the sexy dreams, her body wanted to be mounted, fucked.

And the pulsing between her legs had returned full force. The quick climax she found using her handheld shower massager barely made a dent in the hunger.

She stood naked in front of her closet, her body crying out for release, but everything she'd tried had failed. Determined to make it through the day so she could return home and strip—the furious desires didn't seem quite so bad if she was naked—she searched for something to wear.

The desire that filled her made her feel sluggish and nothing in her closet fit right—it was too loose, or too tight, or covered too much skin. Digging to the far back corner of her closet, her hand landed on a short leather skirt she'd never worn—bought during a "between boyfriends, going out with the girls" phase. Her fingers stroked the supple leather. It was totally inappropriate for the office—even on casual dress Friday—but she wanted to wear it. Wanted that smooth, sexy material caressing her skin. Before she knew what she was doing, she'd pulled on the skirt and slipped into a silky blouse that teased her nipples. The thought of wearing a bra or panties never even crossed her mind.

She stood just for a moment and let the sensuous weight of the clothes press on her skin. The thought that she'd be leaving her scent on the leather — that her wet pussy would leave traces of her on the material — made her groan.

She stepped in front of the mirror, gasping at her reflection. She looked wild and sexual — her lips wet from her tongue's caress, her eyes sparkling with undisguised desire. Four-inch high black stilettos made her legs look long and sexy. Even her hair, usually constrained in a tight swirl at the back of her head, was free and hanging down around her shoulders.

She looked ready to fuck. She couldn't leave her house looking like this. Totally inappropriate for work. At a minimum she needed to put on a bra so her nipples weren't quite so blatantly displayed. Her breasts were too large to spend the day unrestrained.

Her cell phone chimed and she grabbed it, opening it and silently cursing in the same moment. Her partner.

"This is Rebecca."

"Where are you?" The low feminine voice warned that Jessie wasn't happy.

"I'm on my way." She looked at the clock, shocked to see it was nine o'clock. She was always at the office by now. Usually the first one there. But that was before sex had invaded her life.

"*Are* you? Because they are just walking in the door."

Who? She flipped through her mental calendar. Damn. The new clients. All day meeting. Starting two minutes ago.

"I'm really on my way. Stall them." To make sure she wasn't lying, she ran down the steps, grabbed her keys and slammed the door behind her. "I'll be there in ten minutes." It was a twenty minute drive but she could make it. She closed the phone and ran down the short walkway to her car.

Nine minutes later, a little sweaty and breathless, she walked into the office. Jessie met her in the hallway, talking as they walked to Rebecca's office.

"They're here and drinking coffee. We took a quick walk around the office. I made it sound like this was normal when we took on a new client."

Rebecca dropped her bag and scraped her hair back away from her face, listening and trying to calm her breath at the same time. She grabbed the client's files and started for the door.

"Are you sure that was the best choice of an outfit?" Jessie asked, blocking the hallway.

Rebecca looked down. Damn, she was still wearing the fuck-me skirt and top. "I was hot." It was a lame excuse. She grabbed the hanger behind her door and ripped off the black jacket that hung there, just for emergencies like these. Well, not exactly like these. She had never imagined herself coming to work in skirt that barely covered her ass, no bra, no panties.

"Yeah, this new client is going to think you're hot too."

"I'll keep the jacket on. Maybe he won't notice."

Jessie laughed and that was something Jessie rarely did. "Right. The way you look right now, we'll be lucky if Eric Marquez and his brother don't strip you naked and do you on the conference room table."

"Jessie!" Rebecca tugged the edges of her jacket together. There weren't any buttons and there was no way to hide the low dip of her blouse but at least they might not notice she was braless. Very conscious of her breasts, and trying to make sure they weren't bouncing when she walked, she followed Jessie toward the conference room.

Jessie stopped at the conference room door.

"Honey, I think it's a great idea. Use what you got, especially when working with male clients. They'll be so hot for you, they'll sign whatever we put in front of them."

Rebecca groaned. She'd spent her whole professional life trying to be seen as cool and competent. To *not* be treated any differently because of her sex and she certainly wouldn't trade on her sex to get business.

She took a deep breath and ignored the whisper of silk across her nipples. Despite her attire, she would walk in the room and be professional and businesslike and they would wow the client.

* * * * *

"Rebecca, Jessie, I'm more than pleased. You did everything we asked for and more. I like what we've seen. Let's get the contract signed and you can start on Monday."

Eric Marquez—clearly the older and more vocal business partner—smiled and stretched his hand across the table. This was a huge account for their firm. Rebecca fought to suppress a cheer. They'd done it. It had been a long-ass day and Rebecca couldn't wait for it to end. She was practically giddy and only part of it was because they'd landed the deal.

It had taken sheer willpower to keep her attention focused on the presentation and the discussion in the room. Her body still screamed for sex but she'd heard Trey's voice in her head, telling her to control it. It had worked for the most part, but now with nothing to distract her, the need crashed through her body, highlighting every nerve.

With the meeting behind them, she needed to get home and pull out her vibrator. From the past two nights experience, she knew it wouldn't be enough, but it would get her through the night. And then she was definitely calling her doctor. There had to be something wacky with her hormones. Maybe this was her biological clock but instead of ticking it was throbbing, pulsing, pounding.

Heat swelled in her sex and she felt her knees tremble. Just thinking those words made her pussy clench.

"Why don't we take you out for drinks to celebrate?" Jessie offered.

Rebecca heard the words and almost groaned. She didn't want to go out. She wanted to go home. But she knew Jessie was right. Their business was as much about social contact as it was about the day-to-day work they did.

"That sounds great." Tony, the younger brother, turned his smile to Rebecca. "What about you, Rebecca?" There was a hint of sex in his question—enough that she could act on it if she wanted, but not so much that she couldn't easily back away. She'd watched him all day—watched him watch her. The black jacket had come off by lunch—too hot in the conference room—and she'd done her best to keep her breasts camouflaged but she knew it had to be obvious to both men that she was braless. The short skirt had also drawn eyes and attention. Thankfully, once seated at the table, she'd been able to conceal the lower half of her body and focus most of the attention on their business history and training proposals.

She smiled at Tony and nodded. Under most circumstances, she knew it would be just a little light flirtation—she wasn't about to sleep with a client—but these weren't normal circumstances and what happened if she had a meltdown like she'd done last weekend? Based on her recent behavior it was entirely possible that she might give in to the urge to fuck and drag Tony into the backseat of her car and rip open his trousers.

As it had with every other sexual thought throughout the week, her body responded. Her nipples tightened as if a cool breeze was swirling around them. She waited for the jolt of knee-weakening lust but the interest remained on the surface, giving her some hope that this strange desire might be easing.

The group agreed to meet in thirty minutes across the street. It was a little bar that handled business customers during the week, but on Friday and Saturday, it somehow turned into a singles hookup hot spot.

Jessie managed to wait until Eric and Tony had entered the elevator before she screamed and jumped up and down.

"We did it." She threw her arms around Rebecca's neck and squeezed her into a hard quick hug. "You need to flash your tits more often."

116

She said it with just enough laughter that Rebecca couldn't take offense.

Rebecca's mind began to race. "We're going to be very busy over the next three months. We're going to need to hire at least two new trainers." It helped for her to have something to think about so she latched onto the future plans. "We'll want to move Frank over to this account and have one of the new people slip into his job. Though Frank might be willing to do both. We could probably work the schedule..."

She noticed that Jessie wasn't adding anything to the conversation. She looked at her partner.

"What?"

"We just landed the biggest client of our young careers and all you can do is plan? We have to celebrate."

Rebecca nodded and tried to get as excited as Jessie, but after a week of brutally controlling her emotions, it was difficult to let them show. And heaven knew what would happen if she did.

Struggling to maintain that control, she carried her papers to her office. Though the air conditioner was on high, sweat started to form between her breasts. Maybe she was sick. She stared at the phone. It had started last weekend. Maybe she'd contracted some weird sexual disease while she was at Taylor's cabin.

"Let's go, girly," Jessie called from the door. "We're going to party."

Rebecca smiled weakly. "Jess, remember, these guys are clients."

"So, we'll hang with them for a few minutes and then dump them and go find some men. With the way you look, you'll reel them in and I'll take the leftovers."

Considering Jessie was a petite blonde with a flat stomach and perky breasts, Rebecca knew Jessie didn't have to take her leftovers.

With a sigh, she grabbed her purse and followed Jessie out the door and across the street. The noise from the bar slammed into her as they walked inside. The pulsing music seemed to control the rhythm of her heart. She groaned as the sound moved through her veins and rocked into her sex. God, it was too much.

"There's Eric and Tony. Let's go."

Following Jessie through the crowded bar, Rebecca absorbed the overwhelming sensations that assaulted her. Bright lights amid the deliberately dim room pierced her eyes, the music, scents and flavors that seemed to land on her tongue. She licked her lips, capturing the tastes that lingered in the air. It tasted like desire. People out—some desperate, some interested—looking for someone to fuck.

Bodies pressed against her as she pushed through the crowd and it was all she could do not to whimper. God, she thought she would explode soon.

They finally made it to the table and sat down. The conversation was stilted enough that Rebecca had to concentrate—trying to think of something to say, something to smooth the relationship with their new clients. She couldn't ask about business. This was supposed to be social.

"So, do you guys have family in the area?"

The two men looked at each other. Eric laughed. "You could say that."

Tony smiled at the response. It was as though there was a joke between them that Rebecca didn't understand. After a long moment, Tony seemed to take pity on her.

"Actually, we have an extended family. Lots of cousins and aunts and uncles."

That seemed to be enough to get the conversation going.

When drinks arrived, Rebecca gulped down her soda, the little bubbles tickling her throat. Normally she would have gone with a cold white wine, but her senses were already too confused. She wasn't prepared to take any chances with alcohol tonight.

"Want to dance?" Tony's voice was low and masculine and part of her thrilled in the sound. It wasn't the same powerful sensation as when Trey or Deacon had spoken, but still, it was nice. Nice to have the male chasing her. She pushed her hips back, sliding her chair away from the table and stood up. Liquid heat flowed through her veins. Maybe dancing with Tony would be enough.

Maybe fucking Tony would be enough. She considered the idea as she followed him onto the dance floor. She needed a man. Needed a male fucking her.

Trey. Deacon. Her pussy clenched and a renewed rush of moisture teased her pussy lips.

Tony pulled her into his arms, using the crowded dance floor as an obvious excuse for holding her so close. His shoulders were broad and she could feel the tight muscles beneath his shirt as they swayed together. She leaned in closer, letting her breasts brush against his chest. Her nipples were aching. The slick material of her blouse clung to them, conforming to her shape. The light pressure against his chest sent a delicious zing into her pussy.

She moaned and tipped her head back, looking up at Tony. He seemed to be waiting for some sign and that was it. He leaned down and placed his mouth on hers, his hand sliding down her back, pulling her hips against his as he kissed her. He whispered kisses across her lips then opened his mouth, silently asking for entrance. Curious but strangely detached, she opened her lips and let him slip his tongue inside.

The man could kiss. His flavor didn't captivate her the way Deacon and Trey had but he was tasty and her body was practically humming with the need to come. She pressed up against him, rubbing her pussy along his cock. The tight mound in his trousers told her he was aroused as well. His free hand slipped down, touching the edge of her skirt and pulling it up, the back of his fingers stroking her thigh, going higher.

The hunger that had built inside her all week remained, but there was no new sparkle, no frantic surge of need as he moved his hand closer, mere inches from touching her pussy lips. She knew if it had been Deacon or Trey, she would have been squirming to get closer, clawing to get through their clothes. Tony would fuck her, she had no doubt about that, but it wouldn't be enough. She needed that explosive desire satisfied.

Regretfully, she stepped back, noticing that she was breathless. "We should get back to the table," she said and turned away. She wanted to be fucked, have her pussy stroked and kissed—but not by Tony. He was a good-looking, smart, interesting guy, but he wasn't the one she wanted touching her.

She hung around the table for a few minutes—so Tony wouldn't think he'd scared her off—but then made an excuse and slipped away.

Tears pricked her eyes as she stepped outside. What was wrong with her? She wanted sex but when a perfectly good man offered it, she backed away.

Maybe she should call Taylor and ask her to send Trey. She had to do something. The batteries on her vibrator would wear out and all she would get was a weak unsatisfying orgasm.

Feeling drained, irritable and horny, she parked her car in her driveway and trudged up the front walk, jerking to a stop when she realized there were people on her porch. Her motion activated light clicked on as she approached and she saw Trey and Deacon. Trey leaned against the doorjamb, his long hair glowing in the light. Deacon sat on the front stoop, looking far too edible.

A low jolt of hunger shot through her core but it was followed by a stab of panic. This was what she wanted, what

120

her body had been craving for days, but now that they were there, standing in front of her, she wasn't sure she should accept it. "What are you doing here?"

Chapter Nine

ॐ

"What are you doing here?" she repeated when neither answered.

The two men looked at each other, as if both were giving the other a chance to respond. "We came to see you," Deacon finally replied.

That wasn't precisely true, she knew. They came to fuck.

"Together?"

Trey shook his head but again Deacon was the one who spoke. "No, believe it or not, we seemed to have the same idea at the same time."

The center of her body heated up beneath his stare and she fought the urge to crumple before them. She had to focus, had to control whatever this was.

"How did you know where I lived?" She drilled Trey with her stare. He shrugged, clearly not intimidated.

"I asked Taylor."

She turned the determined glare toward Deacon. "I Googled you."

The Internet. Of course.

A light went on next door and Deacon stood up. "Maybe we should talk inside?"

Though she knew she should send them away, she couldn't make herself say the words.

She nodded and walked forward, her shoulder brushing Deacon's chest as her foot hit the first step. The light caress and the delicious male scent that surrounded him was too much for her beleaguered body to resist.

Her knees trembled. There they were. Her lovers. The males to satisfy her. Her body moved without direct command of her mind. She reached out, hooked her hand around Deacon's neck and pulled him close, planting her lips on his, driving her tongue into his open mouth. The hot masculine taste exploded on her tongue. Perfect. His hands clamped down on her hips and he pulled her hard against his body, against his erection.

She groaned and clung to him. The heat invaded her body and she fought the weight of her shirt, wanting it off her skin. Wanting her breasts against him, her nipples teased by the soft hair on his chest.

Another luscious smell pierced the seductive fog around her and she drew back. Trey. Waiting silently. She nipped at Deacon's mouth, silently vowing to return, and stepped onto her porch, grabbing Trey and pulling him to her. He met her with a ferocious kiss, using his tongue to conquer and command. The front of her blouse came apart in her hands, buttons popping and landing on the concrete. She tugged, pulling the edges back. Her nipples sang as they pressed against the rough material of his shirt. She sucked on his tongue. Needing him inside her. Needing —

"Whoa, honey." She wasn't sure which male spoke or which grabbed the silk dropping from her shoulders. "Your neighbors might not like the show."

At the mention of her neighbors, she snapped back, in control and appalled. What the hell had just happened? She stared down. Her shirt was open and her breasts bared. She grabbed the edges of her blouse and tugged them closed.

This was too much. She could understand desire and after the last week, she could even understand *desperate* desire, but stripping on her front porch as she Frenched one man after another? It was insane.

Deacon took the keys out of her hand and opened the door. As she stepped inside, she noticed a strange look on

Trey's face. He looked confused. The confusion turned to irritation.

Trying to act normal—though she wasn't sure what normal was in this situation—she flicked on the lights and put her purse on the entryway table. What happened now? Did she offer them something to drink? Something to eat? *Cookies, steak, me?*

Right. Either way, she had to do something. She refused to let the situation get completely out of hand. She opened her mouth but the look in Trey's eyes stopped her.

"You've been with another man."

Deacon's head snapped up and she felt the pressure of both male glares.

"No."

"I can smell him on you."

She straightened her spine, trying to fight the urge to back up as Trey stalked forward. She lost that battle and took a step backward, ending up against the wall.

He put his fingertips on her lips. "Here." Her throat. "Here." The front of her blouse. "Here. You let him touch you." He blocked her escape with his body.

"We danced. Kissed. That was it," she said, though she wasn't sure why she felt compelled to explain. A new and foreign desire welled up inside her—to drop to her knees and offer herself to these men in apology, to submit to whatever they wanted of her. Her knees wobbled and she had to fight the physical urge to kneel before them.

"Did you let him touch your pussy?" Deacon asked, his voice low and quiet, dangerous.

She fought the compulsion of Trey's gaze and looked over at Deacon. "No."

His eyes tightened as well, watching her with an angry disbelief. "He danced with you. Had those gorgeous tits unbound and pressed against him—and he didn't touch your cunt?"

She shook her head.

Trey sank down, his arm brushing her hip as he inhaled, breathing deep near her thighs. Rebecca held herself still. She knew he was so close he had to be able to smell her pussy, her arousal. Moisture coated her thighs and she knew he sensed it.

"Why do I smell him here?" He touched her skin, just below her skirt hem.

"He tried to touch me, but I stopped him."

"Show me," Trey commanded, standing up and stepping back. "Lift your skirt and show us where he touched you."

Completely on display—she considered making a break for it. Somehow, though their tempers were high right now, she didn't think either man would hurt her. And they'd let her go if she walked away. But the desire to stay was too strong. She liked their power. Liked the way they claimed her.

She grabbed the front of her skirt and pulled it up, raising it a few inches. With one finger, she drew a line across her thigh to show where Tony had touched her.

"Pull the skirt all the way up, baby," Deacon commanded. "We want to see if you let him get close to touching that sweet cunt."

The way he said those words made her pussy quiver. A new dominance, one she hadn't seen last weekend, filled him. The gentle man who'd resisted her seduction was gone and in his place was a powerful intense lover who demanded her compliance.

Swallowing deeply, she inched the skirt up higher, fighting the tight fit, loving the smooth leather against her skin. She lifted it until she was bare, until her pussy was revealed.

"Now, show us."

Again she touched her leg.

"No closer?"

"No." The reply came out soft and breathless.

"I don't like the idea of another man touching your pussy, honey." Trey stepped forward. He reached around her and tugged the skirt back down. Disappointment curled in her chest as he covered her again.

"But I didn't let him."

"You let him get close before you stopped him."

"I was—" She looked between both men, not knowing how to explain. "I needed—"

"What, honey? Did you need to be fucked?" Trey's palm moved over her backside.

She felt her cheeks turn red but she had to answer. "Yes."

"And you went to someone else?" He didn't wait for an answer. "I'm very disappointed. What do you think, Deke?"

"I think she needs to punished, so she understands that *we* fuck that pretty little cunt and no one else."

She shivered at the possession in his words.

"I think you're right." The mere whisper of her zipper sliding down fluttered through the room and the waistband of the skirt came free, dropping to the ground. Trey's hands reached up and pulled the blouse off her shoulders. She stood in the full light of her living room wearing only her high heels.

The thought should have appalled her, but there was no way to deny or avoid the lust in Deacon's eyes. Or the obvious bulge in his jeans. Trey nudged his erection against her hip as if warning her that he was hard too.

"Come here, baby." Deacon held out his hand and waited as she reached for him. He led her into the living room. Thankfully she'd left that morning in such a rush, she hadn't opened the curtains as was her habit. They were isolated from curious neighbors. "Put your hands on the arm of the couch," he commanded. "And bend over." Knowing the high heels lifted her ass, she did as he instructed.

Her heart was pounding in her ears as she eased herself forward, leaning down until her elbows supported her and her ass was tipped upward. Cool air tripped across the inside of her thighs, teasing the wet heat that slipped from her pussy. She spread her feet, instinctively wanting to reveal herself to the two men.

"That's very nice, isn't it, Trey? Like maybe she's done this before." A warm hand caressed her bottom. "Have you had your ass spanked?"

She shook her head, keeping her face hidden in her hands.

"Honey, it's best if you answer aloud," Trey said. "Have you ever been spanked?"

"Not since I was child." *Master.* The word rested on the tip of her tongue but she held it back.

"Well, maybe when we're done, you'll have learned your lesson."

Silence filled the room and the anticipation flooded her core. Her body was primed, ready for any contact. The first sharp smack made her gasp — the bright burst of pain was quickly crushed by the rush of pleasure. It was quickly followed by another smart blow. Not mean, not harsh — but stinging little spanks, flat handed across her bottom.

It burned her skin and the sensation sank into her already wet pussy. Hot long fingers slid into her slit, dipping into her opening.

"So wet," Deacon whispered as if he was pleased with the discovery. "She's drenching my hand."

"I think our little bitch likes having her ass spanked."

"Hmmm, but we can't let her enjoy it too much. She's being punished for letting another man so near her pussy."

"I don't think she'll forget the lesson," Trey said, the low, lazy drawl laced with amusement.

Deacon's hand slipped from between her legs and a harder, firmer spank landed on each cheek. She pressed her lips together to hold back the sound that threatened, not knowing if it would be a plea or moan. But she couldn't stop her hips from moving, pushing her ass back, offering it.

"Oh yeah, honey, that's it. Show us how much you want it."

Deacon took a step back, his mind overwhelmed by the beauty of the scene before him. Rebecca's ass, tight and high, bright pink from the strokes of his hand and Trey's. Deacon's cock was hard, rock solid and he had to fight the temptation to rip open his jeans and pull it out. But he knew as soon as he released himself, he was going to fuck her and he wanted this to last. Not that he wouldn't get hard again. If last weekend was any example, he'd recover faster than a teenage boy.

A low, needy groan slipped from Rebecca's lips and she arched her back, revealing the deep pink of her pussy lips. Deacon licked his lips. He was going to taste her tonight, drive his tongue into her hot little slit.

Trey pushed his hand between Rebecca's thighs. Deacon couldn't stop his groan. Trey looked up, his eyes sparking with the need to fuck. He stared at Deacon for a long time, then pushed two fingers into Rebecca's pussy, sliding them slowly in and pulling back. Her body arched into the slow, sexy finger-fuck.

"I think she's ready, Deacon. And she won't let any other man near our cunt, will you, honey?"

"No." Her answer could have sounded pitiful but instead it sounded hungry.

"That's right." Trey rubbed his hand up and down her slit. The perfume that dripped from her pussy filled the room. "This sweet hole belongs to us."

"Yes," she moaned and moved into his touch. And Deacon thought he'd come right there. He ground his back teeth together and continued the game. He strolled closer, deliberately slowing his walk, knowing that even if Rebecca couldn't see him, she knew where he was. He put his hand alongside Trey's and the other man shifted, not leaving her sex but giving Deacon room to sample.

"But Trey, do you really think she went all week without filling this tight pussy?" He pushed a finger into her passage and felt her clench around him. "We know how much she likes to get fucked." He drove a little deeper, grunting when she fucked herself back onto his fingers.

"You're right." Trey smacked her ass. "I'd be very upset if I thought she'd let another man fuck her." He stroked her sex. "Did you, honey?"

"No." Her red curls shook, falling forward to cover her face as she denied it.

"But you didn't go all week without coming, did you?"

She snapped her head back and looked over her shoulder, a bit of brazenness returning to her eyes. "Did *you*?" she taunted.

"Ooh, our little bitch is getting sassy."

Deacon didn't quite understand why Trey referred to Rebecca as a bitch, but the term somehow came out filled with affection.

"I see that." He eased his hand away and indicated to Trey to do the same. "Maybe she doesn't need us after all. She's got something else that can fill her cunt tonight."

She dropped her head forward. "No, please. I need you," she said, her voice contrite but still irritated. Rebecca wasn't the kind of woman to concede easily. Trey smiled and nodded but Deacon wasn't quite ready to give this up.

"What did you use to make yourself come, baby? Your fingers?" He skimmed his fingertip across her reddened backside. "Did you lie on your bed with your legs spread and drive those slim fingers into this tight cunt?" Again she shook her head. "What did you use?"

"Vibrator." He could almost hear her blushing.

"Sounds interesting," Trey said and he knew the other man was thinking the same thing he was.

Deacon nodded. "I'll run upstairs and see if I can find this toy cock she's been fucking." He thought about the past week and the dreams that had filled his sleep. Hour after hour he'd been teased with the image of his cock sliding into Rebecca's pussy while Trey fucked her mouth. This was his chance to watch and fuck her at the same time. "Maybe you'd want to give her something to do with her mouth."

As Deacon walked out of the room, Trey eased Rebecca upright. She clung to him, accepting his mouth, long drugging kisses. Deacon stood in the shadow of the stairway and watched, his cock hard and ready. The sight of Rebecca's slim curvy ass, pink from his and Trey's hands, made his dick even harder. Her hips pressed forward and Deacon knew she was cuddling Trey's cock between her thighs. Her pussy juices were dampening his jeans.

Trey lifted his head, moving out of reach of Rebecca's seeking mouth. He swooped back in and scraped his teeth across her neck, leaving a faint red streak. Deacon's shoulder heated up where Rebecca had bitten him, as if reminding him how it felt to have her teeth buried in his flesh.

"On your knees, baby. I want my cock in your mouth." It was spoken low, but even from across the room, Deacon heard the command and power in Trey's words. Deacon felt the spike of arousal that shot through Rebecca's body.

"Yes," she whispered, sinking slowly to her knees. Her hands reaching for Trey's belt.

Trey slid his fingers into Rebecca's curls and Deacon turned away, continuing up the stairs.

Tonight was just the culmination of a long, strange week.

Deacon hadn't been at all surprised to see Trey waiting on Rebecca's porch when he'd shown up. Somehow it seemed inevitable, even expected, that the other man would be there. Though Deacon wasn't quite sure how *he'd* come to be here. It had been a compulsion, an impulse, an innate need to find Rebecca and be with her. Fuck her. His cock had existed in various states of hardness all week. It was worse than being a teenager. And it seemed connected to some external source. He knew something was up.

Besides his cock.

He'd parked his car on the road and climbed out, carrying the shopping bags he'd brought along. Was it presumptuous? Probably. But after last weekend, he had a feeling they were going to need what he'd brought. Better to be prepared.

Deacon looked in the door at the top of the stairs and discovered Rebecca's bedroom. He laughed when he saw the pile of clothes dumped on the chair, as if she'd struggled to find an outfit. Well, he approved of the one she'd chosen. Especially the lack of underwear.

Knowing that Trey was downstairs, with Rebecca's lips around his cock, spurred Deacon on. He went to the bedside table and opened the drawer. Two vibrators lay nestled together. Hmm, two. Maybe they wouldn't need what he'd brought after all.

He grabbed the smaller of the two toys—a bright blue, hard plastic vibrator with the faint shaping of cock. So, this was what she'd been using at night. His cock twitched inside his jeans, wanting to be the rod that satisfied her.

Deacon went back downstairs and stopped as he stepped into the living room. Rebecca was back on her feet, bent over, her ass swaying high in the air, her high heels making her tip forward as she buried her face in Trey's lap. The deep pink of her cunt glistened in the weak light. Trey sat on the couch arm, his fingers slowly scraping through the long strands of her hair, a look of pure bliss on his face. He nodded when Deacon entered.

Wanting, needing to be a part of their loving, Deacon joined in, sliding his hand beneath her body and cupping one ripe breast. It fit perfectly in his palm, the tight nipple pressing hard against his skin. She moaned—the sound muffled against Trey's shaft—and arched her back, pushing into his caress.

"Turn your head, baby," he commanded, letting his hunger flow through his words. "Let me see you suck him off."

She lifted her head and looked up at him. Her lips were pink and swollen and she looked a little dazed.

"Did you miss us?"

"Yes."

"Good, now keeping licking his cock, baby. Let me watch you."

She returned to her task, unable to resist Deacon's command—or the temptation of Trey's cock. Mindful of making sure that Deacon could see, she turned her head and cupped Trey's shaft in one hand as she fluttered her tongue up the full length. He moaned and the slow subtle rock of his hips told her how much he liked it.

For a moment, the reality of her situation struck her. Here she was, again, naked with two men, her ass burning from being spanked, a long thick cock in her mouth and she'd never been more turned on in her life. Her pussy clenched and throbbed, aching to be filled.

"Deacon." Trey's hand slid down her back, warm and comforting. "She took her punishment very well, don't you think?"

"I do." Hot fingers caressed her backside, slipping down between her legs. The light touch made her arch her back even more.

"Maybe we should reward her, give her something to fill that pretty cunt."

The loving, explicit way they both spoke made her body shiver.

Deacon knelt down behind her, between her spread thighs, his breath hot against her skin. Rebecca moaned. Her body was vibrating with the desire, the need to come. Energy pulsed between the three of them—Trey to her, her into Deacon, pure electrifying power. She wanted to pull that power—the seductive masculine energy—into her body. "Please," she whimpered against Trey's cock, her lips teasing his skin as she begged. "Fuck me."

"Not yet, baby. Such a pretty little cunt," Deacon whispered, slipping his finger into her. "So wet and hungry for some cock."

"Yes," she moaned, her hips rolling up, trying to ease him into her. He pulled back.

"No, no, baby. You wanted this fake cock. Oh yeah." Cool hard plastic tested the inside edge of her pussy and she tensed. "No, baby, don't move. Let me just coat this so it slides in nice and easy." He rubbed the vibrator along her slit, twirling it, covering it with her pussy juices. "Now, let me push this in." Deacon's voice made her still, holding her breath as he nudged the narrow head of the vibrator into her opening. Slow and steady, he pushed it inside. "Oh, yeah. I like seeing those pretty pink lips spreading to take this inside." He thrust it halfway in then stopped. "I won't go too fast, baby, and you tell me when you're going to come, all right?" She nodded. "Good."

The slim tube slid into her, eased by the hot viscous liquid that drenched her cunt. Deacon held his breath as he pushed the rod inside her, feeling a matching ache in his own cock. Trey grunted and he knew the other man was experiencing the same thing. Deacon pushed the vibrator deeper, slow and steady, trying to gauge the resistance of her body, not wanting to hurt her or wear out her pussy before either her or Trey got to fuck her, but seeing the bright blue sex toy fuck her cunt was too much temptation.

He filled her until she groaned and then slowly pulled back, her moisture coating the thin rod, the scent of her pussy juice filling his head until he was sure it replaced the oxygen in the room. He didn't need it. He could live on her scent alone.

Focusing his mind on her, he drilled the vibrator back inside and used the hard plastic to fuck her. She cried out and he looked up, afraid he'd hurt her, but Trey shook his head, the upward bend of his lips told Deacon she was nowhere near pain. Trey reached beneath her, cupping her breast and drawing out another wicked moan.

Yes, Deacon thought as he eased the vibrator back into her pussy. They would arouse her, fuck her together until she begged to belong to them.

"That's it, baby. Take more." Deacon whispered the words as he spun the end of the vibrator, sending the tool into action. The toy shook in his hand, the slick juices of her cunt making it difficult to hold. He grabbed the end and thrust it forward, savoring the cry that rippled from Rebecca's throat. "Do you want to come with this toy cock inside you?" he demanded. He kept up the steady penetration and retreat, sensing her body's need, knowing this wasn't enough. She needed a real cock inside her, coming inside her.

His cock pulsed against the buttons of his jeans, almost begging to be released. But not yet. Soon, he would fuck her. The sight of her pink pussy accepting the vibrator was so sexy. He slowed down his penetration, making it more sexual than punishing. Her body responded. Tight and slick, she moved against him.

"Is this what you want, Rebecca? Do you want this toy cock fucking you?"

"No." The sound was more moan that actual spoken word.

"Are you sure? You had it before."

"No. I want you."

"What do you think, Trey? Shall we let this sweet cunt be filled?"

"I don't know," he said, shaking his head as if considering a weighty decision. Deacon held back the smile that threatened. It appeared that Trey liked to play as he did —

sensual torture. "It seemed to be enough to satisfy her already. We could leave her —"

"No!" She clutched at his hips, her fingers practically tearing the cloth of Trey's jeans. "It wasn't enough." Her moan was a delicious music to his senses. "Fuck me."

Deacon slipped the blue vibrator from inside her, the slick juices coating his fingers, painting her thighs.

He knelt down and lapped at her cunt, a quick brush of his tongue. Rebecca's cry shattered the room and the delicious tension that zipped through her body made Deacon's cock throb.

"Don't stop sucking him, baby," he commanded against her pussy and seconds later heard Trey's groan. *Oh yes, they were all going to find pleasure tonight.*

Chapter Ten

𝕊𝕆

Trey watched, unable to see what Deacon was doing but feeling the results through Rebecca's body.

"Make him come," Deacon ordered and the dominance in his voice almost made Trey smile. Last weekend Trey never would have expected the human to be a closet Dom, but Deacon controlled the scene. And for now, Trey was content to let him. Of course, knowing his own dominant tendencies, he didn't know how long he could allow the other man to guide their fucking.

The powerful scent of Rebecca's pussy juices flooded the room and it was all Trey could do not to pull her mouth away, spin her around and drive his cock into her cunt. The delicate sucking was incredible, but he wanted to thrust, wanted to pump into her. Coming in her mouth required control on his part that he wasn't sure he had.

Her lips tightened around his cock and she moaned, the sound shivered down his shaft and settled at the base of his spine.

"Oh damn, Deke, whatever you're doing to her, keep at it." He slid his fingers into Rebecca's hair and held her held as he thrust up. She took him, swallowing his cock deep into her mouth. "That's it."

Trey ground his teeth together, fighting the urge to snarl, crushing the surge of jealousy that Deacon was pleasuring her. The connection between Deacon and Rebecca remained strong, the power of her bite and the bond they'd formed by fucking pulled them together and Trey had to push aside his envy that Rebecca had claimed Deacon first.

That she desired Trey, too, was obvious. And she needed him, or her body did. The serum in his cum would help ease her transition, whether she recognized it or not. Once the first full moon had passed, her desires would lessen — at least a bit — and she could think more clearly about who would be her lover. Breaking the bond between her and Deacon wouldn't be pleasant but it could be done.

But that was for later. At least for tonight, he and Deacon were fucking her together, giving her the pleasure she needed.

Deacon stood up, his lips glittering with traces of her pussy juices. Rebecca whimpered at the loss of his mouth and pushed her hips back, silently demanding to be filled. He opened his jeans and shoved the offending material down.

"Make him come," Deacon ordered, pressing his cock along her ass, not entering her but Trey knew it was coming. "Then you'll get fucked, baby."

"I need to come," she moaned. The pleading words slipped around his cock and squeezing.

"And you will, but you should be concentrating on his dick. Show him how much you like having him in your mouth." Deacon smacked his hand on her ass, reminding her of the punishment they'd already given her. She groaned and opened her mouth, swirling her tongue around the head of Trey's cock, licking the drops of pre-cum that were coating the head. "I'm not going to let you come until he spills between those pretty pink lips."

Trey braced himself, knowing she would begin a hard suck. Instead, she kissed his cock and licked, slow, lapping caresses up the full length of his shaft. It was as if she wasn't ready to let go of his cock. Wanted it.

She raised her eyes and pulled her lips away long enough to smile. "I want to taste you," she whispered. "I want you to come in my mouth."

The sensual words were every man's fantasy. And Trey couldn't resist. She opened her mouth over his cock and did the same wickedly slow swallow, taking him to the back of her throat. He gripped her head and lifted his hips, nudging just a little deeper, wanting more. She moaned and took him.

He looked up. Deacon was watching, his eyes trained on her mouth. And Trey's cock inside it. It was strange but just the sight of Deacon watching them made him harder and he pushed his hips up, needing to be a little deeper, wanting to show the other man, share this with him.

"That's it, baby," Trey encouraged, pulling her hair back so Deacon could see. "God, that feels so sweet. Suck me deep, honey."

Her lips tightened around his cock and she drew back, sucking hard and strong, until just the tip stayed in her mouth. The wolf inside him howled and Trey snapped his teeth together, fighting the urge to come. The hot pleasure of her mouth was too tempting. He didn't want it to end so soon. But he couldn't fight for long.

She moaned around his shaft and flicked her tongue across the underside of his cock as she pulled back. The sweet double caress was almost too much. One more thrust. Her lips tightened and he filled her mouth, shooting his cum deep into her throat. She swallowed quickly, lapping at the thick head as if she didn't want to leave a drop behind. He knew his cum tasted different from human males—or so he'd been told—because of his werewolf ancestry. He could only imagine that nature had designed it so the female would fully enjoy her male coming in her mouth.

"Very good, baby." Pleasure fluttered in her chest at Deacon's approval and Trey's caressing hands as he silently expressed his thanks. She only had a moment to savor it. Deacon placed his cock to her entrance, nudging the tip inside, just a hint, just a warning before he held her hips and thrust hard and deep. The thick shaft stretched her almost painfully as he filled her. The slow fuck with her vibrator and Deacon's mouth had primed her pussy and as he pushed into her, she came, crying out as her pussy clenched. Tension shot through her body and her fingernails bit into Trey's thighs as she held on.

"Oh, yeah, she needed to come, didn't you, baby?" Deacon asked, his hips pressing against her ass, his fingers stroking her back.

She nodded, unable to speak, her mind incapable of forming the words.

"You'll come again for me."

Yes. She whispered the word in her head, loving the sexual promise.

"Can you take me hard, baby?" he asked, his hand smoothing down her back, fingers spread wide, pressing deep as he stroked her. "I need to fuck. Watching that toy slide in and out of your pretty cunt has made me so hard. I need to ride you, deep. Can you take me?"

The brutal hunger in his words almost made her come again and she moaned her agreement, pushing her hips back, trying force him deeper. She felt Trey slide out of the way and she grabbed the edge of the couch, bracing herself for the hard, fast fuck that Deacon promised.

His retreat was slow, so slow she felt each individual inch of his cock slide out, until just the head remained, thick and round. He drove in, filling her in one powerful stroke. She groaned and buried her head against the couch.

"Yeah, that's what she needs, Deke. Fuck her." Trey's voice barely penetrated the lust fog that surrounded her. Her world shrunk until all she knew was Deacon's cock pounding into her. As promised, he fucked her hard, his balls slapping her flesh as he filled her. It was glorious. After the long frustrating week, she needed this. She would ache tomorrow but now she wanted him harder and deeper, filling her and marking her body.

She spread her legs and gripped the arm of the couch, bracing herself as he fucked her. His fingers bit into her hips and he pumped faster. A high keening sound slipped into the room and Rebecca realized the noise was coming from her.

"Damn," Deacon grunted. "I'm going to come, baby, I can't stop." His penetration slowed, as if he was fighting his own orgasm. "Help me, Trey. Make her come before I lose it."

A large warm body brushed her side and Trey's hand slid across her stomach, down into her slit, his finger teasing her clit. The touch was light, as if he knew she was hypersensitive.

"Come on, honey, let him feel you come around his cock." His voice sank into her core, a mystical caress that melded with the slow glide of his finger. The delicious hard fucking and Trey's light touch combined, giving her what she needed. He rubbed and it sent a shock through her pussy. Deacon shouted and thrust into her one more time, his cum flooding into her in hot pulses.

She rested her forehead on the couch and listened to her heart pound, her breath frantically straining her lungs. God, she couldn't catch enough air. Deacon was still inside her, softening but hard enough to pulse and tease her well-used flesh. Trey's hand cupped her pussy, petting her mound, soothing her.

Chimes rang through the air and Rebecca slowly lifted her head, dazed, knowing her mouth was probably hanging open. It took her a moment to identify the sound. Her phone. It was her cell phone. The customized ring told her it was Jessie calling. Let it ring, she thought, she couldn't move. Not yet.

"You might want to get that," Trey grumbled. "It's the third time it's rung in the last ten minutes."

She blinked and stared at him, amazed that she could have missed the sound. Her ear was attuned to the ring of her cell phone. It was rarely out of her reach. The chiming continued and Rebecca decided Trey was right. Jessie would just keep calling until Rebecca answered. She wiggled, hinting that Deacon needed to move too. With a reluctant groan and final seductive stroke to her pussy, he slipped out of her. A hot trail of his cum and her moisture slipped down the inside her thighs.

A low growl erupted from Trey as if he could see or sense the other male's seed on her skin. A little shiver went through her sex as his eyes glowed red. She pushed against the couch and straightened, feeling the strain to the backs of her thighs and her lower back. Damn, she was going to be sore tomorrow. But it had been worth it. For the first time in a week, her body was satisfied.

But even as she thought it, she felt the spark of renewed desire. Impossible. She'd just come — hard — several times. Her muscles were trembling, her knees barely held upright but all she could think to do was lie down, spread her legs and beg her lovers to fuck her.

Deacon and Trey stepped back, watching her as she turned and faced them. She opened her mouth, not sure what to say, but was saved by the insistent chiming of her phone. Jessie wasn't giving up.

On shaky legs, she walked to the front door and picked up her purse, conscious of the fact that Deacon and Trey were watching. She grabbed her phone and flipped it open.

"Hi, Jessie."

"Damn, Rebecca, where have you been? Are you okay?"

"I'm fine."

"You looked a little weird when you left the bar."

"I'm fine," she repeated. *I just had sex with two men and I want more but beyond that, I'm fine.*

"Good. And you missed a great celebration party. These guys are so intense. And they loved you. Eric was really impressed by the proposal and wants to see dates early next week. And I swear Tony was drooling when he talked to you." Rebecca nodded, even though she knew Jessie couldn't see her. This was typical after a new client or even just a party. She and Jessie called and rehashed the night's events. But tonight Rebecca had a little more on her mind.

141

Standing apart from Deacon and Trey—and her body satisfied—she could focus on reality.

She'd done it again. She'd had sex with two men. It was the same two men as before but that didn't change the fact that it was *two* men. And she'd loved it, wanted more. Even standing there with Deacon's cum getting sticky on her thighs and the taste of Trey lingering in her mouth, she wanted more. She looked across the room and saw her lovers—Trey's shirt hung open, revealing those tight hard abs she wanted to stroke. Deacon hitched his jeans up and was buttoning them, but she could see the press of his erection. They were both hard again, ready to fuck her.

She licked her lips, almost able to taste them. She whimpered, wanting them both naked and in her mouth.

"Rebecca, are you there?"

"What? Yeah," she answered, but not even Jessie's prompt could hold her attention, the dreams and desires of the past week were too tempting and within her grasp.

"Listen, you sound tired. You should get to bed."

Trey smirked, like he could hear Jessie's conversation from across the room.

"What do you say we meet for breakfast tomorrow?" Jessie asked. "We can get started on the plan and—"

Trey straightened and folded his arms across his chest. The warning in his eyes was clear.

"Uh, Jessie, I think I'm going to be busy tomorrow morning." Deacon raised his eyebrows, daring her. "Probably all day." Both men still stared at her with intense, demanding eyes. "Could be an all weekend thing. Let me just call you, okay? Bye." She hit the off button before she closed the phone—no more calls tonight. The tiny thump as she put the phone on the side table seemed to echo through the room.

Deacon tipped his head to the side and just stared at her. Trey hadn't shifted from his arms folded, towering male pose. Oh, boy. What was she getting herself into? This was so not like her—especially the weird urge to offer her body to these men, to submit to every kinky desire they might have. Of course, if last weekend and tonight were examples, she'd enjoy every minute of those kinky experiences.

Her heart pounded loud in her chest and she decided she needed a moment—just a moment—of being in control.

"I'm going upstairs to take a shower." She strolled toward the stairs, stopping at the first step. "I'll be right back."

The reaction from both men was subtle, just barely visible. Muscles tightened, jaws clenched and she could swear Trey's nostrils flared. What the hell? Submission was all fun and games in bed, but if they expected her to ask permission to take a shower, they were sorely mistaken. The two men looked at her with furious intent. Rebecca glared back. She wasn't backing down on this.

Deacon and Trey turned their stares toward each other and seemed to come to some masculine agreement. Both nodded and started forward, Trey peeling off his shirt as he walked. *Looks like I won't be showering alone.* Okay, she could handle that. The low light in the living room etched intriguing shadows across his chest. She licked her lips, just thinking about running her mouth across every inch of his skin.

"Damn," Deacon muttered as if he could read her thoughts.

Panic threatened but lust was louder, practically howling in her head, drenching her pussy, reminding her that she was hungry, desperate for a taste of her males. The blatant, possessive tone to her thoughts was enough to shock her out of the spell. Resisting the temptation of Trey's chest and the heat burning in Deacon's eyes, Rebecca took the first step up the stairs.

A large hot hand smoothed down her backside, slowing her forward progress. She grabbed the handrailing and held on as Trey's fingers pushed between her legs. He cupped her pussy in his palm and fluttered two fingers across her clit. She groaned but fought the wicked distraction of his touch. "Shower," she whispered. With just that light touch, she knew she couldn't move without Trey's permission.

He continued the delicate caresses and within moments she felt her hips moving, slow pulses against his fingers, silently guiding him where she needed.

"Baby, you're slick and wet, and need to fuck."

"I need a shower more." She tried to sound strong and confident but her words came out as little whimpers, timed to Trey's touch.

He chuckled. "We'll join you." His hand slid back until one finger touched her opening. Then he pushed in. "You can show us how much you missed having our cocks in this tight little hole."

She nodded unable to find the words to reply. Trey's hand slipped away and she whimpered in regret. His soft laughter didn't help much.

"Don't worry, honey, you'll get more." She didn't doubt it for a moment.

Taking a deep breath, she continued up the stairs, strangely unconcerned that she only wore her high heels and that both men could see her bare ass as she walked. Her cheeks heated as she remembered the wicked spanking downstairs. Her bottom was probably still pink, glowing. She led the way to the bathroom and stopped, the practical side of her nature coming to the forefront.

"I don't think three of us are going to fit," she said, staring at the narrow shower she had.

"You'd be surprised what you can fit in a tight space." Deacon's words were laced with sex and made Rebecca shiver. "Now bend over and take off those heels for us."

She stood for a moment, watching the two men. They looked so different in appearance, one dark and one light, but both were strong and dominant. And they wanted her. The lust in their eyes was the only thing that matched.

Feeling like a stripper performing for private clients, she turned to the side and slowly bent over, her ass once again tipping up in the air.

She raised one leg and slipped the tall shoe off, then slowly repeated the process. She didn't need to look at either man to know they were watching with hot hungry stares. Their desire not only inspired hers but gave her a jolt of power.

She straightened and turned away, giving them a clear view of her back and ass. She leaned forward, making sure to keep her legs separated so they could see, and turned on the water. A low growl rumbled from behind her and the sound wove itself into her core, curling through her pussy and settling on her clit.

Fighting the desire in her own body and the lust in theirs, she stepped into the shower, sighing as the hot water splashed across her skin. Slowly she turned to face her lovers. Neither man moved to join her. Trey leaned against the bathroom counter, watching, his shirt gone, his jeans only partially buttoned. Deacon gripped the doorframe as if it was his lifeline. His eyes tracked down her body, stopping at her sex. The sticky residue of his cum lingered on her thighs.

She turned and faced the spray, letting it cascade down her face and breasts, rivulets of water sliding between her legs. It was as if she could feel each drop caressing her skin. And she wanted more.

She pulled the handheld showerhead off the hanger and brought it close, turning the knob until the water pulsed out in a rapid pattern. Mindful of her audience, she faced them, bringing the spray to her breasts. The tiny pulses made her nipples almost painfully hard. A little gasp escaped her throat. Deacon's eyes widened just a fraction as he heard it.

Slowly she worked the showerhead down her stomach, over the tops of her thighs and then between her legs. She moved her feet apart and aimed the spray to her clit. Delicate spikes struck the tight mound of flesh and her breath came in rapid shudders. The last traces of Deacon's cum washed away as she worked the water against her clit. She closed her eyes and focused on the pleasure. Her body was so tuned to sex right now, she could come with just a few more—

A hand covered hers, pulling the pulsing showerhead away. Rebecca's eyes snapped open and she stared into Trey's eyes.

"Honey, for this weekend, you come when we say you can."

She opened her mouth to protest but didn't get the chance. Trey stepped forward, nudging her to the side. Water splashed against the back wall but Trey didn't let that stop him. He lifted the nozzle out of her hand and let it pour down his chest.

Rebecca blinked as water splattered everywhere. She looked and saw Deacon standing there, naked, shaking his head, almost as if he couldn't believe he was doing this.

"One of us is going to be cold," he grumbled as he joined them in the shower, taking his place on Rebecca's other side. He turned her and hooked his arm around her back, pulling her against him, the tight tips of her breasts poking into his chest.

His hand cupped her ass, squeezing and drawing her closer, but Trey didn't let her go far. He scraped his teeth across her neck and shoulder, reminding her that he was there and hungry for her as well.

"Honey, I think you owe us for trying to get your orgasm from some toy."

Blushing, she raised her eyes to Deacon. He nodded, agreeing with Trey.

"What would you like?" she asked, feeling powerful and seductive, even as she offered herself.

"Suck us off, sweet." Trey turned her head and covered her mouth with his. "Use that sweet mouth to make us both come." He bit her lower lip, a touch too hard to be pure pleasure. "And if you're good, we'll let you come again."

Deacon growled his agreement and her insides melted. She didn't understand it. Something about these two men and the wicked way they dominated just drew out the submissive in her—a woman she'd never seen before and barely recognized.

Her gaze bounced between both men then she slowly sank to her knees, her muscles flowing with the hungry need that controlled her body. Hot water continued to splash down on her neck, warming her, cleansing her.

Their two hot, hard cocks waited for her. She groaned as her knees hit the soft padded floor mat. She wanted this. Something inside her wanted to stroke and lick, taste and suck both their cocks. She glanced up. Trey stared down at her, a challenge clear in his eyes. Deacon watched her with a dark hungry gaze. It was amazing—physically they were different but the same dangerous power seemed to fill them.

She curled her fingers around each shaft and slid her hand down to the base, squeezing gently. A sharp hiss escaped from Trey. Both men pushed their hips into her caress.

She smiled and turned first to Deacon, kissing the thick head of his shaft, laving her tongue across the smooth skin before turning and giving the same treatment to Trey's cock. The twin chorus of moans surged through her as pure electric energy.

She worked between the two cocks—back and forth, licking and playing her fingers along their lengths. Deacon was markedly thicker than Trey, but she knew the wicked pleasure of both, knew how good they felt inside her. Hers to play with, hers to tease.

Pumping her fist slowly up and down Trey's cock, she turned and opened her mouth on Deacon, letting inches slide inside, taking what she could, flicking her tongue across the underside of the head as she pulled back, letting him pop free of her lips. She licked the tip with a quick flutter then turned to Trey and worshiped him in the same manner.

Neither man moved. They were barely breathing. The tension in their muscles translated into a sweet flutter in her pussy. Luscious feminine power surged through her body as she sucked and licked them, tormenting them with light strokes. It was delicious and sexy.

"Baby, don't make us wait."

But she wouldn't be rushed. Downstairs and last weekend, they had been in control, but now she had them in her hands—literally—and she wasn't going to be rushed. She wrapped her fingers around both shafts and slowly began to pump, keeping her hands moving at the same rate. Trey shifted, widening his stance and bracing himself as she stroked him. Deacon slipped his hand into her hair and she knew he was fighting the urge to turn her head and drive his cock into her mouth.

She brought their cocks close together, not quite touching and slowly stroked her tongue between them. Deacon cried out as if the sight was too much for him to endure. He thrust against her hand, driving his cock faster and harder between her fingers.

Rebecca shook her head and loosened her grip. "Naughty, naughty, Deacon. You'll take what I give you," she said, using the same words on him that he'd said to her. To give him a little taste of punishment, she turned her head and sucked the tip of Trey's cock into her lips, moaning as she let him sink fully into her mouth. He groaned but remained still and she rewarded him with a several long slow sucks.

Pulling back, she looked up. Deacon's eyes were blazing as he stared down at her. "See what happens to good boys?"

His jaw convulsed and she knew he was fighting his dominant nature. But finally he opened his lips enough to snarl, "Yes."

"Very good." She placed a kiss on his cock head to reward him and went back to her slow methodical strokes, going a little harder and a little longer each time, interspersing flicks of her tongue. Their taste filled her head until all she knew was their flavor and texture, the smooth skin beneath her tongue as she licked.

"Damn it, Rebecca," Deacon growled. His hips rolled forward and she looked up. Trey was staring down, his eyes glowing with a new hunger. She either had to finish this now, or she was going to find herself bent over the edge of the tub.

"Do you want to come?" she asked, her breath hot against their cocks. Both men groaned and she assumed that meant yes. Directing their cocks toward her breasts, she worked their shafts, pumping her hands harder, feeling each man strain to go deeper, wanting their cum, wanting to be the one to give them this pleasure.

Deacon cried out first. His head jerked back and he punched his hips forward, hot streams pulsed from his cock, splattering across her breasts. Trey groaned and moments later his cum poured onto her skin, blending with fading streams of Deacon's orgasm. The scent and sight of their pleasure on her skin was a delicious caress to her soul. Her males had found pleasure with her.

Chapter Eleven

❧

She looked up, captivated by the sight of both men, their strong bodies and tight hard muscles weakened and pleasured by her. She stood up and tipped her head back, arching her breasts into the shower spray. Hot water trickled down her skin, washing away their cum. She scooped her breasts in her hands and held them up, positioned beneath the showerhead.

Deacon leaned in, his mouth on hers, his tongue driving deep into her mouth. Trey hot lips scalded her throat, drawing her attention. She pulled back from Deacon, leaving him with a slip of her tongue and shared the kiss with Trey.

Hot hands and lips moved over her skin. Deacon bent down and sucked hard on her nipple, applying a punishing bite to the tip that made her pussy cream.

Trey's hand slid between her legs.

"Hmmm," he hummed against her neck. "Look whose pussy is soaking wet again." He pushed his finger into her opening. "I think our sweet little bitch likes sucking us both off. Don't you?" She didn't reply, too caught up in the slow thrust of his finger inside her, the way he pressed his thumb against her clit. "Don't you, honey?"

"Yes."

Deacon's hand moved down her body, sliding along Trey's path and easing into her slit.

"Spread your legs, sweetheart, let us touch you." She shifted enough to give them both access. "Damn, you're right, Trey. So hot and slick." He stroked the inside of her pussy lips. "Just waiting for a cock to fill her."

"*Two* cocks to fill her," Trey corrected, his voice low and husky. Rebecca jerked her head up and stared into his eyes. "That's what you want, isn't it, sweet? One of us fucking this tight hole." He pumped his finger inside her pussy. "The other sliding into that sexy ass of yours."

Her pussy reacted to the image, fluttering and squeezing him inside.

"Yes, she likes the idea."

Deacon slowly turned her body until she faced Trey. "Lean forward, baby. Let me see your pretty ass." His fingers skimmed up the split between her ass cheeks, light and teasing, so tempting.

Trembling, not sure what to expect, she clung to Trey's shoulder.

"Do you want me to stop?" Deacon asked, one finger retracing the path he'd just made, pausing to press into the tight rosette.

She looked down, staring at their legs, knowing her cheeks were burning. God, she shouldn't want this, but she did. She wanted to feel both of them inside her.

"Rebecca?" She shook her head. "You need to tell me, baby, or I'm going to stop."

"No." She found her courage and looked up, fearing the laughter or mockery in Trey's eyes. Instead she saw only hunger and pleasure. As if he knew she was on shaky ground, he rubbed her hip and placed a light kiss on her mouth, a brief taste that gave her the comfort. She glanced over her shoulder and saw Deacon watching her with the same desire. "No," she said again. "Don't stop."

Lust rippled beneath the surface of his eyes and he leaned down, kissing her shoulder, his lips hot as his finger pressed forward. The liquid from her pussy coated his fingers and eased his way.

She gasped as he pushed deeper, her body instinctively fighting the penetration. "You okay?" Trey asked and she realized she was probably leaving dents in his skin from her fingernails. She nodded and offered a weak smile.

"I'm just afraid it will hurt."

Deacon's tongue flicked across the back of her neck. "We would never hurt you, baby," he vowed against her ear.

"Never," Trey agreed. "We'll wait until you're ready." He looked over her shoulder to Deacon and she could sense the silent communication between the two men, as if they were agreeing. "Until your body is ready to take one of us back there."

"Yes." Deacon pumped his finger in and out of her ass, slow, almost delicate, letting her absorb the delicious sensations. "We'll wait until you're ready."

Trey lifted her chin, silently urging her to straighten. She found herself trapped between their hard bodies again, Deacon's finger still slowly thrusting in and out of her ass. It was very hard to concentrate with that luscious caress teasing her body. Trey seemed to sense that focus was elsewhere. He looked down and the classic half smile that told her Trey's wicked side was returning curled his lips.

"And to make sure you're ready..." He winked. "Deacon brought you a present."

There was too much mischief in Trey's eyes for her to trust him. "What *kind* of present?"

"The kind you slip into that tight little butt so when we're ready to fuck, you'll let us in."

As if there was some mutually agreed upon signal, Deacon pulled out, leaving her strangely empty. He turned away and washed up. With a final kiss, he climbed out of the shower.

"I'll run downstairs and get her *present*."

Trey backed Rebecca up until she was under the shower spray again, letting it warm her skin for just a moment before he smacked the water off.

"And while he's gone, I'm going to fuck you." He kissed her, a hard, almost punishing, caress. "Your mouth is sweet, baby, but I need to ride you." Her knees trembled at the sensual promise in his words. "Come inside you."

She looked over at Deacon to see his reaction to Trey's announcement. His gaze dropped to her pussy then he nodded as if he could accept Trey's plan.

Left alone with Trey, Rebecca suddenly found herself shy. It was strange that she would feel shy when, if she actually calculated hours that she'd spent with him, they'd spent more time naked than clothed.

He held open a towel waited for her to step into his embrace. She hesitated for just a moment too long.

"Come on, sweetheart, I get so little time alone with your pussy, I don't want to miss a moment of it."

A shiver that had nothing to do with the cool air that had invaded her bathroom raced down her spine.

"Now, come here, sweet, and let me warm you. Deacon's only going to wait so long and I want my tongue between your legs before he returns."

The shiver turned to a tingle and she stepped out of the shower and into his arms. The incredible sensitivity of her skin returned as he rubbed the towel across her arms and back, wiping away the remaining bits of water. He kissed and caressed her even as he slid the towel over her body, making the mundane act of drying her a sensual feast.

Finally, he pulled back, dropping the towel to the ground and lifting her in his arms. Her knees were weak so she was thrilled to be so secure in his hold. Confidently, he strode into her bedroom and dropped her in the middle of the mattress. She had only a moment to thank the heavens that she'd remembered to make her bed that morning. Except for the pile of clothes draped over the chair, her room was fairly tidy.

Not that Trey seemed to notice. He stared at her, a look of disapproval crossing his face. He slowly shook his head.

"We need to begin your proper training," he said.

Training? It was all she could do not to gulp. It sounded ominous and sexual. Her body quivered with the desire to begin.

"I'll let it go this time, honey, because you haven't been told the rules but next time you'll be punished." The word made her heart pound faster. She remembered the spanking downstairs and knew their punishment would be wonderful and dreadful at the same time. "Now, spread your legs so that I can see your pretty cunt."

She looked down and saw her legs were bent, knees pressed together. It was an instinctive feminine and protective pose.

She didn't move. Not sure what to do. Every time she acceded to their wishes she felt herself falling deeper and deeper under the sensual spell but she couldn't stop herself. Didn't want to. Something deep inside her craved these two men.

"Open your legs," Trey commanded again, this time more firmly. Taking a full breath, she slowly lifted her right foot and separated her legs. The blatant act of baring her pussy to him made her cheeks heat up.

"Are you embarrassed?" he asked, his voice low and seductive. She nodded. "Why? Your cunt is pretty and delicious. Shall I show you?"

Again she nodded.

He reached his hand out, easing his fingers into her slit, sliding two into her passage. "So hot." He thrust forward, driving in deep and touching her inside. "Delicious." He crawled onto the end of the bed, positioning himself between her spread thighs. She inched her knees farther apart as he lay between them. "Very good, Rebecca. You know we always want your legs spread when we're around." His approval sent a rush of moisture into her pussy. He leaned forward and stroked his tongue up the full length of her slit, wide and deep, tasting her, leaving behind seductive tingles that made her want more. "I'm going to lick you, honey. Drive my tongue into that hot cunt that Deacon fucked downstairs." He smiled at her. "I'm going to make you scream."

Deacon stood at the top of the stairs and listened to Trey, his promises, his seduction. The few minutes alone had given him time to think. When they'd walked into Rebecca's house, his only thought had been fucking her. That compulsion to be inside her. Now, that he'd come in her and on her, his mind was a little clearer. His cock was still hard. It was as if he was the Energizer Bunny—always hard and ready to serve her.

He wanted to be in there right now, his dick sliding into her cunt, the tight squeeze of her pussy sending him over the edge.

He gripped the doorframe and turned the corner, watching.

Rebecca lay on the bed, her legs spread, her beautiful breasts pink and flushed. Trey's blond head was cradled between her thighs, his face buried in her cunt. Wet hungry sounds slipped from beneath his mouth as he ate her.

She placed one hand on the headboard as if bracing herself. The other she slipped into Trey's hair, holding him, silently guiding him. Deacon watched for long minutes, taking it all in. She was perfect—not model thin—but beautiful, her deep sensuality enhancing her lush sexy form. Pure sexual energy surrounded her as she slowly pulsed her hips, as if Trey was fucking her with his tongue, trying to get deeper into her cunt.

Deacon felt his own cock respond to the shallow thrusts. He wanted to fuck her. Wanted to come in her again. But somehow just seeing her pleasure eased him—even though it was Trey creating the sensations inside her. Deacon didn't understand it, but in the last week he'd come to accept it.

Her groans filled the air and he couldn't hold back, couldn't remain separate any longer. He stepped into the room.

Her eyes were closed and her body stretched and strained, seeking more of the deep caresses of Trey's tongue. God, she was beautiful. Trey's bare shoulders were shoved up hard against the inside her thighs keeping her legs wide and high.

Deacon took his cock in his hand and slowly stroked, moving in time to the slow pulses of her hips as she pushed up against Trey's mouth. He moved closer to get a better view. Years of knowing that he liked to watch culminated in seeing Trey lick Rebecca's cunt.

Her eyes snapped open and she stared at him. The pleasure that shone through her eyes grabbed him by the balls. He wanted to come. Wanted to come when she did. While she twisted and pumped against Trey's mouth.

A blush crept up her cheeks—as if she was embarrassed to be caught with Trey licking her cunt. She didn't understand how hard it made him to watch her come, to see her body twisting and struggling to climax.

"That's it, baby. Fuck his mouth." Deacon sat down beside her, her pretty breasts so available for his hands. He squeezed one firm mound and then moved to the other. "You taste so sweet." He laved and licked her nipples, letting the delicate flavor of her skin fill his senses. "Let him enjoy you."

Her moans and the tight pull of her muscles warned she was close to coming.

He covered one nipple with his lips and sucked, biting lightly, then a little harder as her climax shuddered through her body. She cried out and her back arched, pressing her breasts high. Her orgasm washed from her body to his and he groaned, feeling his cock tighten. Not enough to come but fuck, he could pound nails with his dick.

Another sweet seductive shout escaped and he felt another wicked tremor moved through her. Her muscles tightened for a moment then relaxed, almost collapsing to the mattress.

Deacon drew back, turning and watching as Trey raised his head. Rebecca's pussy juice surrounded his lips and the scent was captivating. Trey's eyes caught Deacon's and Deacon had the strangest urge to lean down and kiss the other man, to lick those sweet juices off his skin, sharing Rebecca's taste before driving his tongue into Trey's mouth.

The image was so clear in his mind that Deacon flinched, jerking his eyes away. What the fuck was he thinking? Kissing another man? Sure, he'd shared Rebecca with Trey but that was different.

He glanced at Trey and saw the same confusion on his face, not quite meeting Deacon's eyes.

Trey sat back, kneeling between Rebecca's spread thighs, his hands pressed on the insides of her knees, keeping her open and on display. He traced in invisible path up her thigh, skirting close to her pussy but not quite touching.

"What do you think, Deacon?" Trey asked as he repeated the leisurely stroke of his fingertip. Deacon tipped his head in question. "She's had you—inside her. And I've licked her cunt." He ran his tongue across his upper lip. "Delicious by the way." His index finger teased the entrance to her pussy. "Do you think she's had enough?"

Deacon listened and immediately knew Trey's game.

"Maybe," he said. "Check her pussy. Is she still wet?"

Rebecca didn't move as Trey slipped his finger into her entrance, just teasing the first inch. Deacon watched, seeing the delicious tension that moved through her body. She wanted more. Could take them each again. He fingered the new butt plug he'd purchased. Memories of that night on the lakeside had haunted him—the possibility of both men fucking her.

Trey pumped his finger in slowly. "She's still wet and slick, Deke, but we wouldn't want to wear her out. Maybe we should leave and—"

A small squeak of protest slipped from Rebecca's lips. Deacon dragged his stare away from the slow pulse of Trey's finger inside her cunt and looked at her face. Her cheeks were flushed, her lips wet and open. And the light in her eyes was painted with panic.

Trey leaned over her, holding himself inches above her.

"Do you want more cock, honey? Do you want me to fill this sweet cunt?"

"Yes." Her breathless answer was pure desperation but she couldn't worry about it. She needed this too badly.

He kissed her, then pressed his teeth into her lower lip, a sharp painful nip. "Do you? Do you want my cock?"

"Yes, please, Trey. Fuck me."

Conscious of Deacon's presence, she glanced at her other lover.

"Don't worry, honey," Trey said, the edge of his mouth curling up in a half smile. "He likes to watch." His hand slid between their bodies and he cupped her pussy. "And I'll bet he wants to see more of this. Shall we let him? Shall we let him watch my cock slide into your pussy?"

It seemed deliciously wicked and she nodded. Trey rolled off her and onto his back.

"Come over me, sweet."

Her body felt drugged by sensation—and by the idea that Deacon was watching. She quickly shot her gaze to him, to make sure he wasn't upset. He looked aroused. Hungry. Holding his gaze for just a moment as she cupped her hand around Trey's hard shaft and caressed it. Deacon licked his lips and his eyes blazed with desire.

She turned her attention back to Trey, slowly sitting up, and easing the thick crown of his shaft into her. Slightly sore from the hard pounding that Deacon had given her, she took it slow, letting Trey in just an inch or two before she pulled back. Knowing that Deacon watched added a yummy layer to the sensations surging through her body. She pushed down, sinking Trey's cock into her.

"Yeah, baby, take him inside you." Deacon's encouragement sent a sweet caress into her pussy. "Damn, baby, that's sweet."

She slowly began to move on Trey, long languid strokes in and out. The drive to come was a distant goal. Right now, she just wanted to feel him inside her, pleasure Trey and herself. And Deacon.

Knowing that she had captured the attention of these two men only made the experience more sensual. She ran her hands across Trey's chest, bending down to nip her teeth into the tight pec. God, he was delicious. His hands gripped her hips, guiding her up and down, working his cock in and out of her pussy. Despite his words in the bathroom, he didn't seem to have the driving urge to fuck her hard. He raised and lowered her slowly, letting every inch of his cock slide through her pussy, almost pulling out each time. It was delicious, building the tension in her cunt until she was sure she would come.

She just needed a little more, a little faster. She tried to thrust down, tried to drive him harder into her pussy but she couldn't break his grip.

"Please, Trey. Let me..."

Instead of freeing her, Trey eased her down slowly one more time, and held her in place. "I think she's ready, Deke."

His voice interrupted her sexual climb. She shook her head and looked first at Trey, then to Deacon. Deacon placed one knee on the bed and crawled over to them, kneeling behind her.

"Lean forward, honey." With Trey's command she remembered. Deacon had brought something. Something for her. Blindly she followed Trey's instructions, leaning down.

Trey's hands cupped her ass, pulling her cheeks apart. The motion completely opened her up. She gasped as cool slick fingers teased her butt.

"Easy, honey. Let him get you ready."

One slick finger slipped into her ass and she grabbed Trey's shoulders.

"Relax, baby. He'll start you off slow, just a little tonight."

She knew what was coming, that soon she'd have much more than a finger there. If she didn't stop it. But did she want to stop it? The slow easy penetration of Deacon's finger felt good. It slipped away and she suddenly missed the sensation.

But then it returned, only it wasn't his finger. It was thinner then slowly widened out as he pressed it inside.

Trey rolled his hips, shallow thrusts of his cock inside her, reminding her that he was there, still filling her. His fingers teased her clit distracting her from the pressure that built in her ass. It wasn't painful, just a little weird, making her feel full.

"That's it." Deacon smoothed his hand across her ass. "We'll just leave that there for a bit." He kissed her shoulder, pressing his chest to her back. "Get you used to having something in your ass before we fuck you."

She whimpered, and rocked against the cock that filled her.

"That's good, honey. We won't do more than this tonight," Trey assured her. "But we are going to enjoy you like this." He rolled her over, easing her onto her back, shifting the tiny butt plug within her. She cried out and clung to Trey, feeling him pump inside her, shallow and slow. "Yeah, she feels it."

She gripped his shoulders, adapting to the new sensation.

160

"You okay?" Trey asked as he settled deep in her. She nodded because she couldn't speak. "Good. Let us know if it hurts. It shouldn't hurt." Nodding again, she agreed. "Very good, honey. Now, let me have this sweet cunt I've been dreaming about fucking all week."

He pulled out, again slow and steady. Rebecca bit her lip to keep from begging. She needed more. She needed him hard, coming inside her. His fingers bit into her hips, holding her in place. He held himself still for a moment, long enough for Rebecca to take a breath, then he plunged in, driving hard and deep. God, just what she needed. Her pussy clenched and she cried out, the orgasm shooting through her core.

"Damn, I love watching her come," Deacon whispered.

Trey growled his agreement and continued to ride her, each stroke harder than the last. She was going to ache later but now it was perfect, her body making the climb again, savoring every thrust. The sensation of the butt plug in her ass a constant reminder of what was to come.

Trey drew back, pulling up on his knees, lifting Rebecca's hips high on his thighs, his cock still buried inside her. She pressed her head into mattress, trying to slow her racing heart but the fire in Trey's eyes gave her no relief. Now he held himself still and worked her pussy on his cock, sliding her across his shaft, each stroke whispering across her clit until she thought her eyes were going to cross.

"Trey—"

"Soon, honey, I just want to enjoy being inside your pussy for a little longer. So sweet. You take us so well. Oh yeah."

From the left, she sensed rather than saw movement and saw Deacon standing beside the bed. His cock was hard and he was watching, watching her pussy and Trey's cock.

"Deke, man, suck on her tits. I want her screaming when she comes again."

Deacon slowly nodded but didn't pull his gaze away, as if he was completely captivated by the sight of Trey fucking her.

He got back on the bed and lay down beside her. Dragging his eyes away, he looked at her face.

"You're so beautiful. Watching you get fucked is so fucking beautiful." The dazed sound to his voice soothed her ragged nerves. He bent down and kissed her, soft and sensual.

His hands slid across her body, cupping her breasts, pinching her nipples. The delicate pain seemed directly connected to her clit and every stroke was another wicked burst of pleasure.

"Oh yeah, Deke, she's about to come. I can feel her squeezing me."

Deacon raised his head, looking at her. "Come for us, baby." As he spoke, he teased his finger into her slit, a delicate touch. He pressed a little harder, small slow circles around her clit, so she was trapped between the hard drive of Trey's cock and Deacon's finger. The shock went through her body and she cried out, arching up, moving into Trey's thrust.

"That's it." Deacon's touch lightened but he didn't stop, as if he was drawing out every last vibration of her orgasm.

Trey's pace increased and seconds late a long hot splash poured into her pussy. Taking his cum into her body sent another shiver of pleasure through her core and Rebecca groaned.

Her strength gave out and she collapsed onto the bed, Trey still inside her but softening. Deacon's mouth licking and biting her breasts.

Completely sated, she could only absorb the sensations, let them filter into her body. The idea of sleep hovered but so did the questions. Why was this happening? Did she want it to stop? So relaxed and satisfied, her body shouted out a resounding "no" to that question.

Trey pulled out of her and she whimpered. Her pussy was going to be sore. He disappeared and returned seconds later with a warm washcloth. Gently he spread her legs and wiped between them, clearing away his cum, soothing her with the gentle moist heat. She sighed and spread her legs wider, wanting more. It felt so good.

He finished tending to her and came back to the bed, lying down beside her, his hand joining Deacon's as they stroked her body.

"You okay, honey?" Trey asked, placing a soft kiss on her shoulder.

She barely found the strength to nod.

"Good. We'll let you rest for a bit."

A bit? How about forever? She was sure, absolutely sure, that she wouldn't be even interested in sex for a long while. Then she opened her eyes. Deacon was watching her, his gaze filled with heat and satisfaction. She looked to Trey. His stare was much more shuttered—the desire was there but also something she didn't recognize. It looked like concern or worry.

Seeing that in his eyes made her want to soothe him, ease him. She placed her hand behind his neck and pulled him gently down, meeting his lips with hers, gentle hot kisses just for the pleasure of tasting each other. As he drew back, she turned, wanting to share the same with Deacon.

Trey's lips moved to her shoulder even as Deacon slid his hand down her body. His touch was delicate as he cupped her pussy. She moaned and felt her hips rise to meet his caress. Low, deep inside her core, a new rush of heat gathered. She tipped her head back, gasping for air. It didn't seem possible but damn, she wanted more, wanted one of her males to come in her.

Both men shifted, their muscles tightening as she pulsed her hips upward. She dared a glance at Deacon and saw the hunger in his eyes.

No, her night was far from over.

Chapter Twelve

 જી

Rebecca pulled the edges of her robe tighter together. The nervous action gave her hands something to do. Just as pacing kept her feet busy.

She did another slow loop around her living room, taking the brief moment of solitude to gather her thoughts. It wasn't much working. She was too stunned, shocked, amazed by her own behavior. Sex with Deacon and Trey. All night. Just thinking of it made her pussy throb. She smoothed her hand down the front of her robe, letting her fingers whisper across her mound, unable to deny the sensitive flesh some caress. By rights she should be impossibly sore but instead her muscles were loose, her sex wet.

It didn't make sense. She was used to her body behaving in a certain way. She could handle sex, actual penetration, once, sometimes twice a night. After that her pussy was sore, her clit too sensitive to touch let alone press against, and the insides of her thighs were usually strained.

But last night, she'd taken them time and again. They'd spent stretches of time when they *weren't* inside her but the majority of the night she'd been pierced by one cock or the other. Her knees wobbled as she thought on it. Damn, even her memories were physical sensations.

The hum of the upstairs shower caught her attention— reminding her of last night and her sexy suck of her two men. The splashing sounds also reported that Deacon was up there. Naked, wet. She spread her hand wide across her belly, trying to quell the desperate need that surged inside her.

She swung past the kitchen and caught of whiff of the ham and sausage Trey was frying. She didn't know where it had come from—she was a long time vegetarian—but he was in there cooking it. And man, did it smell good. Her stomach growled and she forced her feet to walk her away. Trey must have brought it with him. She had a vague memory of him carrying a bag last night as well. Deacon's had been filled with sex toys—she squirmed as she remembered the butt plug they'd slipped into her ass—but Trey had brought food.

Hmm, I wonder if this is a glimpse of our future relationship. She scoffed as the question formed in her mind. *We don't have a relationship. Hell, we don't even have conversations. We have sex.*

Well, no more. At least not until they talked. Until she found if this was a perfectly normal situation for both of them and she was the only one a little freaked out. Trey seemed comfortable with it. Deacon...Rebecca shook her head. Deacon had looked a little wild around the eyes when he'd finally crawled out of bed this morning—as if what they'd done all through the night had finally hit him as well.

So, that was it. No more sex until the three of them sat down—maybe over some of that sausage Trey was cooking—and talked. Her fingers curled into fists as if to silently support her determination.

The scent of meat drew her toward the kitchen but a soft knock on the front door stopped her. Rebecca hesitated. Was it Jessie? Had Rebecca's strange behavior last night caused her to worry and stop by?

She glanced at the kitchen, hoping Trey stayed there and Deacon stayed upstairs. She didn't want to have to explain having two men in her house.

She peeked out the side window and gasped. It wasn't Jessie on her porch. Oh, this was so much worse.

Taking a breath, she pulled the door open a few inches and put her face in the opening.

"Taylor, hi." She nodded to the two men flanking her friend. "Mikhel, Zach. What's up?"

Taylor bit her lip, a sure sign she was nervous, and glanced at Mikhel. He nodded, giving her silent encouragement. "Can we come in? We need to talk to you."

"Uh, now's really not a good time." She forced a laugh. "I'm not dressed."

"That's okay. It's important—"

Rebecca mind worked to come up with a logical reason not to let Taylor inside but she never got a chance to use it.

"Is that Mikhel?" Trey called out. She waved him to be quiet but he ignored her, coming close and leaning over her shoulder so his face appeared in the same small open space. "Good morning. Welcome."

Taylor looked surprised to see him. Mikhel did not. Great. The guys were talking about her. Not good.

Not seeing another choice—since Trey had showed himself—Rebecca backed up and let the door fall open. Taylor stepped through the opening, sending a stark questioning look to her friend.

"You and Trey?"

And Deacon, Rebecca added silently. She shrugged weakly.

Taylor's eyes dropped down to a squint. "This happened last weekend, didn't it?" Then she stepped back and looked Rebecca up and down. With a resigned sigh, she said, "I guess it was inevitable."

The press of Mikhel and Zach through the door urged the women into the living room. Rebecca glanced toward the stairs, praying that Deacon would at least remain upstairs. It was all well and good for Taylor to have sex with two men. Rebecca had come to accept that. But to have Taylor know *she'd* been sleeping with two guys, that was just too weird to comprehend.

Seizing control of the situation, before Mikhel could, Rebecca stepped to the middle of her living room and stared at her guests. She noticed that Trey went and stood beside

Mikhel, leaving Rebecca feeling very alone, vulnerable. She lifted her chin and stared back at the eyes watching her.

"So what's up?"

Taylor opened her mouth then seemed to lose her nerve. She glanced at Mikhel. Even from the other side of the room, Rebecca could see the command in his eyes. Taylor seemed to take strength in what she saw there and she turned back.

"Well, it's like this. Last week, when you were at the cabin..." Taylor's words drifted away and Rebecca couldn't stand the suspense.

"What?"

Taylor took a deep breath and started again. "Last week, at the lake, you were bitten."

"Yes."

"Rebecca, you were bitten by a werewolf."

Rebecca fully admitted she was exhausted. She'd gotten little sleep last night and it just compounded the lack of sleep from the week before. But even as exhausted as she was, she couldn't have heard Taylor correctly.

"A what?"

"A werewolf, and now, you're turning into one."

She looked at the serious faces aimed her direction. "I'm a little slow this morning so you're going to have to explain the joke to me because I'm not getting it."

"It's no joke." This was from Mikhel. "A rogue werewolf bit you and the venom from his fangs has infected you."

Ignoring the solemn man speaking to her, she drilled Taylor with her gaze. "Taylor? What's going on?"

"It's true. Trey's spent the last week trying to find out who bit you but so far, he's drawing a blank."

Anger turned to fury and exploded into rage and she glared at Mikhel, including Zach in her stare. "What kind of freaky drugs have you been giving her?"

Mikhel straightened and the corners of his mouth tightened as if he was fighting the urge to snarl.

"Rebecca!" Taylor's gasp was the only thing that could have distracted her. "It's not drugs or hallucinations. It's true. You've been bitten by a werewolf."

"And you know this why? Because *you* guys are werewolves?" She scanned the small crowd. They all nodded. When she saw Taylor's head moving, she stopped. "Wait. I've known you for ten years and spent many nights with you and never once did you become furry."

"Well, no." Taylor took a few steps forward, as if she wanted to touch Rebecca, comfort her, but Rebecca backed away, a little too freaked out by all of this. "I just became a werewolf eighteen months ago." The pain on Taylor's face tugged at Rebecca's heart but she couldn't quite let go of the weirdness. "She's not going to believe us. Someone is going to have to change." She looked at the three men and then pointed to Trey. "You."

Trey grimaced but reached for the buttons of his shirt. "Why me?" he groused but Rebecca noticed he didn't stop undressing.

"Because she's seen you naked." Taylor tilted her head and Rebecca could almost imagine her flirting with Trey. "And so have I."

Trey's cheeks turned red and he lowered his stare to the ground. It took him only seconds to strip off his clothes and toss them over the arm of her couch. Rebecca remembered quite clearly how she'd leaned against that couch as Deacon fucked her, Trey in her mouth. The memory heated her skin and she wanted to join Trey in stripping off clothes.

When he was naked, he stepped into the middle of the living room.

Her mind was a blur. They all truly believed this. They actually thought Trey was going to turn into a wolf. She backed toward the stairs, giving Trey some space and getting a little closer to Deacon. Surely he was still sane.

Rebecca looked around — trying to maintain some semblance of serenity — and saw Taylor watching her. Her eyes filled with concern and love. So, even if Taylor was crazy, she was still Rebecca's best friend. She vowed to visit Taylor and Zach in the mental ward. She wasn't so sure about Mikhel. He was a bit too cranky.

That resolution held in her heart, she watched Trey. He rolled his shoulders back and cracked his neck like a fighter ready to start the next round.

"With your permission, Alpha?" He directed the question to Mikhel. Mikhel nodded.

Okay, one more crazy she was going to have to visit.

With a breath, a calm seemed to settle on Trey. For a moment, he was perfectly still. The air in the room stopped...and then his body began to change. His face stretched forward, sharp long teeth erupting from his gums. The distinct sounds of bone crunching echoed in the room. Trey fell and Rebecca reached out to catch him, only to jerk her hand back. By the time he hit the ground, his hands were paws and a gray and black wolf stood before her.

The scream burst from her throat before she had the chance to stop it.

Deacon turned off the shower and stood in the tub, letting the water drip from his skin. He looked down. He was hard but that was expected — at least after the last week, it was.

The night had been amazing. Standing there, soaking wet from a cold shower and his body could remember what it felt like to be inside Rebecca. To slide in and out, every time he filled her, the sweet grip of her cunt squeezed him. The center of his stomach hollowed out and he slapped his hand against the wall, trying to hold himself upright as his knees weakened. Damn, she was sweet. Responsive and just submissive enough.

Enough so that she defied them and they had the chance to punish.

It was strange that after the night—and last weekend if he was honest—he'd begun to think about fucking Rebecca as a group activity. As something "they" did. He and Trey. Last night, watching Trey ride her, fill her...Deacon groaned, remembering how hard he'd been. And when Trey had finished with her, had come inside her, Deacon had fucked her.

And she'd welcomed him. Her body eagerly accepting him deep and hard.

Fighting the memories, he climbed out of the shower and grabbed a towel. Trey had muttered something about breakfast as he'd crawled out of bed. Deacon's stomach rumbled in agreement with his mind.

He didn't hurry downstairs. He didn't think Rebecca or Trey would let him starve—and he wasn't quite sure what he would say when he got there. After last night, what was Deacon supposed to say to Rebecca, except "thanks"?

He dragged his jeans on, deciding next time he'd be a little less focused on sex toys—though the butt plug had been a perfect addition to their play—and a little more focused on bringing an extra pair of pants.

His hand was stretching out for his shirt when he heard Rebecca's scream.

Deacon bolted down the stairs, skidding to a stop behind Rebecca. He immediately gathered her in his arms, holding her close, ready to comfort, protect, whatever she needed. She was trembling. Her body shook against his even as she turned her face into his neck. Deacon tracked the line backward, following her shoulder, into the living room. A huge timber wolf stood in the living room.

"What the hell?" Keeping his arms around Rebecca, holding her even closer, he looked at the crowd that occupied the living room. "What is that...wolf doing here?"

"It's Trey."

The words were muffled against his chest. He hitched his fingers beneath Rebecca's chin and raised her face.

"What?"

His question seemed to shock her out of whatever trance she was in and she straightened. "That's Trey." She pointed to the wolf. "He turned into a wolf. Right in front of me."

She looked as confused as he felt.

"What?"

One of the men turned to the woman and said, "Great, didn't know the human was still here."

The distaste in his voice when he said "the human" put Deacon's nerves on edge.

"What the hell is going on?" As he asked the question, the wolf sat down and looked up at him. Then slowly it began to change. It grew taller, pinker and the face shrunk back into a human face. Trey's human face. Deacon tightened his grip on Rebecca. "Oh my God." He looked at the strangers. "What are you?"

"Werewolves, human," the pissed one in the center said. "And I'd watch your tone."

That sent the hair on the back of Deacon's neck standing straight up. "Listen, buddy, I don't know who or what—"

"Okay, enough." The woman raised her hands. "Rebecca and I have a lot to talk about."

Deacon looked at Rebecca, his curiosity winning out over the irritation. "Rebecca?"

She looked stunned. Her mouth hung open and she kept blinking, as though she expected the scene before her to change. "Uh, I guess I'm turning into one of those."

"What? How?"

"That's what bit me last weekend." That statement seemed to give her a jolt of energy. She spun around and stared at the small group. "You don't know who bit me?"

"No," Trey answered. He was pulling on his jeans. "Like Taylor said, we've spent the week trying to find out, but we're having no luck."

"But why would..." Her question faded away and she looked at the woman.

"We don't know. Listen," she said, turning to the men who had arrived with her. "You guys go have breakfast or something. Rebecca and I are going to have a talk."

With that, the woman, whose name Deacon still didn't know, led Rebecca up the stairs. Leaving Deacon alone with several pissed off...werewolves?

The big one in the middle stepped forward, his chin going up, his lips bending in a crooked, cruel line.

"Now, we have to decide what to do with the human."

Rebecca followed Taylor upstairs. Her mind was so overwhelmed that she didn't even worry that her room looked like a scene from an orgy. Hell, it was a scene from an orgy.

They stopped inside the door and Rebecca found the courage to look her best friend in the eye.

"You're really a werewolf?"

Taylor nodded. "I couldn't tell you. I mean, who would believe it? Unless you actually saw it happen."

The friendship question would have to wait until later. For now, Rebecca needed hard, cold facts. "So you actually turn into a wolf?"

"No." Taylor shook her head. "And you probably won't either. Females, particularly when they are created and not born, typically don't physically make the change."

Rebecca forced her mind to work through what Taylor had just said. "So, nothing will change."

"Not exactly. I mean, your senses will become sharper." Taylor winced. "And you'll probably need to eat meat. Your wolf is going to crave it."

"I can handle that."

"And there's the sex thing."

"What sex thing?"

"Well, I mean, haven't you been feeling really, you know, aroused, wound up. Horny?"

"A little." A lot.

"Well, that's from the werewolf bite. Mikhel says that after the first full moon, some of that will ease, but let me tell you, it doesn't really go away. And since you bit Deacon, he's going through the same thing you are."

Rebecca finally gave into the weakness in her muscles and dropped down into her chair, still piled with yesterday's discarded clothes. That explained so much. It hadn't been her attracting Deacon. She'd bitten him and somehow infected him with this lust. Wow, didn't do much for her ego.

"But what about Trey?"

"What about him?"

"I didn't bite him. At least, not that I can remember. Why's he been here, so willing to, you know, service me?" She squinted her eyes and peered at Taylor "Did Mikhel tell him to come?" she asked suspiciously.

Taylor laughed. "Oh honey, I don't think either of those males is here under duress. Trey, and I'm sure Deacon, is here because they want you."

Rebecca shrugged. Not sure that she believed that.

But then she remembered the night before. Neither man had seemed at all reluctant. They'd both wanted her. But were they attracted to her or the werewolf growing inside her?

Chapter Thirteen

ε⌒)

The trees opened up before him and Deacon stepped out onto the beach. Two weeks ago, he and Trey had fucked Rebecca here. They'd taken turns riding between her thighs, feeling her cunt glove them as they filled her.

His cock twitched at the memory and he shook his head. At least knowing what was causing his perpetual state of arousal helped. It was the bite that Rebecca had given him that first night. It had connected them. Bound them. From what he could gather from Trey, each time they fucked, the bonds between them grew stronger. The idea probably should have panicked Deacon, but in the past week since this little revelation about the existence of werewolves had been made, Deacon had spent a lot of time with Rebecca — both having sex and not.

He could agree that his body responded to her arousal, her level of need controlled his, but there was something else. He liked her. Liked the way she thought, the bold way she spoke.

He'd also taken the opportunity to spend some time with Mikhel. The Alpha werewolf — and from what Deacon could see, Mikhel was all Alpha — had decided that Deacon could live. At least for now. Deacon knew that as long as he remained silent, he would live. One word about their existence and Deacon had no doubt he would have a mysterious accident that would leave him dead.

Curious about the existence of werewolves, Deacon had peppered Mikhel with questions. Surprisingly, Mikhel had answered most of them, explaining that the werewolves came in three forms — human, wolf and *were*. The *were* being the

174

most dangerous. Both Mikhel and Trey believed that a werewolf in his *were* form had attacked Rebecca, but there was no way to tell who had done it. Trey was still investigating.

Tonight had been a "Pack Meeting." Rebecca had been invited. Deacon hadn't. He'd walked her over to Mikhel's house and handed her over to the care of Trey, who said he'd escort her back to Deacon's cabin later.

After he'd fucked her, no doubt.

There was little jealousy in Deacon's thoughts. The three of them hadn't fucked together since that Friday night, a week ago. Rebecca had spent alternating nights with him and Trey, trying to ease the growing wolf inside her.

The nights she'd spent with Trey had been pure torture for Deacon. Not because another man was fucking her but because he could feel her rise to pleasure, even knew when she was coming, but he wasn't there to see it. He wanted to be there, to watch as she came, as she took Trey's cum inside her.

With a groan, Deacon started across the beach. The trees muffled the dim light of his front porch but the moon was bright. There was another week before the full moon but the clear skies gave him enough light to see his steps.

A noise caught his ear as he started down the beach. The forest was usually quiet. No large animals lived in the area. Now he knew why — the werewolves were very territorial and, according to Trey, marked their territory well. Nothing else would dare enter.

Another rustle sounded behind him. The little hairs at the back of his neck stood up as the forest became silent. Oh, that was never good.

He turned and looked over his shoulder.

Pain splintered his head and the world disappeared beneath him. Seconds later, the earth returned — hard against his shoulder. He groaned and tried to roll over but a heavy weight landed on his back, shoving his face into the dirt. Lights swirled in his eyes as he fought to stay conscious. Huge hands gripped his shoulders and pushed him down. Just from the weight and size of the creature on top of him, Deacon knew this had to be the *were* that had attacked Rebecca.

"So you're the one fucking my pretty werewolf bitch." Vicious claws raked across Deacon's spine. "You want to be one of us, human? Or maybe you just want to be fucked by a real werewolf." The snarling voice paused for a second and then Deacon felt it—four sharp spikes in his shoulder. The *were* growled as he sank his teeth into Deacon's flesh. Fire burned from the wound and flooded Deacon's chest, flowing through his veins, burning until he thought his heart would explode.

Fighting the fire in his wounds, he barely felt it when the *were* flipped him over, ripped open his shirt and scraped his claws down his chest. Deacon arched up into the pain, his cry filling the night. The *were*'s weight held him to the ground. Deacon was in good shape and strong for a human but he was no match for the werewolf's power.

He opened his eyes and saw the beast kneeling above him. The creature was gray and had the face of a wolf. But the eyes were pure human—filled with fury. The *were* backhanded Deacon across the cheek. Blood spurted across his face.

"That bitch belongs to me. And now, so do you. I made you." The words were muffled—spoken through a wolf's jaw that wasn't designed to form human words. The *were* punctuated his sentence with his fist across Deacon's face. Deacon groaned, though the new pain was just a layer on top of the old one. He didn't know how much longer he could remain conscious. "You like to fuck her? You like coming inside her?"

Movement between them captured his focus and he saw the *were* was stroking his own cock, masturbating on top of Deacon. Deacon's stomach roiled at what was happening and he increased his struggles, his body finding new strength. His head throbbed but he twisted his shoulder. The *were* drove his knuckles into Deacon's chin, knocking his head back against the river rock.

Dazed and unable to command his body to move, he could only lie there, repulsed and violated.

The creature pumped his fist up and down his cock, working his shaft hard until it grunted and hot streams of semen splattered across Deacon's stomach. He put his hand flat against Deacon's stomach and rubbed the semen into his skin.

"You belong to me. I've changed you and marked you. Now I'm going to fuck your ass, so you'll never forget that I own you. You're mine."

Bile rose in Deacon's throat. He fought the urge to vomit, knowing he needed to keep his senses, keep aware.

The *were* lifted his hips, freeing Deacon's hands, and Deacon's body came to life. He swung out, slamming his fist into the animal's jaw. The wolf head snapped back and Deacon moved, throwing off the *were* and grabbing the ground to escape. Claws tore as his back as he ran but Deacon refused to give up. The *were* landed on him again, sending him into the ground, driving the breath from his lungs.

A growl erupted behind them and the *were* looked back. A wolf leapt out of the brush and landed on the creature, his teeth sinking into his thigh. The *were* cried out and swiped his hand down, knocking the wolf free. Blood dripped down the beast's leg as he limped off, running into the trees.

Deacon's heart was pounding so loud in his ears it took him a second to gather his wits. He looked into the darkness and saw Trey — naked and pushing himself up off the ground. Deacon tried to do the same but pain held him down. His head ached, his shoulder throbbed. He took a breath and the smell of blood and the *were* covered him, infiltrating his chest. Invading his soul.

"Are you okay?" Trey knelt down beside him.

Deacon tipped his chin down, hiding the wound on his shoulder. Blood dripped down his shoulder from the *were* bite. He knew enough to know what that meant. He was going to become a werewolf. *You belong to me.* Without wanting to, he looked down. Traces of the *were's* semen clung to his skin. The creature had marked him.

Finding his courage, he turned his head and showed Trey the *were* bite.

"Son of a bitch," Trey muttered.

Then he inhaled, and Deacon knew he smelled the scent of the *were* on him.

The *were* was right. He was marked.

* * * * *

Deacon sat on the couch and stared into the fireplace. Trey or Rebecca had started the fire. He didn't know which one but he knew why. They were trying to warm up the room. The physical temperature was comfortable but there was no mistaking the chill that occupied the space surrounding Deacon. He bent his fingers into a fist, wishing he could curl his body into ball and hide. But he didn't allow himself that luxury.

Instead he just stared ahead and felt the poison flowing through his body.

He knew what was going to happen. Trey had explained it all two nights ago after they'd cleaned up and bandaged up from the *were's* attack.

The full moon was less than a week away and, at that time, Deacon would turn into a wolf. A werewolf. A fucking werewolf. All because some rogue bastard had attacked him.

It was the same *were* that had attacked Rebecca, but the creature had vanished. Trey had stopped to check on Deacon and the *were* had escaped, leaving no trace of his identity. Mikhel was furious that a second werewolf had been created. He'd been polite to Deacon but his irritation at having another nascent werewolf thrust upon him and his pack was obvious.

He'd turned to Trey and demanded he find this rogue *were* and figure out what the fuck the animal was doing. And why he was doing it.

Deacon could have told him that. It was revenge or anger. He was trying to get back at someone. Based on what Rebecca remembered of her attack, it was likely directed at Trey.

But Deacon hadn't mentioned any of that to Trey or Mikhel. He hadn't wanted to talk about it. Didn't want to now. He just wanted to be left alone.

With any luck, Rebecca and Trey would both leave tomorrow. They'd stayed an extra day, past the weekend, because they were worried about him.

"Are you all right?" Rebecca's voice — soft when he knew she wanted to rail at him for being such an ass — interrupted his thoughts and he nodded.

"I'm fine."

She sat down on the couch and reached toward him.

The light press of her fingers on his shoulder made him flinch.

"Don't." He shrugged, knocking her hand away. Her hurt radiated from her eyes as he backed up, hating himself but unable to bear her touch. "I'm going to go take a shower."

As he walked from the room, he felt Trey's weighted stare.

Deacon shut the door and leaned against the back, knowing he was being an asshole but unable to find his center. It wasn't just the fact that he was turning into a werewolf. He wanted to believe he would have handled that. It was the way it was done. The attack raged in his brain, repeated and replayed until it was all he could see, until he could feel it again and again.

His stomach turned and he bent over the toilet, retching up the lunch he'd just eaten. He rinsed out his mouth, stripped off his clothes and climbed into the shower, letting the hot water beat on him, almost burning him, but still it wasn't enough.

The water turned cold and he continued to let it pound him, hoping it would numb him out but nothing worked.

Finally, he turned off the tap and dried off. He looked at the crumpled pile of clothes and knew he couldn't put them back on. It was as if they'd been tainted somehow by being on his body.

He wrapped the towel around his waist, the cold easing from his core. Just part of the werewolf heritage. The heat, similar to what Rebecca had experienced, burned beneath his skin, but while desire had accompanied hers, the fire only reminded him of that night.

He opened the door into the bedroom and stopped. Trey sat on the edge of the bed, waiting. He looked up, the reprimand in his eyes intermixed with pity and Deacon had the urge to cover himself. Hell, the man had seen him naked more often than most of his lovers. But that didn't stop the urge. Deacon crossed his arms over his chest and braced his legs apart, needing aggression to keep from losing it.

"Yes?" he demanded.

"Rebecca didn't deserve that."

Deacon nodded, pressing his lips together to keep back the scream. When he was in control, he said. "I'll apologize."

"Do one better. Get over it."

"Fuck you."

That got Trey to his feet. "So you're turning into a werewolf. Life will go on."

"This isn't about fucking turning into a werewolf. I could handle that." Trey's eyes widened just a bit and Deacon mentally cursed, wishing he'd kept his mouth shut. But now that he'd said the words, Trey was going to want the rest.

But he didn't ask the question that Deacon was expecting. Instead Trey nodded. "It's because of how it happened."

That simple statement released the flood inside him.

"It's like I can still feel him. It's poison flowing through my veins." He wanted to pace, to move, but his body was locked in the memory. "Fuck, I can still smell him on me. I feel like I've been raped." His lips pulled back from his teeth, curling into a snarl—another trait that had appeared since the attack. "When he was on top of me, he told me he owned me. That I belonged to him and, damn it, he's right. I can't break free. I still feel him."

The understanding in Trey's eyes was too much to handle. Deacon looked away, staring at the carpet, thinking about escape. Getting the hell away from all of them.

But that meant leaving Rebecca and he couldn't do that. The connection between them was still strong, still compelling. Even if he couldn't bear the thought of anyone touching him.

"It's because of the violence of the attack."

No shit. Deacon kept the words to himself, his outburst drawing off some of his anger. He really did need to apologize to Rebecca. It was just...he felt dirty, used. And he didn't want her to see that, to see the claim that bastard had on him.

"There might be a way to change it."

That caught Deacon's attention.

Trey winced. "It won't make you any less werewolf. There's nothing to do to change that. In a week's time, you're going to turn furry." The hint of a smile and the possibility in his words reached into Deacon's chest and gave him hope. "But I might be able to break the connection between you and the *were* that changed you.

"When he bit you, he marked you. The wound is gone but the spiritual mark is still there. We sense it. You feel it." Deacon nodded. "I talked to Mikhel and as far as we know, we can't erase the mark."

Deacon wasn't sure how he felt about the Alpha wolf knowing about his situation, but obviously Trey had been worried about it. Or Rebecca's concern had prompted the conversation.

"If you can't get rid of it, then what good is it?"

"We think I can change it. Replace it. Basically overwrite it."

"How?" Deacon asked suspiciously. Something wasn't quite right.

"By biting you."

Revulsion shot through his body, rejecting the idea. Another bite. He could still feel the first one. Even though the wound and scar were gone, he could feel it.

But this was Trey and if it would replace the memory, hell, even dull the memory, Deacon was willing to try.

"So, bite me." He tipped his head to the right, baring his neck, wanting this to be over. Trey didn't move. Deacon held himself still, his eyes staring at the wall, drifting down to the bedside table.

A bottle of lubricant and a condom sat beneath the lamp.

The realization made him straighten.

"You don't mean just bite me."

Trey shook his head. "It wouldn't work. When the *were* bit you, the violence, the energy was channeled into the bite. For this to work, there needs to be the same intensity." He shrugged. "And sex is probably the best way to create the same amount of power."

"You want to fuck me?"

Again Trey shrugged. But he didn't say no.

"Where's Rebecca?" Deacon asked. If he did this, he didn't want her around. Didn't want her witnessing this.

"She went out."

Relief filled his chest. That was good. She wouldn't see— hell, was he actually considering it? Let another man fuck him? He took a moment to think about what would happen.

Somehow he knew it would involve penetration. Heavy petting wasn't going to cut it. He was actually going to let another man fuck him.

No, Trey. He was going to let *Trey* fuck him. Trey, who shared Rebecca with him. The two of them had worked together to bring her to orgasm a dozen times. She'd loved and fucked them both. That was a bond they shared.

Could he do it?

Did he have a choice? Because he couldn't live like this.

"Fine." He added a nod to show his intention.

"You're willing to try it?"

"Yes. Let's just do it."

He saw Trey tense, straighten, pull his shoulders back, as if he was preparing for battle. Good. Deacon didn't want to be the only one nervous as hell about this.

"Okay." The muscles in Trey's throat convulsed as if he was swallowing.

Deacon braced himself as Trey took the final three steps to him, until they stood inches away from each other. Intimate inches that lovers shared.

When this was over, Trey would be his lover.

Trey looked at him, staring intently into his eyes as if to confirm that Deacon was really going through with it. Deacon raised his chin and forced his arms to his side, baring his chest. Trey nodded, as though he'd received the silent signal and leaned down.

Deacon's heart pounded, filling his throat and his ears as he waited for Trey's lips to touch his, but Trey turned away, opening his mouth on Deacon's shoulder. His lips touched the place the *were* had marked, zeroing in on each wound. He licked his tongue out, tasting, soothing.

Deacon's hands curled into fists as Trey kissed his shoulder and moved down. Large, rough hands touched his side, stroking the muscles covering his ribs.

183

Trey continued to lick and kiss his skin, his mouth going lower, opening over Deacon's nipple. The slow, upward stroke sent a warning to Deacon's cock, making it harden. Fuck. Was he really going to get hard for this?

Trey lingered, his tongue tormenting Deacon's flat nipple, sucking it, working it until Deacon couldn't hold back a groan. It felt good but it wasn't right.

The pleasurable sensation stopped him. Something wasn't right. As Trey worked downward, his fingers reaching for the towel that hung around Deacon's waist, it came to him.

"No," Deacon said. He clamped down on Trey's hands, stopping him from freeing the towel. At his statement, Trey backed up, instantly giving him room. Giving him the space he needed.

Deacon looked at Trey. He was a man who women loved. His face was strong and his hair was gorgeous. Long and blond, making him the envy of females everywhere.

But beyond that, he was attractive. Just a basic beauty that called to Deacon, even if he wanted to deny it.

"You want me to stop?" Trey asked and Deacon knew that if he turned away, if he backed away, Trey would understand.

"No," Deacon said. Trey paused for only a moment, then he stepped closer, bending to continue his slow, seductive exploration of Deacon's chest. Deacon shook his head. "No. If you're going to fuck my ass, the least you can do is kiss me on the lips."

The edge of Trey's mouth pulled up in a smile. It was a classic Trey look—amused, arrogant and in command. The sight soothed the strain in Deacon's chest.

"I didn't want to freak you out."

"Yeah, well, that ship's already sailed. We might as well do this right."

Trey nodded and leaned in. Deacon pulled back.

"Have you ever done this before?"

"Fucked another man?"

"Yeah."

"No. You?"

"No."

Again that half smile appeared. "I assumed we could figure it out."

Deacon found himself grinning in response. "Probably. And I guess…I guess, if I was going to get it up for any guy, it would be you."

Trey nodded. "Back at'cha."

That was all the warning Deacon got. Trey moved in, meshing their lips together. The shock moved through his body, translating into a hard cock that he hadn't expected.

Trey's mouth was only content on the surface for a moment. He parted his lips, giving Deacon the signal to open his. He hesitated for a moment, suddenly wanting to taste the man who stood before him.

He opened his mouth and Trey drove his tongue inside. The foreign, masculine taste wasn't unpleasant and after a few licks, Deacon decided he liked it. But being passive had never been a part of his makeup.

Trey dominated the kiss, subtly urging Deacon's submission. Deacon yanked his head back, letting the low growl rumble from his throat. He reached out, grabbing Trey's sides and pulled him back, taking his turn to control the kiss, to command, as Trey accepted the penetration of his tongue. It was strange kissing a man taller than Trey was, but he adjusted, moving so he matched Deacon's body.

As Trey drew back, Deacon scraped his teeth along the other man's lower lip, biting down just a shade too hard, warning that he wasn't going to be easily overpowered.

Trey snapped his head back. "Puppy." He followed the curse with another kiss, taking control. Deacon tugged on the shirt that covered Trey's chest, wanting him to be naked, wanting that flesh beneath his hands. Strange desires filled him but he was too caught up, too captivated, to analyze them. He merely followed the direction of his body and his body demanded that Trey be naked.

The buttons snapped in his hands and he tugged the material down, baring Trey's chest. The voice inside his head that he recognized as the wolf growled its pleasure. His teeth stretched as he imagined sinking his canines into the tight hard flesh of Trey's chest, scoring him with his claws. Marking him.

The desires ran through him and he knew this would work. This would be enough to break the connection to the *were* that marked him. *More. More. He needed more.*

"God." Trey snapped his head back. His breath was as harsh as Deacon's. His lips were wet and swollen and Deacon couldn't resist kissing them, biting them, loving the scrape of Trey's claws on his shoulders.

Deacon leaned down and dragged his teeth across Trey's neck, letting his incisors break the skin just enough. Marking him.

Trey growled and clamped his teeth around Deacon's neck, hard, but without penetrating. The bite moved through him, making his cock throb. Fuck, he wanted more. He wanted Trey inside him.

The foreign desires should have shocked him, but the passion and need flowing through his core was too much. The violence and strength as they touched each other was so different from making love to a woman.

Trey reached down and stripped away the towel. Deacon's cock rebounded, standing tall and full. Breathless, the two men stared each other. This was it. They were crossing a line that could never be reversed.

"Do it," Deacon commanded.

With a sharp nod, Trey's fingers—rough from hours working in the sun—curled around Deacon's erect cock. He heard the grunt and it took a moment to realize the sound had come from him. Trey stroked up, stopping just before he reached the tip and sliding back down.

"Damn." He traced the same path. "You *are* thick."

Unable to stop himself, Deacon leaned forward and kissed Trey's mouth.

Trey pulled back after a short taste. "No wonder Rebecca cries out when you fuck her."

A strange distance filled the space between them. A distance that Deacon felt compelled to cross.

"She loves to have you fuck her too."

Trey nodded. "But you bear her mark."

The words were hollow and low…and followed by a slow stroke of Trey's fingers. Deacon tried to grab at the thought, to retain it in his brain, but the strong steady pump of Trey's hand zapped all coherency from his mind.

It was like masturbating—only better. Another hand was touching him, who knew just how to touch, how to stroke, harder, a little stronger than a woman would dare.

He dropped his head back, letting his head bang against the wall. "Oh fuck."

"Good?"

Trey accompanied the question with a harsh scrape of his teeth.

"God, yes."

He continued to stroke him, sliding his fist back and forth across Deacon's cock until Deacon was meeting each stroke with a thrust of his own.

"Don't come." Trey pulled his hand away. "I don't want you coming before I fuck your ass."

Deacon moved, biting at Trey's mouth, needing that one connection, the final taste. He sank his tongue into the warm mouth waiting for him and savored the groan that flowed from Trey's chest. They were two dominant males, fighting for control, each trying to top the other.

Trey snapped his neck back and tilted his head toward the mattress.

"Get on the bed."

It took a moment for Deacon to realize the command had been directed at him. He'd spent most of his life commanding women, ordering them to his bed, and now he was the one.

Part of him rebelled but another side, something he never would have imagined, pushed him onward, sending him forward, until he was in the center of the mattress on his hands and knees, his ass up and open. God, he was actually offering himself to another male. Offering himself to be fucked.

The thought stunned him but his body was compliant. He wanted, needed to feel Trey inside him.

Hot, seductive hands slid over his ass, touching his skin, freeing him. The warmth shuddered through his body, adding to the heat that already filled him.

His back arched as the first finger slid into him, testing his readiness, the slick glide of lube easing his way.

Deacon dropped his head between his hands, tilting his ass upward. Trey's hands wandered across Deacon's skin, distracting him from the fact that one—hmm, now two fingers were sliding into his ass. The steady determined thrust dragged Deacon's head back. His ass, only ever penetrated by a single female finger, was full, stretched as Trey slid his fingers slowly in and out.

He never could have imagined it feeling so good.

"Oh, yeah," Trey groaned. "You're going to take me. Squeeze me hard."

"Yes." There was no other answer to give. He needed this. Needed to feel Trey sliding into his ass.

"That's it. Let me in."

The fingers disappeared and the hard, blunt head of Trey's cock filled the space. Part of Deacon's mind returned, enough that he realized what he was doing. The panic started as Trey penetrated, the sweet strain of his ass jerking him back. He dropped his forehead to the mattress and closed his eyes, letting his other senses take over, feeling the slow slide of Trey's cock, every inch filling him, stretching him, taking him.

Deacon grabbed the edge of the mattress and held on, fighting his scream as Trey entered him, the pleasure laced with pain.

"Okay?" Trey's voice managed to pierce the seductive fog and Deacon nodded, arching his back, allowing Trey's cock to sinker deeper. "Yeah, that's it. Let me in."

He sank in and then slowly started to withdraw.

The retreat was more glorious than the penetration as Trey whispered, "That's it, Deke. Feel me inside you. I'm going to fuck your ass, mark you." He nipped the skin across Deacon's shoulder blade. "You'll belong to me."

The possessive words sank into his soul and he moaned, pushing back as Trey slowly thrust forward. It was gentle and dominating and incredibly sexy.

"Yes," he sighed as Trey continued his slow steady penetration and retreat. A hot, hard hand curled around Deacon's cock, stroking in time to the intoxicating ass-fucking he was receiving.

"Oh yeah, Deke. You're hard, thick."

Trey's voice caressed him. It was good, so hot. Only one thing could have made it better.

Even as he thought it, he sensed movement beside him. He turned his head and looked at the open door. Rebecca filled the space watching them, her mouth was open but it didn't look like shock that held her frozen in the space.

Deacon dropped his head between his forearms, hiding his face, wanting her but not sure he wanted her to remember this. But even with that concern, he couldn't stop the slow rocking of his ass, pressing back as Trey fucked him.

"Hmm, Deacon, I think our little wolf wants to play too." Trey spread his fingers across Deacon's back and slowly scraped his claws across the smooth skin. The tiny bit of pain made him arch and moan—every inch of his flesh was alive. "Don't you, Rebecca?"

"Yes." Her voice was low and husky and filled with hunger. Deacon recognized the tone of her response, could smell the sweet scent of her cunt from across the room. She wasn't disgusted by what she saw. She was aroused.

"Shall we let her join us?" Trey sank into him and stopped, holding his cock deep inside.

"God, yes." The answer popped out of Deacon's mouth without his command but he knew it was the right choice. He wanted her to be a part of this. He turned and looked again, meeting her eyes for the first time in days, seeing the worry and love glowing back at him. And the desire. They'd use that for now and later he would apologize for being such a prick. She undid the buttons of her shirt and let it drop the ground, leaving her naked. Part of his mind registered that she hadn't just returned from outside, that she'd been preparing for this entrance, but the sight of her naked body, the tight nipples crowning those delicious breasts, pushed the irritating thought away. She strolled to the end of bed and climbed onto the mattress, leaning in first to kiss Trey, their bodies moving together. Their tongues entwined together and seemed reluctant to part, lingering as she pulled away. Deacon watched, craving that same contact. She curled down, offering her mouth to Deacon.

He accepted, driving his tongue between her lips, subtly tasting Trey on her. He didn't know if that was a product of turning into a werewolf or because he'd kissed Trey himself and recognized the taste. Didn't matter. It was good, it bound the three of them together.

"I want to taste you," she said, whispering the words into his mouth.

"Yeah, that's good, honey," Trey said. "Because he is hard and needs to come."

Rebecca glanced up to Trey and smiled, licking her lips as if already anticipating Deacon's cock in her mouth.

Trey shifted back, giving Deacon some room. He pushed up, allowing Rebecca to wiggle under their bodies. It was awkward and not the least bit sexual but within seconds she was beneath him, on her back, her head between his legs, her wet pussy open beneath his mouth.

"Oh yeah," he groaned, bending down and plunging his tongue into her slit. The hot seductive taste of her cunt was addictive and he always wanted more. He bent his head and tried to sink his tongue into her passage, needing to be inside her. As he licked the tight entrance, her lips closed on his cock.

He arched back, his head snapping up.

"Our little wolf does have a way with her mouth, doesn't she?" Trey chuckled as he pulled his cock back.

"Fuck yeah." He could feel Rebecca's smile but after a second, didn't care. She licked and kissed the full length of his shaft, squirming to get closer. Deacon clamped down on her hip, not wanting her sweet cunt to get away. He lapped at her clit, loving the way her groans vibrated into his cock, even as Trey sank deep into him.

Deacon realized he had a new definition of paradise — Rebecca's mouth on his cock, her wet pussy open to him and Trey slowly fucking his ass.

He buried his head between her thighs and tried to concentrate on making her come but the combined strokes of Trey's cock and Rebecca's mouth sapped all his attention.

She opened her mouth and again sucked Deacon's cock inside. He couldn't help but thrust down, needing to fuck, to driving his cock into her. He hoped he wasn't hurting her.

He gripped the mattress and tried to hold himself still, fighting the orgasm that was approaching like a speeding train. His fingers stretched and he looked at his hands, seeing the claws reach out and pierce the mattress. He tipped his head back and growled. Wanting it, wanting to come. Wanting his lovers to make him come.

Rebecca squeezed his cock with her hand as she sucked back and it was enough. He cried out, punching his hips forward, his cum shooting down her throat.

Trey's body covered his, strong hands holding him in place. A bright sharp pain entered his shoulder as Trey's teeth sank into his flesh.

The fire shot through his body—the pain turning into pleasure as it raced down his spine—and another orgasm slammed through his cock.

* * * * *

Deacon opened his eyes and looked up at the ceiling. What the hell? He must have passed out for a moment. Rebecca was curled up beside him, her eyes wide with curiosity and concern, her fingers stroking his chest, her leg entwined with his.

"You okay?"

He nodded not sure his voice would work. He'd never come like that before.

"Did I hurt you?" He stroked her cheek. He hadn't been able to control his thrusts toward the end.

"No. You were perfect." She licked her lips. "Yummy." His cock twitched and she slid her leg down, rubbing against the thick shaft.

He looked around. Trey stood beside the bed, his eyes dark, the set of his mouth serious.

"Feel any different?"

Deacon did a quick check of his body. The vile poison that had been flowing through his veins was gone. The memory of the attack seemed almost a dream. When he thought about being bitten, he remembered Trey's cock inside him, Rebecca's mouth on him. The loving words and sexual pleasure.

"Yeah. It's gone." Trey nodded but the look on his face didn't change. Deacon looked down and saw Trey was still hard. The condom was gone and he'd obviously cleaned up while Deacon was passed out but he hadn't come. "Come here."

Trey hesitated for a moment but then Rebecca held out her hand. He wrapped his fingers in hers and he crawled onto the bed, moving up beside Deacon.

As if they could read each other's thoughts, Rebecca and Deacon reached for Trey, their hands meeting and curling around his cock. Rebecca leaned over and licked the tip. Trey tensed and Deacon looked up. There was still some distance.

Staying flat on his back, he put his hand behind Trey's neck and pulled him down, stretching up enough to meet his mouth, starting with a gentle kiss and then driving his tongue inside.

Trey lashed his tongue around Deacon's, both males again fighting for control. When they finally separated, they were both breathless, their lips wet and stung from the harsh kisses.

Trey sat up and turned, capturing Rebecca's mouth, sharing a deep kiss with her.

With them involved, Deacon put his hand around Trey's cock and began to pump, needing this, realizing there was one final part to completely block the *were's* attack from his mind.

Trey groaned and straightened, his hips rolling to meet Deacon's strokes.

"Good. Yeah. Do it."

Rebecca knelt beside them, watching, not physically touching either man but still a part of this.

Deacon worked Trey's cock, feeling the rising tide, knowing he was close. With a shout, Trey punched his hips forward and hot cum splattered onto Deacon's stomach. He kept stroking, drawing the last bit out, wanting to be marked by Trey's seed.

Trey raised his eyes, the distance was gone and all that was left was a silent amazement.

"No part of me belongs to him," Deacon announced.

"None." He leaned down and kissed Deacon. The caress was soft and loving, almost careful. With a final lick of his tongue, he pulled back and lay down beside Deacon, propping his head up on his hand, staring across the male body before him to Rebecca. "Now, we've both come. I think our little wolf needs to be fucked."

Deacon nodded. "Fucked long and hard."

A rush of scent filled the room and Deacon knew Rebecca's pussy juices had to be coating her thighs.

He looked at Trey, knowing he sensed her arousal as well.

Rebecca backed away, inching toward the edge of the bed.

Deacon looked at Trey.

"She can't seriously be thinking of running."

"I wouldn't think so."

Rebecca's feet hit the floor and she ran for the door.

As a unit, Deacon and Trey moved, chasing their woman.

Chapter Fourteen

∞

Deacon tapped his fingers on his thigh and forced himself to take a sip of the beer he held but didn't want. The back of his neck prickled, as if every tiny hair was standing on end. He just wanted the night over with.

The full moon was on the rise and tonight he would make his first change into the wolf form. Trey had assured him repeatedly in the past week that it wasn't hard. His body would instinctively know what to do. What he really wanted was to be back at his little cabin, Rebecca and Trey nearby. But no, Mikhel's pack—which it appeared Deacon had become a member of—was meeting for a full moon run. Made extra special by the fact that Deacon was making his first transition.

In addition to Taylor, Mikhel and Zach, Mikhel's brothers and parents, and a few members of their pack had decided to come to the lake for the full moon.

Great, just what he needed—an audience for his first time.

As the week had progressed, Deacon had sensed the rising moon, feeling the wolf come alive inside him. Thank God Trey had been around. They hadn't fucked again but they'd spent hours together. Rebecca had returned to the city each morning for work but she'd come back to the cabin at night and the three of them had talked and made love. But the tension, the anticipation was wearing on Deacon's nerves.

I'm about to become a wolf. That's one for my diary. If I kept a diary, which I don't. Maybe I should start one. My life as a new werewolf. It could make a great book.

Realizing that his nervousness had translated into internal babbling, he scanned the room. Trey was standing on the far side of the room, talking to a cute little blonde werewolf who belonged to Mikhel's father's pack. She tipped her head to the side and smiled at something he said, her eyelashes fluttering, attracting Trey's gaze. Trey returned the smile and the blonde stepped closer.

Oops, bad idea.

From his position by the window, Deacon watched Rebecca leave her conversation with Taylor and stalk over to Trey's side. She didn't open her mouth. She just looked up at him, silently speaking with a stare. His eyes widened in surprise, as if he was shocked that she would be jealous. Fool. Deacon shook his head. Rebecca considered them her personal property. She wasn't going to let another woman poach.

Confusion crossed Trey's face as she faced the petite blonde werewolf and glared until the woman backed away.

How did Trey not understand that Rebecca thought they belonged to her?

Then he heard Trey's voice in his head. From the night they'd been together. *You bear her mark.* Deacon remembered the sadness, the pain in that simple phrase. He hadn't had time to acknowledge it then—he'd been a little distracted—but now, he realized that Trey might not believe that Rebecca had claimed him. Of course, to hear Trey talk, the connection between them would ease after the rise of the first moon.

Deacon felt a strong pull both to Rebecca, and after last week, Trey. Rebecca obviously experienced the same sensations. Trey seemed to feel nothing in return. The last few days, he'd been withdrawing. Not only from Deacon but from Rebecca as well. The threesome had been tense as they'd arrived at Mikhel's house tonight. Rebecca's little fit of jealousy probably wasn't going to help.

Trey worked his way across the room, taking up the space next to Deacon. The urge to lean into him, to rest his shoulder against Trey's was strong but Deacon knew it wouldn't be welcome. Not only because of Trey's distance but because of the presence of so many others. Even Zach and Mikhel, who

Deacon had learned were lovers, showed no signs of the intimacy that Deacon had seen at other times.

Rebecca followed Trey across the room and stood beside Deacon, turning her back to him, almost as if she was keeping watch over her males, making sure no other female came near. The subtle scent of her shampoo made Deacon's cock hard. He shifted, trying to ease the tension in his groin. He didn't want to be the only werewolf with a hard-on. And he was going to have to get naked with these people in just a few minutes.

"I wish we'd get on with this," Deacon muttered.

"We can't until Mikhel calls for us to go. He's the Alpha."

"What's he waiting for?"

"He's the Alpha," Trey repeated.

Deacon pressed his lips together to keep from snarling. He took a deep breath, inhaling through his nose, gathering the multilayered scents in the room. Rebecca's arousal was the strongest but there were others. One that was familiar...

Deacon froze and he felt Trey tense. He recognized it too.

"He's here."

"Who's here?" Rebecca asked, spinning around as if she'd caught the tension of the two men.

"That bastard who bit us."

Trey's body tightened, straightened, going into warrior mode.

Deacon sniffed the air, following the stronger scent.

"He's that way." He nodded toward the back deck.

"Let's go."

"No, I want to face him."

Trey's eyes closed down into a squint and Deacon was sure he was going to protest but his friend nodded. "Fine. You start it off."

Deacon knew Trey was giving him a chance to face the bastard, but he didn't for a moment think he was going out there alone. That fact gave him extra confidence. Deacon knew just how strong the *were* was. He wasn't sure his strength was equal to the creature. Not yet.

He opened the back door and stepped onto the deck. For a moment he thought he was alone but then he saw the man standing in the shadows.

"I knew you'd follow," the voice said just before he stepped forward. For a moment Deacon thought it was Trey but quickly realized though the man had the same hair and the same basic body shape, that's where the similarities ended. This had to be Trey's cousin Marcus. "We didn't get to finish what we started. Come here."

Deacon felt a strange compulsion to walk across the deck but the urge passed almost immediately and he shook his head.

"Puppy. You think to defy me. I own you. You belong to me."

Deacon laughed. The guy tried to sound so commanding, so menacing that it was actually funny.

"I don't think so."

Marcus stepped forward, his nose twitching as he sniffed the air. "So my cousin decided to mark you. Doesn't matter. I was still the first. I made you—" He stared across the deck. "You and that little bitch will call *me* Alpha."

As his hands reached out, a low dangerous growl echoed from the lawn. Deacon looked over and saw a wolf—the same wolf who'd stood in Rebecca's living room two weeks ago. Its lips were peeled back, revealing long white teeth. Its eyes glowed red. Without further warning, Trey leapt forward.

But Marcus' body changed as well—not dropping into wolf form but expanding, his chest broadening. He grew taller and his skin turned a steel gray. The long wolf snout stretched from his face. This was the *were* form that Trey had told him about.

Deacon watched as Trey struck, his teeth sinking into the werewolf thigh. Marcus swung his arm down and slammed his hand into Trey's body, knocking him free. The scent of fresh blood combined with the fury that Marcus would harm his mate and clouded Deacon's mind.

A fierce growl erupted from his throat as he looked up at the *were*. Way up.

Part of Deacon's mind rebelled at the sudden change. He was three feet above the ground, on all fours. He'd changed into a wolf.

But even with the human panic running through his brain, the wolf's instincts came to life. He knew precisely where to strike. As the *were* turned away, stalking after Trey, Deacon attacked, going for the flank muscle, sinking his teeth into the strong flesh. Blood filled his mouth but he didn't release. He bit down, pulling with his body. The *were* screamed, tipping his head back and howling at the full moon.

The bare neck gave Trey the perfect target and the wolf lunged, leaping high and clamping down on the *were*'s throat. The scream died and became a gurgle. The *were* clawed at Trey's back trying to pull him free but Trey held on. Deacon tugged backward, dragging Marcus to the deck.

Deacon's sensitive ears heard the final beats of the *were*'s heart as the combined wounds drained the life from his body. Marcus collapsed and Trey staggered away. Through his wolf eyes, Deacons saw Trey struggling, stumbling off the deck.

The bright glow of fresh blood covered his chest, deep vicious wounds left by the *were*'s claws. Deacon ran to Trey's side, using his hypersensitive nose to investigate.

Sounds warned of others approaching. Deacon spun around, placing his body in front of Trey's fallen form. He dragged his lips back and growled, daring any to come near.

Deacon didn't know the large wolf that approached but when the animal growled a warning, Deacon knew he couldn't back down. He wouldn't let anyone harm Trey.

The wolf came closer.

You would challenge your Alpha?

The voice rang inside his head—a wolf version of Mikhel's voice.

I would to protect my mate, Deacon replied, finding the strangely formal words came naturally to his mind. The other wolf seemed to hear him.

We don't want to harm him. He's hurt. Let us help him.

A human body approached and Deacon immediately recognized the scent. Rebecca. She cried out and ran forward, dropping down beside Trey.

"Deacon, help him."

It took him a moment to realize he was still in wolf form—and didn't know how to become human again. He wasn't sure how he'd become the wolf. He looked at Mikhel, needing help. A foreign picture filled his mind, like a movie projector on his brain, giving him the instructions on how to make the transition. He dropped his head and followed the guidance, pushing the wolf back, reforming the human in his head.

Pain crackled through his limbs as they stretched and straightened, bending at different angles, leaving him kneeling on the ground beside Trey's body.

"Is he okay?" Rebecca asked as she crouched next to him.

"Let me look." Deacon inspected the wolf. "Most of it looks pretty shallow. He's probably just stunned."

"Should we wake him? Get him back in human form?"

Deacon shook his head. "I'm going to be able to treat him better like this."

"Why?" That question came from behind him—probably Mikhel but he wasn't positive.

"Because I'm vet."

Rebecca leaned back. "You're a vet?"

"Yeah." He ignored her shock. He hadn't deliberately misled her but she'd felt so comfortable with him after he'd taken care of her wound, he didn't want to ruin it by saying most of his patients walked on fours legs. But at this point, many of his friends did as well. "I need my kit. It's back at the cabin."

"I'll get it," Zach said, pulling off his shirt. "I can get there faster on four legs than two." He opened his jeans and dropped his pants, glaring at Mikhel. "But no Lassie jokes." With that, he changed, dropping into his wolf form with the ease of someone used to the change.

The rest of the group was milling around, whispering, muttering. Mikhel looked around.

"Dad, can you lead the rest on a run while we take care of Trey?" He glanced at the fallen *were* body. "And him."

Rike nodded and guided the remaining crowd off the porch into the backyard. Under the light of the full moon, Deacon watched as body after body changed from human to wolf. There was a strange beauty in it.

I did that, he realized as he watched. *I became a wolf. Even if it was only for a little while.*

Rebecca knelt down beside Deacon, her eyes worried.

"Is he going to be okay?" she asked, putting her hand on Trey's chest, her fingers gently stroking his fur.

"I think he'll be fine."

Deacon's jeans landed on the ground next to him. He mumbled his thanks to whoever had tossed him his clothes and stood up to drag them on, blushing when he realized Mikhel, his pack and their friends were watching.

"You're really a vet?" the Alpha wolf asked, closing the top button of his jeans.

"Yes."

"Good. We need a family doctor."

Before that conversation could continue, Zach returned, Deacon's bag in his jaw. He dropped it and ran over to Mikhel's side, sitting beside his Alpha as if waiting for instructions.

Feeling in his element, Deacon opened his kit and pulled out the antiseptic and some gauze pads. "Okay, let's get Trey patched up."

* * * * *

Seven hours later, Rebecca was amazed at the transformation. Trey was alive and well. Human again. Deacon had worked on him in his wolf form, stitching up the biggest cuts, cleaning and bandaging the rest. Finally he'd given Trey some sort of animal sedative that had knocked the wolf out for hours.

The werewolf healing had taken care of most of the damage and two hours ago, Trey had awakened and returned to his human form, crawling into bed.

By that time, the house was almost empty. Mikhel's family and friends had gone home after their run and Rebecca had made it through her first full moon. She hadn't really noticed, she'd been so worried about Trey. Despite Deacon's assurances, she'd continued to hover. Her hands were sore from twisting her fingers together.

But now, Trey sat up, looking calm and cool. Too cool. She wondered if maybe he was hurting more than he wanted to let on.

"You sure you're all right?" she asked, reaching out to stroke his shoulder.

He subtly shifted away, sliding from beneath her touch. "I'm good. Chest is sore but I'm glad we got that bastard."

Rebecca nodded. Mikhel had taken care of getting rid of Marcus' body. She didn't know what had happened to it and didn't want to. Zach and Mikhel had been grim when they'd returned from that little errand and neither seemed inclined to talk about it.

"Trey, you should be resting," Deacon said as he entered the room. "I mean, I know I deal with animals mostly but you did sustain a head wound earlier and some fairly major cuts."

Trey didn't smile. He barely reacted. If Rebecca hadn't seen them together, she never would have known the two men were lovers. Or that Trey was her lover.

He looked at them—he wasn't avoiding their eyes. It would have almost been better if he did. Then maybe she wouldn't have seen the complete lack of interest. It was as though an invisible wall had been constructed between them—and Trey had no intention of tearing it down.

"I'm fine," he said with a shrug. "I'll keep it slow today. I should be back to full strength tomorrow."

Again there was that distance, that chill to his words. Something was definitely wrong. Rebecca didn't need the wolf's instincts to know she wasn't going to like what happened next.

Trey looked down at his hands and then up at Rebecca and Deacon. He hated to do this, everything in him rejected the idea, but it had to be done. And it had to be done now.

"How did you two make it through the first full moon?"

Both nodded.

"Mikhel helped you transition out?" he asked Deacon. The desire to reach out to the other male, to pull him close, let their skin touch, their bodies meld together, pulsed through Trey's veins but he expected that. The power of his bite would linger for months but it would fade. As long as the contact between them was broken.

"Yeah, he was somehow in my head."

"It's an Alpha thing." Trey shook his head. "I don't really understand it." He took deep breath. "So, this is it."

Rebecca looked at Trey, then at Deacon, wondering if she'd missed something, then back to Trey. "This is what?"

"I told you that after the full moon, the connection between us would weaken." That hadn't exactly occurred. He still wanted to fuck Rebecca and hell, maybe even Deacon again. But he had to go with what he knew. "The three of us can't meet again. At least not for a while."

"How long's 'a while'?" Deacon asked.

"Six months, a year." *Whatever it takes.*

"What? Why?" Though Rebecca didn't speak, Trey could see the same questions in her eyes.

"The connection between you two…and between Deacon and me, is purely driven by our wolves. It's not real."

"It feels real."

"It's lust," Trey said. "In this case, purely animal lust. If you two met on the street, you'd probably never even look at each other. And I sure as hell wouldn't have fucked Deacon."

Deacon straightened, obviously offended. Trey was sure when Deacon's pride wasn't involved, he would admit the truth to that statement.

"I don't understand why we can't see each other," Rebecca said, jumping into the conversation.

He pressed his lips together and forced his breath through his nose, desperate that they grasp what he was saying. "What you're feeling isn't real. Your wolves want to fuck. They are connected through the bite you shared and they'll do anything to keep that connection going."

"And why is this a bad thing?" Deacon asked, his body shifting, taking on the aggressive stance of a challenged male.

"Because the connection between your wolves will grow. The bond will become unbreakable. Think about it. Your human side won't be able to resist. It won't matter if you love or hate each other, you'll have to fuck. And in ten years, you'll wake up, look at this person you've been fucking for a decade and realize you don't even like them. But by then your wolves will be so bound together you can't break free. You'll be trapped and miserable."

Neither spoke. Finally Trey sighed.

"Trust me. I speak from experience. My parents met — typical case of full moon lust. They let their wolves dictate who they mated with. Eventually they realized they hated each other but they couldn't be apart." It had been hell living in that house. The only time there had been peace was when his parents were fucking.

He looked at his lovers, hoping they understood how important this was. He didn't want to consign anyone — himself or either of them — to the kind of hell his parents lived through.

"The first full moon is past. The cravings and desires shouldn't be as strong. Now's the time."

Both Rebecca and Deacon reacted, ready to protest. Trey shook his head. He had to end this and it had to be now — before he wanted more, before he wanted to stay with them forever.

"As of this moment, all contact between the three of us has to be broken." Neither moved. They stared at him with stunned, hurt eyes. It was too much. "I'd really like you both to leave my room."

For a moment, he thought they would ignore his request. Rebecca pressed her lips together and Trey could see tears forming in her eyes. She nodded and turned away, too proud to let her tears be seen.

Deacon just looked pissed. He glared at Trey and followed Rebecca from the room.

As the door closed, Trey flinched — and listened to his wolf howl.

Chapter Fifteen

ʂɔ

Deacon stared at the phone, willing it to ring. Dreading that it would. Dreading that it wouldn't because then *he'd* be the one making the call.

But part of him was able to wait, just a little longer.

It was Rebecca's turn.

He'd made the first call late Sunday night—after more than three weeks of being separated from her and Trey.

During the week, he could distract himself with work. He'd continued to come to the cabin each night instead of sleeping in his house in town. Even knowing it was just torturing him, he wanted to be near the memories, remembering Rebecca at his table, in his bed. And Trey—the strong powerful body that had dominated his. Deacon dropped his head back, the memory making his cock hard.

Weekends and nights were the hardest.

Last Sunday, the day had been endless—maybe because he'd seen Trey across the lake but knew better than to approach. And Deacon had turned to the one person who would understand—Rebecca.

Trey was right, the pull between them was strong. Intense. He'd claimed that the impact of Rebecca's bite would fade after that first full moon but Deacon hadn't noticed a change. He still felt the compulsion. Felt the need to be with her, talk to her. Fuck her.

So far, he and Rebecca had managed to resist making physical contact but after that first phone call, they'd spoken each night, conversations that lasted hours, until one or both were falling asleep. Then they said good night.

Deacon found his dreams filled with Rebecca—dancing naked before him, moonlight covering her skin.

But they weren't alone. Trey was there. Joining Deacon, touching him, kissing him, their male bodies pressed together as Rebecca moved with them. A sensual feast. Lips and tongues, hands and fingers. Cocks and a sweet wet pussy that both men tasted.

Deacon groaned and pressed his hand to his erection. His logical mind agreed with Trey's explanation but damn, something had to give soon. He didn't know if he was strong enough to fight it.

The phone shattered the grim silence and Deacon sighed, relieved that Rebecca would distract him. Funny, that talking to the woman he wanted would distract him from fucking her.

He picked up the receiver and said, "Hello."

"Hi."

Rebecca. "How're you, baby?"

She moaned as if his low sexual tone teased her. "I'm okay. Same as last night. Hot, restless. Horny, though I hate to use that term."

Deacon chuckled. "I know what you mean." And hearing her voice only made him harder but God, he didn't want to hang up. Didn't want to lose the connection to her. "So, let's talk about something else. How was your day?" Then he remembered their conversation last night. "Did you talk to that client? You were dreading that."

"Goodness." The disgust in her voice made him smile. He could picture her—rolling her eyes, shaking her head and squishing her lips together. "What an idiot…"

Deacon stretched out on the couch and listened as she described the meeting. That topic flowed into another and when he finally looked at the clock it was past eleven. They'd been on the phone for three hours.

"Damn, baby, you need to go to bed." She needed a full eight hours of sleep or she was cranky the next day. He'd figured that out Tuesday night when she'd been a tad bitchy during their shortened conversation.

"Oh, you're right. But I'm not going to be able to sleep."

"Me either."

She paused and he knew her mind was going the same place his had been. "I miss seeing you," she said. "Touching you."

"I know. Me too."

"So what do we do? Is this making it worse? Talking like this?" She laughed. "I don't suppose Trey would approve."

"Probably not but since he won't see me I can't ask him."

"Maybe he's right."

Deacon nodded even though she couldn't see him then said, "Maybe he's not."

"What?" The hope in her voice urged him on.

"I understand what he's saying. I can feel the pull of the wolf. It's a definite desire to fuck you. But that's not all I feel. This isn't some mindless bond. If it were, I don't think I'd've been able fuck another woman."

"You've *fucked* another woman?" The question crackled through the line like a shot.

"No, not exactly."

"Not exactly?" The precise way she spoke left no doubt about her feelings on the subject.

"Not at all." He took a breath. "Saturday night, I couldn't stand it anymore. I was about to come out of my skin I needed to fuck so badly." Rebecca was silent on the other end of the phone but he could feel the tension zipping through the phone line and knew she hadn't hung up. "I went out to this hick club down road. Had a few drinks, danced a bit. There was this woman—" The growl that rumbled through the earpiece warned him to speak cautiously. And quickly. "We danced and she was rubbing up against me. We made out a bit and she suggested we go outside. Part of me thought, 'Ah hell, just do it. Get it out of your system'. The wolf was all for it. Ready to fuck.

"My cock was hard, she was cute and wanted it. I could have done it."

"And…"

"And I didn't." He scraped his fingers through his hair and stared at the floor. "I just kept thinking, 'She's not Rebecca'. I didn't really want her. I wanted you." He chuckled. "Then I thought, 'Damn, Rebecca will kick my ass if I fuck this woman'. So, I came home and took a cold shower."

Silence greeted him but it was a friendlier sound than before.

"Rebecca?"

"I'm here. I'm just trying to decide how I feel about that. I mean, I'm glad you didn't sleep with her and yes, I would have been supremely pissed."

"I know."

"Maybe you're right. Maybe there's something besides the pull of the wolf."

"I think it's something we need to explore. Talk about." He took the next step. "Face-to-face."

"Then we should do it in public, just in case."

"Good. Tomorrow, I'll meet you for lunch."

"Okay. Sounds good."

A knot loosened inside Deacon's chest. This was good. Seeing Rebecca was the first step. Where they would go from there remained to be seen.

* * * * *

Deacon peered out the window, watching Trey for a second before he let him in. The werewolf was tense tonight — his eyes staring off, as if he was considering making a run for it.

The smile that tugged on Deacon's lips couldn't be stopped. Trey was about to stop running.

Checking the room one more time, he opened the door.

Tension vibrated off Trey's body as he slowly turned and faced Deacon. Deacon felt the pull of his wolf, the connection that Trey had told him about. They hadn't seen each other in over four weeks and his wolf was anxious for contact with the one it considered its mate.

"What's up?" Trey asked, not making any move to walk into the cabin.

But Deacon was determined.

"Come in. I need to talk to you for a second."

Trey again turned his eyes to woods. He was struggling with the pull of their wolves as well. He shook his head as if shaking off a bad decision and walked inside. Deacon stepped out of the way, giving him space, silently guiding him into the middle of the living room.

"So, what's up?" Trey asked again, his impatience laced with irritation. Or more likely frustration. "I'm trying to get some stuff done for—" His eyes squinted down until they were almost slits. "Rebecca's here."

The words were an accusation but Deacon didn't bother to deny it. He just smiled and nodded. Trey sighed and glanced at the bedroom door, in time to see Rebecca walk out, dressed in Deacon's shirt. And nothing else.

"Fuck," Trey cursed.

"Not yet," Rebecca said. "But later, hopefully."

"Definitely," Deacon added.

"No." Trey slashed his hand down and backed up, so both Deacon and Rebecca were in front of him. "You two can't keep doing this. You're going to screw yourselves, badly."

"That's what we wanted to talk to you about."

"There's nothing else to say. You are connected, bound to each other because of Rebecca's bite. You need to break that bond now and the only way to do that is to stay away from each other."

Rebecca's lips tightened and Deacon could tell she was near her explosion point. But that would ruin their plan. Tonight was about seduction so Deacon spoke. "But we don't want to stay away from each other." He winked at Rebecca, trying to tease her back into good spirits. She rolled her eyes and tipped her head to the side, giving him a slight nod.

"But that's the problem. It's your wolves. It's not real. And if you don't break this bond now, you'll wake up some day..." He shook his head. "You'll be miserable."

Deacon knew Trey was speaking from personal experience but he and Rebecca had talked about it. They'd talked about everything and while the pull of the wolf was strong, so was the human connection.

He even felt it with Trey. He'd never have considered taking another man as a lover before the werewolf bite but now that he'd crossed that line, he wanted more. He wanted the freedom and sexual power to touch Trey, fuck Trey. And have Trey fuck him. But it was more than the clamoring of his wolf, more than a physical need. God, he couldn't believe he was even thinking it, but he was pretty sure he was falling in love with Trey.

But they'd deal with that later. Tonight he needed to strengthen, not weaken the bonds that held them.

"Well see, we'd like to test this theory of yours," he said, moving closer to Trey, blocking his access to the door. He wasn't ready to let him escape just yet.

"What theory?" Trey folded his arms on his chest and set his chin into a firm hard line.

"The theory that the only thing pulling us together is the connection between the wolves." He was close now. Close enough to touch. So he did. He rubbed his hand down Trey's back, letting his palm rest on the upper curve of his ass. Trey tensed and for a moment Deacon thought he'd move away but the man stayed still. "See if that's the case, then I want to fuck Rebecca because she bit me."

That was Rebecca's cue. She nodded and strolled forward until she was positioned in front of Trey. She looked tiny in Deacon's shirt. Tiny but not helpless. There was a strength and sexuality about her that drew the attention of every male in the area. Deacon could only thank God that she'd chosen them as her lovers.

"Yes," Trey said but the word was tight and strained.

"And I want to fuck you..." Deacon continued, letting his hand tighten on Trey's ass. "Because you bit me."

"Exactly."

"Then there should be no reason why you should want to fuck Rebecca. Nothing that pulls you to her."

Deacon moved around behind Trey while Rebecca moved up close, until he was caged between the two of them.

"Is that true?" Rebecca asked. "You don't want me?" She ran her fingers up the front of Trey's shirt, opening the top two buttons and spreading the sides apart. She leaned in and placed a kiss on his chest. "You don't want to come inside me?" Another kiss. Deacon moved closer so his body pressed against Trey's back, his erection bumping against Trey's ass. "Don't want that hard cock sliding into my pussy? Or into my mouth?"

Heat exploded from Trey's body. The warmth filtered into Deacon's and he moved even closer, blatantly rubbing his cock against Trey. Rebecca continued to open buttons and kiss her way down Trey's chest. Deacon watched over his friend's shoulder, loving the sight of Rebecca's lips on Trey's skin, sensing the supreme control moving through Trey's body, the way he was fighting the desire to grab her and fuck her.

Rebecca opened the last button and dragged Trey's shirt back, down his shoulders until it fell between their bodies. Trey hadn't moved since they'd begun. His hands were curled into fists as if he was resisting every sensation.

Rebecca spread her fingers across his chest and bit the nails gently into his skin, slowly scratching down, leaving ten thin pink lines across Trey's flesh.

When she reached his stomach she backed away, letting her hands drop to her side.

"Hmmm, I don't know. Maybe he's right, Deacon," she said as she stepped backward. She fluttered her eyelashes like a wide-eyed innocent. "Maybe it is just the call of the wolf."

Deacon wrapped his arms around Trey, one hand sliding across his chest, the other easing down between his legs. Trey tensed as Deacon's hand closed over his cock, hard and pushing against the thick material of his jeans. "Well, baby, something's made him hard." Deacon squeezed gently, still amazed that he had his hand on another man's cock and was enjoying it.

There was a catch in Trey's throat, so low that only Deacon could hear it. He stroked his tongue across Trey's shoulder, rewarding him for the quiet sound.

"I think, Rebecca, you should show him what he's missing."

Rebecca stared at Trey and slowly sank into the recliner. She draped one leg over the arm and pushed the other leg wide, baring her pussy to the two men. Trey's cock jumped in Deacon's hand.

"Oh yeah. That's one sweet little cunt, isn't it?"

Trey nodded and licked his lips. Deacon could understand the reaction. His mouth was dry, watching as Rebecca's fingers meandered up the insides of her thighs until she reached her pussy. Deep pink and glistening with sex juice.

She toyed with her pussy lips, her fingers dancing across the moist skin. Trey's breath changed as she dipped one finger into her pussy and then raised it to her mouth, letting her tongue flick out and capture a single taste. Her eyes were locked on Trey's as she pushed her hand back between her legs and slowly thrust two fingers into her tight opening.

The scent of her cunt filled the room and Trey heard his wolf howl inside his head.

Heat incased his cock and he realized Deacon had opened his jeans and was stroking his cock. God, didn't they realize what they were doing? They were making the bond even tighter. They had to stop. But God he couldn't move. Couldn't step out of Deacon's hold or look away from Rebecca's pretty cunt. He wanted this. Wanted Rebecca. And Deacon.

"Oh, yeah, that's it, baby," Deacon whispered. He placed a kiss beneath Trey's ear, soft and sensual, followed by a tiny bite, as if the slow sexual way of making love wouldn't work between the two males. "Doesn't she look hot?" He pumped his fist up and down Trey's cock.

"Yes."

"Yes." He snagged Trey's ear lobe in his teeth, leaving another tiny wound. Trey felt the gentle bite sizzle down his spine and tighten his cock. The wayward organ leapt in Deacon's hand. "Oh, yeah, you like that. You like to have your skin marked. Like it when we bite you."

He didn't bother to deny it. He couldn't. He'd always liked a little bit of pain with his pleasure but he'd always been so careful with his lovers. Now, his lovers were the ones pushing him.

Deacon's hand tightened on his cock and slid up until his fist was resting against Trey's groin. For a moment, he thought Deacon was just stroking him but then the grip held, pressing Trey back, as Deacon rubbed his cock against him, his shaft slipping between the split in his ass. The thick—very thick— cock pulsed against him even as Deacon kissed his neck. The heat that crept through his ass made his dick ache. He wanted more.

The sensations—and the wicked sight of Rebecca finger-fucking herself—were too much for his strained body. He'd thought, dreamed, fantasized about these two for weeks now. And they were with him, wanted him. Even though he knew it was wrong, that they would regret it, he couldn't fight it.

"Yeah, you want to fuck her, don't you Trey?" Deacon's lips continued to caress him, whispering across his ear, his neck, his shoulder.

"Yes."

"But you want more than that, don't you?" Deacon did a slow stroke of Trey's cock, from base to tip. "You want more than just to come inside her." Another long pump. "You want to feel her pearly white teeth sink into you." His teeth nipped Trey's ear. "Have her mark you, claim you."

"Yes!" The response was ripped from him, a visceral reaction that came from deep inside his soul.

Rebecca pulled her fingers out of her pussy, liquid coating the slim digits. She swung her legs down, closed. Trey felt a growl well up in the back of his throat at the loss of her pussy. He needed it. Wanted it. It belonged to them.

The strange phrase filled his mind and he realized that he was claiming her cunt for both him and Deacon. They would be the males who pleased and satisfied her. He'd kill any other male who touched her. Except Deacon.

Rebecca pushed herself up, slow and sensual. As she stood, she opened the shirt she wore and pushed it down, leaving her naked. Her nipples were tight and hard and Trey licked his lips, wanting those tight peaks in his mouth.

Letting her shirt trail behind her, she strolled across the living room and turned left, past them, toward the bedroom.

Deacon's hands seemed to slip away from him as Trey followed Rebecca into the bedroom. He stepped inside and she was on the bed, lying on her side, her leg drawn up, giving him just a hint of her pussy.

"Trey." She said his name—part command, part plea— and the sound drew him forward. He shoved his jeans and shorts down, leaving a short trail of clothes to the bedside.

He lay down beside her, his hands immediately reaching for her, pulling her close. There was no hesitation as she rolled with him, raising her leg and opening her pretty sex to him. Part of him wanted to dominate, to climb on top of her and pound into her but another part wanted to be taken, claimed. Ridden.

He hooked his hand around her hips and pulled her near, thinking to draw her top of him, but she resisted, giving him only enough so he could enter her. The tip of his cock slipped into her passage, sinking in as though he was meant to be there, meant to fill her. She rolled her hips, pressing forward and Trey shifted, adjusting so he could push into her pussy.

Still on his side, he couldn't fuck hard and deep nor would he be ridden.

He looked up and Rebecca was there, her eyes alight with heat and desire and something else. Something more.

He pushed in deeper, taking her until she engulfed his cock, swallowing him in that hot tight cunt of hers. God, he wanted her, he loved her. He kept the words to himself, knowing it was too much, sure that it couldn't be real. That it was the connection of the wolf that was pulling them together. Except she hadn't bitten him. He wasn't marked. Wasn't claimed in any way.

He slowly pumped, a deep gentle rocking inside her pussy. He ground his teeth together and fought the urge to come. He wanted to feel her. Wanted to feel her orgasm grab him.

He bent down and covered her mouth with his own. She was there, ready to greet him, taste him. Their lips completed the connection between them and Trey had one bright, shining moment when he realized this was more than wolf-to-wolf desire. He wanted this woman. Wanted to fuck her. Wanted to be a part of her. Wanted to fill her.

And he wanted more.

Even as he bent down and latched his lips around her nipple, he felt the heat return to his back. Deacon. The hot hard cock that had teased him before was bare and sliding between his ass cheeks. The warm press of Deacon's chest, his hand moving down, between their bodies, stroking Trey and Rebecca. Deacon's lips on his neck, his shoulder.

Unable to deny the need, Trey turned his head and met Deacon's mouth. Deacon drove his tongue between Trey's lips, licking and seeking.

Trey punched his hips forward, the temptation of Rebecca's pussy was too much for him to resist. Deacon's warmth covered him from behind as he sank into her cunt. God, it felt as if he was being fucked.

Hot and intimate. The three of them moved together, touching, skin against skin. Deacon's hot hands stroking his hip, sliding over and cupping Rebecca's firm breast, then slipping down her back to cuddle her ass closer, sinking Trey's cock deeper into her cunt. A groan erupted between them and Trey couldn't resist thrusting, shallow pulses deep inside her. Because of their positions on their sides, he couldn't get much leverage so he just worked his cock slowly in her. He kissed and sipped at Rebecca's lips, trying to maintain some control. Deacon scraped his teeth across Trey's shoulder as he slid his cock against Trey's ass. Not trying to enter him, just rubbing and touching.

The wolf inside him growled its demand, wanting more of his lovers.

Trey dug his fingers into Rebecca's hip and drove his cock forward, his orgasm too powerful to resist.

He felt her mouth on his pectoral muscle just seconds before her teeth sank in, biting down, claiming him. The mark was so intense it jolted through his body and he thrust, coming again inside her even as her teeth gripped him. The second climax hadn't cleared his body when he felt the next bite, hot and wet, at the base of his neck.

Deacon.

The sharp, hot werewolf teeth clamped down on his neck.

He cried out as another orgasm slammed into his body.

* * * * *

Time passed. He opened his eyes, almost stunned to find himself on his back...staring up at Rebecca and Deacon. His lovers.

His mates.

Claimed by both of them, he could feel their energy, their need running through is body.

Rebecca dipped her head and laved her tongue up his chest, teasing his flat nipple as she passed.

"You okay?" she asked when she looked up.

Trey nodded, not sure his vocal cords were working yet. But the rest of his body was alive and well. Very alive. He turned his head and looked into Deacon's hot eyes. He leaned down and kissed Trey's mouth, soft and exploring, obviously waiting for Trey's response. He pushed up, deepening the kiss, opening his mouth to accept Deacon's tongue. Rebecca's teeth nipped at his neck and Trey growled. It was like being a part of a delicious sexual game. Too many temptations to experience at once.

Hands surrounded his cock, slow stroking fingers. He didn't know who was touching him but decided it was both Deacon and Rebecca.

Deacon's cock pressed against his hip and Trey eased back from the kiss.

"You're not fucking my ass," he said, placing another fast kiss on Deacon's mouth before he could get away.

Deacon smiled. "I hadn't intended to, even though it would only be fair since you did mine."

Rebecca rested her chin in her hand and watched the interchange between the two men. They were pressing each other, subtly fighting for position and power. She would let it go for a bit but if it went too far, she'd step in and distract them. Thankfully, her men were very easy to distract.

The wolf inside her growled its pleasure. *Her males. Yes. They both belonged to her now.* Her teeth had penetrated both of them.

"Which you loved," Trey pointed out, his voice conveying affection as well as teasing.

Deacon's cheeks turned red as he nodded once, briskly.

"But I was thinking..." His voice trailed away as he bent down and placed his lips against Trey's ear, whispering so low not even Rebecca's supersensitive hearing could pick it up. Her lower lip curled out into a pout. Whatever they had planned, she wanted to be a part of.

Then both males directed their stares toward her.

The heat from their gazes ignited a fire of need and trepidation in her core. Instinct took over and she started to back away, her body taking power from the wolf as she retreated.

Low warning growls from her males made her freeze. She looked at her lovers. Her mind tried to take command but the wolf was in control and pure visceral need seized her body. Large hot hands reached for her, pulling her close. Awash in the sensations that surrounded her, she met the hot lips that touched hers, accepting Deacon's tongue into her mouth, only to have it replaced by Trey's. The flavor of the two males was distinct but each so delicious that she wanted more, wanted to immerse herself in their taste.

As Trey commanded her mouth, his tongue sliding along hers, she felt the seductive bite of Deacon's teeth on her neck. The wicked pain shot into her pussy and she groaned. Deacon and Trey pulled back. The two males looked at her and she could only imagine what they saw. There she was naked, kneeling at the bed, Trey's cum on her thighs, her hair wild, the tips of her breasts were tight and pink. Deacon and Trey looked at each other—seemingly in some silent communion—and nodded, pleased with what they had created.

They reached for her, pulling her until she was snugged between their bodies, Deacon's cock pressing against her from the front and Trey's from the rear. Neither entered her but both were so close.

The delicious temptation they offered drew her on and she raised her leg over Deacon's hip. She knew his thickness, knew how his cock filled her, stretched her. He pressed forward, sliding his erection along her slit. She gasped as the delicate caress of his cock whispered across her clit. Breath caught in her throat and she wanted more. Wanted him inside her.

Another hot, hard cock slid between her legs. Trey.

Deacon groaned as Trey pushed forward, their cocks rubbing against her, and against each other. Trey's breath was hot on her neck as he pumped between her thighs.

"Fuck, we need to get inside her or I'm going to come all over both of you," Trey growled. His words barely penetrated her mind. Feeling wicked and deliciously sexual, Rebecca squeezed her thighs a little tighter, not hard enough to hurt but her subtle movement drew powerful groans from both males. With a siren's smile, she twisted her head around and offered her mouth to Trey. He was there, accepting her gift, driving his tongue between her lips even as Deacon licked and nibbled on her neck. She let the sensations cover her, seduce her until she was liquid, malleable and flowing in their arms.

"Deke, I think our sweet little wolf is ready to be fucked." There was an intensity to Trey's voice that she hadn't heard before. Hands and lips continued to stroke her skin, spreading warmth through her body, until she felt as if she was on fire, the heat inside her consumed her.

"I think you're right, Trey. She's ready to take us both."

His words finally penetrated the sensual fog. Both? At the same time? Even as she thought it, four hot hands guided her forward, urging her over, until she straddled Deacon's hips. His cock was hard and lying against his stomach, still damp from her pussy juices when he'd teased her with it.

"Deacon?" Her voice trembled as her imagination took off. Deacon ran his hands soothingly up her arms, even as Trey's back pressed against her.

"It's time, baby. You've been prepared for it. We're going to have you. I'll fill your cunt. Trey is going to fuck your ass."

The center of her stomach fell away. She'd known from the start that this was possible, now it was happening.

"Will you let us in?" Trey whispered, his lips teasing her ear. "Let us have you, honey."

They offered her pleasure, temptation, something wicked and a little dangerous. But she felt so safe in their arms.

She nodded and she felt the first prodding of Deacon's cock to her pussy. He eased her down as he entered her.

She followed the line of his gaze, staring between their bodies, his cock, thick and hard, pushing up into her sex. It had been weeks since he'd been inside her and his thickness stretched her pussy, almost an ache but so sweet she didn't want it to end. Her cunt eased, wet and hot, ready for more, as Deacon slowly pushed up. Hot hands grabbed her breasts, squeezing just this side of pain until she wanted more. As if he could hear her need, Trey's hands moved across her skin, tightening as he reached her nipples.

She cried out but couldn't contain the sweet pleasure that jolted through her body. His thick hard cock pushed into her pussy and Rebecca shifted, letting it fill her. She groaned, loving the way Deacon's cock invaded her.

"That's it, baby. Take me." His teeth scraped across her neck and she groaned. "Now Trey's going to sink into that sweet ass."

Part of her wanted to rebel but she couldn't find a direction to pull away. Everywhere she looked either Trey or Deacon filled the space. She wanted these men. Wanted them to fuck her, fill her in every way. She heard the crinkle of a condom wrapper and knew she was seconds away from being penetrated.

"That's it," Deacon whispered and she realized he was pulling her ass cheeks apart, giving Trey access to her. "Oh, God, it's going to feel so good when he puts himself inside you."

Even as he said it, Trey pushed forward. His cock was slick but still it was thick and hard. Delicate pain shot through her ass but the soft whispers of her lovers eased her. Heat and love surrounded her. Deacon's voice whispering. His words invading her mind as delicate little caresses, telling her how beautiful she was, how sexy she was. The power she held in her body.

Trey continued his slow penetration. Gentle and persistent, he slid into her until his groin was flush against her backside, his cock completely buried in her ass. Rebecca panted, trying to deal with the overwhelming sensations. She was full, completely surrounded and engulfed by these two men.

"Too much, honey?" Trey asked. "Am I hurting you?"

She shook her head. "Feels good. Feels…" She couldn't find the words. It was strange, foreign, but she liked it. Slowly, Trey began to retreat and Rebecca gasped. She barely had time to absorb the delicious sensations when he pushed back in. As he entered, Deacon pulled out, his withdrawal perfectly matching Trey's penetration.

Overwhelmed by sensation, she clutched Deacon's arms, clinging to them as she opened her body and heart to these two men.

"Yeah, that's it. God, you feel good. I want to come in you."

Pleasure upon pleasure moved through her as they both rode her, sometimes meeting deep inside her, sometimes countering each other with strokes until Rebecca couldn't contain it anymore. She cried out—letting her orgasm jolt through her body. Deacon's followed seconds later and as if that had been what Trey was waiting for, she heard his grunt of satisfaction as he slid into her one more time.

Long moments later, Rebecca found herself on her back, her lovers on each side, her body tended to and eased, but lingering little aches reminded her of their loving.

Her body was sated but her heart was on shaky ground.

Silence reigned as each male stroked her skin, languid caresses that just savored her skin.

Finally Trey raised his eyes. Rebecca braced herself, ready for the reprimand, the anger. Instead he smiled.

"Are we okay?" she asked.

He nodded. "I don't know what will happen but I do know I've been miserable the last few weeks." He looked at her then up at Deacon. "I've missed both of you. A lot."

Rebecca smiled. "We'll just see how it goes and if one of us starts to panic or we can't find a way to make it work, we'll figure it out then."

Deacon nodded but Rebecca could see the truth in his eyes. He wasn't planning on letting either of his lovers go any time soon. The heat in his stare warmed her heart. Trey was still a little unsure but she didn't doubt that once he made the commitment, he'd be steady and loyal.

She could wait—and between her and Deacon, they'd give him a place to come when he figured out where he wanted to be.

Also by Tielle St. Clare

ဢ

eBooks:

Wolf's Heritage 4: Jackson's Rise
Wolf's Heritage 5: Shadow's Embrace

Print Books:

Christmas Elf
Ellora's Cavemen: Dreams of the Oasis III *(anthology)*
Ellora's Cavemen: Jewels of the Nile IV *(anthology)*
Ellora's Cavemen: Legendary Tails II *(anthology)*
Ellora's Cavemen: Tales from the Temple II *(anthology)*
Enter the Dragon *(anthology)*
Feral Fascination *(anthology)*
Irish Enchantment *(anthology)*
Shadow of the Dragon 1: Dragon's Kiss
Shadow of the Dragon 2: Dragon's Fire
Shadow of the Dragon 3: Dragon's Rise
Shadow of the Dragon 4: Dragon's Prey
Through Shattered Light
Transformations *(anthology)*

About the Author

80

Tielle (pronounced "teal") St. Clare has had life-long love of romance novels. She began reading romances in the 7th grade when she discovered Victoria Holt novels and began writing romances at the age of 16 (during Trigonometry, if the truth be told). During her senior year in high school, the class dressed up as what they would be in twenty years—Tielle dressed as a romance writer. When not writing romances, Tielle has worked in public relations and video production for the past 20 years. She moved to Alaska when she was seven years old in 1972 when her father was transferred with the military. Tielle believes romances should be hot and sexy with a great story and fun characters.

80

The author welcomes comments from readers. You can find her website and email address on her author bio page at www.ellorascave.com.

Tell Us What You Think

We appreciate hearing reader opinions about our books. You can email us at Comments@EllorasCave.com.

Why an electronic book?

We live in the Information Age—an exciting time in the history of human civilization, in which technology rules supreme and continues to progress in leaps and bounds every minute of every day. For a multitude of reasons, more and more avid literary fans are opting to purchase e-books instead of paper books. The question from those not yet initiated into the world of electronic reading is simply: *Why?*

1. *Price.* An electronic title at Ellora's Cave Publishing runs anywhere from 40% to 75% less than the cover price of the exact same title in paperback format. Why? Basic mathematics and cost. It is less expensive to publish an e-book (no paper and printing, no warehousing and shipping) than it is to publish a paperback, so the savings are passed along to the consumer.

2. *Space.* Running out of room in your house for your books? That is one worry you will never have with electronic books. For a low one-time cost, you can purchase a handheld device specifically designed for e-reading. Many e-readers have large, convenient screens for viewing. Better yet, hundreds of titles can be stored within your new library—on a single microchip. There are a variety of e-readers from different manufacturers. You can also read e-books on your PC or laptop computer. (Please note that Ellora's Cave does not endorse any specific brands.

You can check our website at www.ellorascave.com for information we make available to new consumers.)

3. *Mobility.* Because your new e-library consists of only a microchip within a small, easily transportable e-reader, your entire cache of books can be taken with you wherever you go.

4. *Personal Viewing Preferences.* Are the words you are currently reading too small? Too large? Too... ANNOYING? Paperback books cannot be modified according to personal preferences, but e-books can.

5. *Instant Gratification.* Is it the middle of the night and all the bookstores near you are closed? Are you tired of waiting days, sometimes weeks, for bookstores to ship the novels you bought? Ellora's Cave Publishing sells instantaneous downloads twenty-four hours a day, seven days a week, every day of the year. Our webstore is never closed. Our e-book delivery system is 100% automated, meaning your order is filled as soon as you pay for it.

Those are a few of the top reasons why electronic books are replacing paperbacks for many avid readers.

As always, Ellora's Cave welcomes your questions and comments. We invite you to email us at Comments@ellorascave.com or write to us directly at Ellora's Cave Publishing Inc., 1056 Home Avenue, Akron, OH 44310-3502.

ELLORA'S CAVE

Romanticon

Annual convention
for women who
refuse to behave

www.JasmineJade.com/Romanticon
For additional info contact: conventions@ellorascave.com

*Discover for yourself why readers can't get enough
of the multiple award-winning publisher
Ellora's Cave.*

*Whether you prefer e-books or paperbacks,
be sure to visit EC on the web at
www.ellorascave.com*

*for an erotic reading experience that will leave you
breathless.*

CPSIA information can be obtained at www.ICGtesting.com
Printed in the USA
LVOW08s1457170814

399566LV00001B/151/P